THE WOLF AT THE DOOR

KATE WILEY

Storm
PUBLISHING

Ebook ISBN: 978-1-83700-163-7
Paperback ISBN: 978-1-83700-164-4

Cover design: Blacksheep
Cover images: Shutterstock

Published by Storm Publishing.
For further information, visit:
www.stormpublishing.co

ALSO BY KATE WILEY

Detective Margot Phalen Series

The Killer's Daughter

Her Father's Secret

The Killer Instinct

In the Blood

Out of the Woods

Margot Phalen FBI series

Tell Me Her Name

As Sierra Dean

The Secret McQueen Series

Something Secret This Way Comes

A Bloody Good Secret

Deep Dark Secret

Keeping Secret

Grave Secret

Secret Unleashed

Cold Hard Secret

A Secret to Die For

Secret Lives

A Wicked Secret

Deadly Little Secret

One Last Secret

The Genie McQueen Series

Bayou Blues

Black Magic Bayou

Black-Hearted Devil

Blood in the Bayou

The Rain Chaser Series

Thunder Road

Driving Rain

Highway to Hail

The Boys of Summer Series

Pitch Perfect

Perfect Catch

High Heat

As Gretchen Rue

The Witches' Brew Mysteries

Steeped to Death

Death by a Thousand Sips

The Grim Steeper

The Lucky Pie Mysteries

A Pie to Die For

To anyone who works at the Body Farm and knows how to coordinate author visits, I can be there any time.

ONE

Once upon a time there was a man.
The man knew a lot about the woods.
The man liked to hunt.
The man was very good at hunting.
*One day, the man was caught hunting something he should not have
been, and he was locked away for a long, long time.*
But the man left many bones behind.
*Because a good hunter knows, you have to be careful where you bury
your kill.*

Special Agent Margot Phalen had been sleeping on an
uncomfortable motel mattress for three nights, but it was the skeletons in the woods that were keeping her awake.

She was also being sorely reminded that she was no longer in
her twenties.

Normally, the FBI sprang for at least a semi-decent hotel, but
normally they weren't working in the middle of nowhere, specifically a town called Trumbull, Tennessee with only one motel to
offer.

So far, nothing about this case had been going the way it was meant to, and that was saying something considering how decidedly *abnormal* the work Margot and her team did was.

They were used to working out of prisons, doing interviews, and in their own office, where at least the chairs were comfortable. But this case had taken an unexpected turn, one that meant their *field* work was a lot more literal.

Margot didn't mind that part, honestly. Being out of the office and in a new environment—one that didn't smell like a prison—was an exciting change of pace. But she could have done without this bed, which had her googling the symptoms of sciatica.

And once she was awake, there were the victims to think of. Victims who, until very recently, had been buried like so many other secrets.

The dead were always at the heart of the work Margot did.

Giving up on sleep for the night, she decided to get up and prepare for the day. She called home, despite how ungodly early it would be on the West Coast. She knew Wes would answer, because Wes Fox always answered.

"Good morning," he said, though there was a faint edge of grogginess to his words.

Margot smiled into the receiver just hearing his voice. "And here I thought you just stayed up all night on the off chance I *might* call," she said.

"As if I could sleep with that damned cat of yours pining away for you."

Poor Lucy. Margot's beloved calico had gotten a lot clingier over the past year thanks to a near tragedy the previous fall. While she remained an outgoing and bossy cat, she now solely slept in their bed, like she needed to know where Margot was even in the night.

"Poor girl."

"No, poor Wes. Wes," he grumbled and she could hear the shuffle of sheets, the creaking of their old bed frame. If she closed her eyes, she could picture the whole scene and find herself there, rather than this dire motel room where the bathroom mirror was cracked and permanently fogged from age.

"Poor Wes," she commiserated.

"Thank you. That was almost believable."

"You all set for today? Feeling okay?"

This wasn't a topic she liked to broach, especially not when she was so far away, but the day demanded it. The previous year, Wes had been arrested under suspicion of the murder of a teenaged girl at the high school where he coached. He had been cleared of all wrongdoing, but the real killer had never been found, something that bothered Margot whenever she had the time to think about it.

The school had brought him back on, but under a strict six-month probationary period. They wanted to make sure there would be no uproar from parents, or they were covering themselves in case Wes did anything that would reflect badly on them.

That six months was now over, and today Wes was meeting with the school, as well as the school board, to determine if he would remain employed.

"I'm okay," he said. "I know I've done everything right, and as far as I know no one is chomping at the bit to see me fired. Even Whitney's parents wrote a letter of support, from what I understand." His voice hitched when he said the girl's name. Margot's chest tightened. She knew he still carried a lot of personal guilt about the night she died, considering he had dropped her off at home after a softball practice at the school.

There were a lot of *what if* questions for the people left behind in situations like that. Wes had asked them all, time and time again.

"You'll do great. Let me know how it goes?"

"Of course. And you've got your big trek today?"

"Just call me Margot of the Mountains."

"I will not."

"Buzzkill."

He chuckled. "Take a selfie in all your REI glory, please. I want to include it in the Christmas letter."

"Rude."

"Not rude," he protested. "I bet you'll look really cute." He paused. "You feeling ready to see that?"

The skeletons were long gone, so it was just a crime scene. Margot was no stranger to a crime scene, even if she'd been off the homicide beat for a long time now.

"Like riding a bike."

They said their goodbyes, and as she hung up Margot realized she felt both better and worse. Her day was always vastly improved when she got to speak to Wes first thing. But knowing how far away he was, and that she couldn't be there for him on a difficult day, made her feel queasy, an almost guilt-like sickness. He was a much more positive person than she was, though, and if he said he was okay, he meant it.

She wasn't sure *she* was so convinced that she was ready for the day ahead. Especially not if these victims had to do with the man she thought they might.

Margot grudgingly began to get ready, having used up all her excuses to avoid it. She'd already showered before calling Wes, but now she went through the routine of brushing her teeth and slathering herself in sunscreen. She was a pale person, and this case was requiring a lot more outdoor time than usual for her and the team.

Under the usual circumstances, her team investigated cold cases, and tried to tie imprisoned serial killers to potential murders they hadn't previously been connected to. They did good work, had closed dozens of cold cases over the course of six years, and had a good system of research and direct interviews with the killers that worked well for them.

Those interviews were why Margot had been recruited to the team, and why she had been granted more flexibility in her job than most other agents. Her work before the FBI was as a homicide detective in San Francisco. But her expertise in serial killers ran a lot closer to home.

When she had been fifteen, she'd learned her father, Ed Finch, was one of the country's most notorious serial killers: the Classified Killer.

With some external pressure, she had come out of hiding two decades on and interviewed him for almost two years to help close his final unknown victim files. Then she had killed him.

Though, in fairness to her, he hadn't left her much of a choice.

Her skill in getting information out of killers had opened doors for her in the FBI. Her tragic backstory and somewhat complicated mental health meant she was able to do much of her work from home instead of the FBI office in San Francisco.

But there were times she had no choice but to be on site, and this was a situation unlike any she had experienced before in her new job.

Margot donned a pair of shorts to combat the sweaty humidity of Tennessee, but then felt absolutely stupid trying to figure out how to put a gun on with them. She had to be armed, it was part of the regulations of being an agent, but there was simply no way to look cool or authoritative when pairing a gun with shorts.

She settled for a hip holster and a button-down shirt over her tee, to at least make the gun a little less obvious but give her access to it if she needed it. Her badge she slipped in her back pocket. Another thing that felt useless to carry on a hike but was still necessary. She slid some latex gloves into the pocket of her FBI windbreaker in case she needed to handle evidence at some point.

Before donning her clunky hiking boots, she took her files for their current case to the small table by the window.

Three unearthed skeletons found on one remote patch of the Appalachian trail had been more than enough motivation for the local Tennessee police to call in bigger guns.

Margot's team wouldn't typically be the first line of contact for a case like this, except the location of the bodies and some of the photographs of the skeletons sent alarm bells up the chain, that this might be the work of someone their team was already acquainted with.

One of the cases they had been circling around for over a year was that of Wyatt William Holmes. Though he shared a name with the infamous 1920s Chicago serial killer H.H. Holmes, the connections really ended there. Wyatt didn't have a house of horrors, he took his show entirely on the road.

Or the backroad, more precisely.

Holmes lived in an off-grid cabin in the Tennessee wilderness, and, in a dangerous combination for a killer he was both a skilled hunter, and a paranoid schizophrenic who believed that a pack of wolves that roamed the hills near his home were speaking to him. He worshipped them like gods.

He believed they were telling him where to find prey. He would go out at night, to where he thought the wolves were telling him to go, and he would hunt. Except he wasn't hunting deer, or rabbits, or any of the game available to him in those woods.

He was hunting hikers.

Specifically, hikers on the Appalachian Trail, which was already a treacherous and difficult undertaking without having to fend off serial killers. He singled out solo hikers typically, though he had on more than one occasion taken out a couple. What made him so difficult to find, despite the fact he had used the same killing ground for almost thirty years, was that he had no problem stalking his prey for days, or even a week, at a time. He was careful to always make sure there were no other hikers within a certain distance of his chosen victims—he would often hike ahead of them by as much as a day to make sure he knew where others might be on the trail, giving himself the most time possible before he finally struck.

So while his victims were all found on the same hiking trail, they weren't all found in the same *place*.

Sometimes they weren't found at all.

That's what had brought Margot's team in for this particular case. First, they had the most immediate knowledge of Holmes and his crimes since they were already working his case. They'd be the best equipped in all of the FBI to know if these unsolved homicides were related to his work.

Second, they had been in touch with the prison he was housed in, making it that much faster and easier to get in to talk to him.

Margot chewed her thumbnail. While she was good at what she did and confident in her abilities to talk to any killer, including Holmes, a small part of her appreciated the reprieve of getting to do something different, a little change of pace. It could wear a person down, talking to killers all the time.

She flipped to a map of where the new bodies had been found and compared it to a map of where Holmes's previous victims had been located. The connection was definitely possible.

She slapped the case file closed, her mind now filled with thoughts of wolf gods and open graves. She hadn't even had a cup of coffee yet, but wasn't sure it was a good idea, given the circumstances.

Now Margot was preparing to do her two least favorite things in the world. Sit across the table from a killer.

And go for a hike.

TWO

Margot, despite her better judgement, stopped for a coffee at a diner close to the motel. While her room did have a small single-cup brewer, she had a lot of doubts about the overall cleanliness of the space they'd been given, and she preferred to leave the coffee to professionals.

She bought a second cup and returned to the motel, where she knocked on one of the adjacent rooms on the main floor. Andrew Rhodes answered.

He sported a pair of khaki cargo pants and a plaid short-sleeve shirt not dissimilar to the one she was wearing, just with shorter sleeves.

"You couldn't figure out how to hide the gun, either, I take it." She handed him the second coffee, which he took. He did not comment on her assessment.

"Alana already left with Sydney and Greg. You ready?" he asked.

"As I'll ever be." He locked up his room and they got into the rental car parked outside his door. There were a surprising number of cars in the lot, which made Margot wonder if she had too high standards for where she slept. The motel seemed to do steady business.

The drive to the trailhead wasn't far, and normally Margot would have tried to fill the silence with small talk, but instead she just let the morning news drone on from the radio. There was a story about the bodies, because it was big news locally, but Andrew shut it off.

When they arrived at the trailhead, there were two other cars waiting for them: another rental almost identical to Andrew's and a dust-covered pickup truck.

They'd teamed up with a local guide to take them out to the location where the skeletons had been found. A small team of forensic anthropologists—mostly students—were working the surrounding area to see if any bone fragments had been missed, or any new remains were waiting to be found. That team was camping on the trail. Margot and her crew were living the fancy federally funded life in the worst motel in history, not counting the Bates.

Frankly, Margot would take a mommy-obsessed, knife-wielding weirdo over this place if it meant not having springs dig into her back every time she rolled over. She had briefly considered sleeping on the floor before reminding herself of the untold horrors the floor might hold.

She was ready to head to Nashville early to get the interview going, because it would mean a real hotel, with real towels, real hot water, and no mysterious stains on the carpet and ceiling that made her want to open a brand-new cold case file to see what they might be from.

Plus the whole place smelled of stale cigarette smoke, and she was worried the longer she stayed there the harder it would be to get the smell out of her clothes and hair.

For the first three days they'd been in town they had interviewed the local police, visited the remains at the morgue—or what counted as a morgue in a place this small, which was really just the cold storage locker at a nearby funeral home. The skeletal remains would ultimately be transferred to an anthropology lab for further investigation. Now, on the dawn of day four, Margot was lacing up a pair of hiking boots that her common law partner, Wes, would later say *I told you so* about telling her to take along, and just being grateful she wasn't in Alana Yarrow's shoes, literally.

Alana was a high-heel woman to her core. Her feet were probably shaped like Barbie's when she took her shoes off at night. She looked wildly out of her comfort zone in her brand-new boots and khaki cargo pants.

As Margot and Andrew joined the small group of agents gathered together at the trailhead, where they would begin their hike up to the crime scene, Margot went over and joined Alana, who was shuffling from foot to foot, like having her feet flat was causing her legitimate discomfort.

"You're going to destroy your feet in those," Margot commented, pointing to Alana's boots. They were so new she wouldn't have been surprised if they'd still had a tag on them that morning.

"Well, it's these or my Tom Ford Angelinas. Which I think I might actually enjoy hiking in more." Her white-blonde hair was pulled back in a small ponytail at the nape of her neck, but she was sporting her signature red lipstick.

Margot smiled. Alana had once explained that she justified buying thousand-dollar shoes on an FBI salary—which was not very high—on the basis that they were a lifelong investment piece. A few classic-colored pumps could be worn with anything, so her cost-per-wear had been whittled down over the years. She was probably the only person Margot knew who wore Christian Louboutin heels to her underpaid FBI job.

Margot wore ankle boots. All day, every day, if she was on the job. If she was working from home, she had yielded to the siren song of basic bitch comfort, and wandered around her ranch in Uggs. Wes often teased that she might soon need to invest in cowboy boots, but Margot didn't think she would ever see that day come around. Though, admittedly, she had also never thought she'd see the day she owned a ranch, had chickens, lived with a man, and occasionally walked alone at night without pepper spray.

So, anything was possible.

Margot nodded a greeting to the rest of the team milling around the trailhead, waiting for their guide to arrive: Special Agents Gregory Howell and Sydney Onyema. It was a point of pride to Margot that their team was one of the few in the FBI where women outnumbered men.

And with Andrew set to retire in the next year, their dynamic was likely to shift again.

The FBI had an archaic rule by which agents were forced to retire at fifty-seven. It was a rule that dated back to the Hoover years, and, despite efforts to change it, it remained staunchly in place.

Andrew had managed to dodge it, using the excuse of establishing his cold case team, and then, somehow, by getting lost in the bureaucratic process after that. He'd been "out of sight, out of mind" with his specialty team in San Francsico and it had seemed like the higher-ups either forgot, or chose to ignore, that his fifty-seventh birthday had come and gone some time ago.

But they'd figured him out recently, and had given him one last year to do his work. Margot wasn't clear if that meant that when Andrew retired the team would be disbanded and shuffled to other projects, or if the year was to allow Andrew the rare opportunity to select and groom his own successor.

Margot sincerely hoped Alana would get the job. There was no one else on the team who commanded as much respect as she did, and the position was of no interest to Margot because it would put the kibosh on her unique work-from-home situation.

It felt impossible that Andrew was leaving the FBI. Andrew Rhodes was the first agent Margot had ever met. He was also the man who had finally tracked down her father after his decades of menacing the Bay Area. He was good at what he did. So good that he'd evaded his own retirement. Margot wasn't even sure he would know what to do with himself outside the FBI. He didn't talk about his home life much, though she knew he had a wife and two kids. Would he be excited to spend more time with them? His kids were already finished college at this point, something that stunned Margot whenever she thought about it.

She still imagined them as the little boys she'd seen in a picture in his wallet when she was fifteen. But they were in their thirties by now, weren't they? Doing the mental math was jarring because to Margot they would always be the little boys with chubby cheeks in a photo he'd shown her a long, long time ago.

Andrew looked just as at ease in this environment as he did anywhere else. His appearance, as ever, was that of a college professor, with his salt-and-pepper beard and tortoiseshell glasses.

As Margot assessed her colleagues, she couldn't help but smile despite the grim scenario that had brought them out to the Tennessee wilderness. Sydney was practically bouncing with enthusiasm. Over the previous six months she'd been getting her feet wet in more offsite work for the unit, and she was proving to be just as smart and observant in the field as she was when poring over old case files. Her black braids were pulled back in a thick ponytail, and she wore a denim shirt and khaki shorts under her FBI-issued windbreaker. She looked like *she* was prepared to guide them into the backwoods. Margot watched her scanning their surroundings as if she was desperate to point out different types of trees or let them know what kind of bird was making such a racket this early in the morning.

Next to Sydney, Greg appeared to have switched into Boy Scout mode, something Margot had never expected from him. He was sporting a small day pack over his windbreaker, and had an FBI ball cap obscuring his eyes, his red hair peeking out from underneath. He looked almost as eager as Sydney to get going, which wasn't what Margot would have predicted. She thought if anyone here might match Alana for discomfort, it would be him.

Greg, who had once been called "Gory" by his colleagues because of his unsettling enthusiasm for talking about killers, and his general lack of people skills, didn't strike Margot as outdoorsy. She used to imagine he never left the FBI office, because it was so hard to picture him anywhere else. Evidently, she was very wrong.

He had an actual trail guidebook out and was offering up tidbits of information to anyone who would listen. Margot loved Greg, but she was going to need more coffee to handle a lecture on trail history.

A man climbed out of the pickup truck, evidently having been waiting for them all to arrive. He was probably in his late twenties, and full of the kind of pep Margot found annoying now that she was over forty. She hoped he and Sydney could bounce their energy off each other.

The man was good-looking, with the kind of face that would likely look young until he was very, very old. He had dark hair, and warm brown eyes, and under different circumstances Margot could have pictured him being quite the lady-killer.

Of course, given where they were and why they were here, being a lady-killer wasn't something that anyone wanted to be. Still, it didn't escape Margot's notice that Sydney stared at him a little longer than might be polite. Margot smiled to herself.

The man clapped his hands together, and rocked back and forth on his feet like he was going to run the whole way up the trail.

"All right, folks, I'm Spencer Nguyen and I'll be your guide today. I know you're not here for fun, but for work or play it's important to be prepared on the AT. I hope you all brought some water, and you aren't breaking in new shoes."

Margot looked over to Alana, who let out a frustrated sigh. "Like everyone just *has* hiking boots," she muttered gloomily.

"Let's get going," Spencer said. "No one wants to be out in these woods after dark if they don't have to be."

THREE

The part of the trail where the bodies had been found was within the Great Smoky Mountains. The only connection Margot had previously had to those mountains—and to Tennessee at all—was a love of Dolly Parton that had endured with her through childhood into adulthood.

She had never been to Tennessee before though, and, aside from a vague awareness of Nashville, knew very little about the state.

What she was learning, as she paced along the trail behind Spencer, was that Tennessee was stunning. The trees were dense, but in a way that was new to her. She had spent a lot of time in the Muir Woods area back in San Francisco, which was its own unique canopy, but the trees of the Great Smoky Mountains felt completely different. Her own property in Elk Creek, California, was so sparse when it came to trees that they seemed like fun little surprises whenever she came across one, but here the trees seemed to have come up in the thousands.

Millions, possibly.

The area seemed dominated by spruce and fir trees, but there were also an almost impossible number of oaks. Margot took it all in, and understood for the first time why people hiked, and why they traveled to do it. That old line about not seeing the forest for the trees missed the whole point of a forest.

The enjoyment of the forest *was* the trees. The joy in seeing how many different kinds there were, how they shaded the well-worn path, the way the needles of the evergreens scented the air. If not for what was waiting for them at their destination, Margot might have almost found the hike enjoyable.

This was something she would have never allowed herself to do only six years earlier. Back then, her father's warnings had cast a shadow over every part of her life. She was constantly afraid, forever paranoid that any kind of routine, any kind of slightly dangerous environment, was as good as asking someone to stalk and kill her.

It was a thrill to find out she was able to enjoy this for what it was.

But that voice—Ed's voice—still lingered in the back of her mind, telling her this wasn't safe at all. That the reason they were there was hard evidence that killers could and did lurk everywhere, especially where you couldn't see them.

There's always someone watching, buddy.

She smiled despite herself. Even though the fucker was dead, she couldn't manage to escape him completely.

Spencer wasn't a mind reader, but he might as well have been. He fell in step beside Margot and gave her an encouraging smile.

"You look like you're almost enjoying yourself," he said.

"I'm not sure I'd go that far, given the circumstances, but let's just say I'm not hating it as much as I thought I would. Certainly not as much as other folks." She glanced back down the trail to where Alana was bent over, fidgeting with her boots, probably swearing under her breath. When she straightened up and started hiking again, she whistled to herself, almost like she needed the motivation to keep going.

Spencer's expression changed when Alana started to whistle; he stiffened slightly, a frown taking over from his formerly golden retriever vibe.

"Everything okay?" Margot asked.

He shook himself off. "I'm sorry, old superstitions."

"Oh?" Margot wouldn't mind a little distraction from the ache of her own feet. As lovely as the scenery was, this was more physical exertion than she was used to, especially after sleeping so poorly.

"You must know about Appalachian folklore," Spencer said, smiling. "I thought it had made the rounds on social media a few times by now."

"That assumes I have social media." Margot smiled back.

Spencer did a double-take. "I didn't think it was possible to *not* have social media. Like, are we talking you just don't have things like TikTok, or are we talking like, you don't even have Facebook?"

"None of it. So you have a completely ignorant audience. Tell me all about it, it'll make the hike go faster."

He looked briefly hurt that she would want a hike to go faster, but rebounded quickly.

"I used to run this company with my pop before he passed, and he knew so much Appalachian lore, but I'll give you the high-level overview. Basically, in these woods, nothing is ever what it seems. These are old woods, with their own history, and we're the ones trespassing here. Some of the dwellers in the trees don't mind that so much, they'll leave you alone if you leave them alone. But there are others that aren't quite so friendly. You want to respect the rules."

Margot was going to laugh at this, but he seemed serious. "What rules?"

"Don't stare into the woods at night. Don't whistle at night."

"Whistle? Seriously?"

He nodded. "Don't follow any mysterious lights. And *any* time of day, if you hear something calling you, it might sound like someone you know, might sound like a baby, but if you hear anything off the trail, don't go following it."

He followed this with a broad smile. "Don't let any of the locals get started on talk of skinwalkers either, that'll just convince you we're all lost causes." He chuckled.

Margot laughed with him, feeling some of the tension ease. Spencer would have been excellent at telling ghost stories around a campfire; now she couldn't help but imagine glints of light among the dark trees.

The team was quiet as they hiked, except for the sound of heavy breathing and the occasional curse when someone would trip over a rock or exposed branch. The elevation escalated quickly and, while everyone on the team was relatively fit, three of them were over forty and Andrew was on the other side of sixty. Spencer, however, barely seemed aware that they might be having difficulty trailing behind him. He continued on, his pace steady, and told them little tidbits about the forest as he went. It wasn't meant to be a guided tour, but it seemed like old habits died hard for someone who was paid to share the woods with his companions.

When they finally got to the crime scene about three hours later, Alana was limping but hadn't said a single word about her pain, and Margot felt certain that, collectively, they had not brought enough water with them.

She had expected to find police, or possibly park rangers—the Great Smoky Mountains were a national park, after all—up here, but the only thing that marked the place as being anything remotely exceptional was the yellow crime scene tape cordoning off a large rectangle of woods.

She could make out the sound of voices nearby, and Spencer led them a little further off the path and through the trees, to what, based on the little circle of tents, seemed to be a designated campsite.

There were three people sitting in folding camp chairs—something Margot couldn't have imagined hauling this far up the trail willingly—eating out of small zippered bags and chatting in upbeat tones. They all looked a little dirty, but there was a rosiness in their cheeks and expressions that told her there was nowhere else they would rather be. When Margot and her crew came up, they seemed briefly startled to see other people, then waved a general greeting.

A tent nearby unzipped and a woman came out. She was older than the other three, probably in her early fifties, and had an undeniable aura of authority. Andrew must have read that same vibe because he approached her with his hand extended.

"Dr. Langstrom?" he asked.

She shook his hand, a firm grip from what Margot could see, and gave him a quick nod of agreement. "You can call me Ava. Or Dr. Ava if you insist, like the youths do." She gestured with a hand towards the three people sitting in chairs. Two young men and a young woman.

"Ava," Andrew agreed with a smile. "I'm Supervisory Special Agent Andrew Rhodes. These are Special Agents Margot Phalen, Alana Yarrow, Gregory Howell, and Sydney Onyema." He gestured to each of them in turn. "We've been working the Holmes case for some time now and are very curious to see if you've made any additional headway."

Ava smiled absently at Margot and the rest of them, then pointed at her own team. "These are Beckett, Lieberman, and Jones, my best students."

"Theo, Grace, and Chip," clarified the one Ava had introduced as Beckett.

Margot felt fairly certain that, if anyone on that hillside was quizzed later about the people they'd been introduced to that morning, there would be a worse than fifty percent recall rate on any of their names.

"Let's let them finish their lunch," Ava said. "We've had a busy morning."

Without another word she left the small campsite and crossed the trail they'd come up on, ducking under the yellow tape and vanishing into the woods.

Margot and her colleagues stared after her, unsure of what to do next.

"You'll want to follow her," Beckett said, eating something that might have been ground beef out of his bag.

Andrew was the first to do so, and the rest of the team traipsed after him. Margot could tell, just from the soft grunt of pain, that Alana had hoped they might be able to take a break from walking for a bit, but no such luck.

Still, she didn't complain, and Margot didn't know whether to be proud of her or tell her to go sit down with the others. But Alana wouldn't miss this because of sore feet. She wouldn't miss this if her leg was cut off at the knee.

Margot followed her team, and the moment they stepped off the trail was a stark reminder that they were deep in the wilderness. The trees, which had been so lovely to look at from the well-traversed path, were now clustered together, blotting out the sun, creating a damp and chilly cavern for them to wander through. The ground under their feet was rough, bits of rock breaking away under their feet, skittering down the hill.

This wasn't an easy walk. Margot slipped several times, catching her balance on a nearby tree once and another time falling directly on her ass in the damp underbrush. Greg was kind enough to help her back to her feet, and no one laughed at her, because they were all too focused on staying standing themselves.

Margot guessed they'd walked quarter of a mile off the path. Ava moved at a much more confident clip than they did, having been navigating this terrain for three days already; that quarter of a mile might as well have been ten for the rest of them. When they finally found themselves in a small, open area, they were huffing louder than ever and Margot needed to sit down on a nearby boulder to catch her breath. Her brow was sweaty, and she cursed every potato chip she'd eaten in the last fifteen years. She had thought she was in good shape, but it was very clear that the Great Smoky Mountains were telling her otherwise.

Sydney plopped down beside her on the rock and pulled a bottle of water from her pack, sucked back a huge gulp of it and then gasped for air. The zeal she'd shown earlier had worn off.

"I was looking forward to this. I thought the hills in San Francisco would prepare me, but I was so very, very wrong. I'm kind of wishing we could have just stayed at the office and looked at pictures," she wheezed.

Margot offered a thin smile, but her throat and lungs felt too raw to give any real reply. Besides which, she agreed with Sydney in that moment. She knew in-person was always best for understanding a case, but she was hard-pressed to imagine any reason they actually *had* to be there.

Then she heard a little "*Oh!*"

She looked over to where the noise had come from—Greg, standing at the edge of the treeline—and pushed herself up to her feet to get over to him. When she reached his side, she let out her own raspy gasp.

There were four skeletons.

These were new; the first three had already been bagged up and removed from the trail. There was a grid of wooden stakes and string marking off squares across an area the size of a small swimming pool, and the four skeletons were on the periphery of that grid, close to the trees under a makeshift canopy, in what appeared to be two sets of two, the skulls nestled, plain as day, in the soil.

"When did you find these?" Andrew asked, his tone calm but his expression as stunned as the rest of them.

"Uncovered the first one yesterday, been digging the rest out over the past twenty-four hours." Ava wasn't looking at them, she was staring at the exposed scar in the landscape that had once been someone's private burial ground.

Margot frowned as she took in the details. Holmes had disposed of his bodies in a number of ways. Occasionally he left them on the trail for someone to find. He was also a fan of dragging the body a few yards off the trail and leaving it for the wildlife to dispose of. Of the bodies he had buried, he'd never put more than one in the same place, and never this many all together.

Seven bodies in the same grave was wildly out of character for

Holmes. It raised red flags for Margot, even though the hunting ground was right. It just didn't feel like him.

But perhaps that was the point.

If it had been more in line with his known kills, then it was unlikely it would have gone unnoticed for so long. This could be his early work, or perhaps a period of heightened activity they had never noticed before.

"Were they all buried at the same time?" she asked.

Ava gave her a quick, assessing look. "No. We'll need to have a look at them to give you a more accurate representation of when they were buried, but I'd hazard just by looking at this that you have at least four distinct burial sites. Two different ones in the first batch, two in this batch."

That was bold for Holmes, as well. But it might help them narrow down the identities of these victims faster. Couples or friends who went missing at the same time were sure to draw attention.

But then, people made friends on the trail. Sometimes they would walk together for a few days, or a few weeks, without ever having known each other in the outside world.

There was little to no hope of there being any physical evidence of Holmes left on those bodies, so tying them to him without a confession would be almost impossible.

Margot stared into the open pit, looking at those four skeletons. The only way they were going to get any answers was from Holmes himself. And that meant it was time for her to do what she did best.

FOUR

Margot opened her fourth bottle of water since returning to the hotel room and collapsed on her bed. She had showered, washing off most of the sweat and grime from the hike, but she still felt dirty.

That was a problematic side effect of the work.

It had been a long time since Margot had been around human remains. Her work these days tended to consist of studying photos of old bodies, long since buried, sometimes in unmarked graves. Bodies she didn't have to look at in person.

As a homicide detective, she had often been one of the first people on the scene after a death. Since moving to cold cases, those extra-distasteful parts of the job had become something she no longer had to think about. Margot just needed to read the notes, to look at the photos with a dispassionate eye.

She'd changed into her pajamas after the shower because the idea of lying on her motel bed in just a towel was too unpleasant, no matter how tired she was.

She pulled out her phone and called home.

Wes answered on the second ring. "Hey, babe. So, did you get a trail name?" She could hear him laughing and switched the phone to a video call, because she wanted to see him smile at her, even if it meant he needed to look at her in a deeply unflattering position since she refused to sit up. He accepted the call and his tanned, smiling face appeared, his dark-blond hair mussed like he had been lying down. He wasn't wearing a shirt, which still managed to make her cheeks flush even after all these years.

"A trail name?" she asked, trying to steer back to the topic at hand.

"Didn't you watch *Wild*?" he asked.

"If it's not about a cartoon hamburger shop, or something that was released in the 1990s, I probably haven't seen it."

He snorted. "Your trail name is the name other hikers know you by on the big trails like the AT and Pacific Crest. It's like a cheeky nickname."

Margot mulled this over for a moment. "Mine would probably be Skid Mark, thanks to falling on my ass, but at least I'm not Alana, who is probably calling herself Bloody Toes right about now."

"Aren't you glad I told you—"

"No. No *I told you so*, thank you very much. You know perfectly well that you were right."

"I will take *you were right* as a victory, and I want you to picture me pumping my fists in the air like Rocky."

"I'm going to hang up on you," Margot threatened.

"You wouldn't dare."

"How is everything there? How did the meeting go?" She felt a pang of longing for her home. Not just for Wes, though he was certainly a major factor in her homesickness. But she'd done the unthinkable when they'd bought the ranch, and had become a pet person. She had developed a penchant for rescuing senior dogs, and as a result there were now five of them wandering their property, as well as six cats, and a gaggle of chickens. Was that the right word for a bunch of chickens? She wasn't sure.

They'd had to rebuild the barn on the property over the winter as the previous one had burned down, and now that it was finally complete, she and Wes had been debating doing some livestock rescue by adopting goats.

Margot had not allowed herself to get close to anyone or anything for such a huge part of her life, but in letting herself learn to love Wes she had unlocked a previously unknown capacity for empathy and love that seemed like a bottomless pit now. One that she just kept filling with more and more animals that needed to be loved.

It seemed harmless, but the costs associated with feeding and medicating all those animals—especially the seniors—was no joke. Margot was never going to be able to retire if she kept this up.

"Everyone is alive and well. Lucy has accepted me as a temporary substitute, it seems. She sat with me for breakfast."

"And the meeting?" she urged, noticing he'd skipped over that.

"It went fine, I told you it would. Probation is over. It was... emotional, but by and large positive." He paused, and she decided to leave it alone. She was happy enough knowing Wes's job was on track again, and it was nice to have the reprieve of chatting about lighter topics, like trail names and the cats.

Things that weren't mass graves in the Great Smoky Mountains.

Wes, ever attuned to her, read something in her silence that she hadn't said in words. His expression changed, softening, showing a sympathy and understanding that only a decade together could achieve.

"This one is rougher than you predicted, isn't it?"

She let out a little sigh. Wes had also been a career homicide detective, but he'd left the police department not long after she did, after the corruption they had uncovered about the chief of police made it untenable for him to continue working there. When they'd moved, he could have looked for other police work, but he'd decided to become a high school coach instead.

So sometimes Margot felt guilty for bringing him back into the world he had willingly left behind him. Wes had been an incredible detective, but he didn't live and breathe this work the way she did. He could leave it behind without issue. Margot wasn't sure she'd ever be able to do that.

"It's not great. There were four more bodies up there by the time we got to see the grave, that's on top of the three already recovered. The team working at the site think that's it, at least, but it certainly muddies the waters a lot more."

A lot more, if she was being honest with herself.

Margot was used to uncovering one or two more victims they could link to the killers they were working with. That happened often and was part of what was so satisfying about the job. Of course, in the cases of many serial killers that would be a normal victim count.

The killers whose counts were in the dozens were a rarer breed, though they were the ones most often featured in popular culture. Margot understood that someone who had killed a hundred people was much scarier and more interesting than those who had only killed two or three—the threshold considered by most experts to be where the definition of a serial killer began.

Famously, when authorities told Ted Bundy how many murders he was being held accountable for—thirty-six—he'd said, "Add a number to that and you'd be correct." This intentionally vague statement might have just been part of his own myth-building, but it could also have meant that his victim count was anywhere from thirty-seven to three hundred and sixty. *Those* were the kind of unsolved case numbers that kept Margot awake at night.

Seven new bodies was enough to have her pondering the worst question of them all: how many more had been missed? There was no guarantee these victims were all Holmes's handiwork, and if they weren't, that meant there was an entirely different killer who had once stalked the Appalachian Trail—and might still be out there.

They were going to need to talk to Holmes soon, something Margot was feeling more tense about than usual. She was eager to see if he lived up to the almost mythological status that had been established by those who had interviewed him before her. He wasn't a typical killer. He was actually delusional, and that would mean breaking him down and getting him to open up would be a lot more difficult than with some of the other killers she spoke to.

"You've got this," Wes said after a moment, giving her an encouraging smile. "No matter how bad it gets, you've had worse. You can do anything."

Margot couldn't help but smile back. There was a reason she'd kept him around for all these years. She might keep him around forever, at this rate.

"It's easy for you to be Mr. Pep Talk when *you* don't have to solve the cold cases." She rolled her eyes, trying to add some levity to a conversation that was veering towards being too grim.

"That's very true, but you didn't have a fourteen-year-old boy vomit on you today after running drills, I bet."

Margot shuddered. "I think, perhaps, I'll stick to the dead bodies."

"Lean into your strengths, my father always says."

"Your father also says *full fat everything because I'm going to die someday anyway*."

"See, a very wise man." He grinned.

Neither of them mentioned her father. They didn't bring Ed up often, if they could help it. Margot didn't tell Wes how often in a week she heard her father's voice in her head, how difficult it could sometimes be to separate his voice from her own inner monologue.

"What's tomorrow for you?" Wes asked. He had gotten up and wandered through their house, ending up at the fridge, where he was digging out something to snack on. Wes was a big evening snacker.

"Back up the trail, just to get a better sense of the crime scene, check the area, see what else the team up there has found. Then I think the plan will be a day or two in Nashville to see if Holmes will talk to us."

"You going to go to a honky-tonk?"

"Absolutely not."

"But you've got friends in low places." He crunched on a pickle and she felt hungry.

"You're my only friend in low places, buddy."

"I'm honored. Hold on a sec." He padded into a different room, then, in a sweet voice, he said, "Lucy, say goodnight to your mother."

The phone shifted angles and her calico cat blinked up at her sleepily, then gave a little meow.

Margot smiled.

Life was garbage a lot of the time.

But sometimes it was magic.

FIVE

The hike back to the grave was no easier the second day. If anything, the residual muscle pain from the previous day made Margot's legs feel more leaden, and the lumpy mattress she'd been sleeping on made everything about ten times worse than it might have been otherwise.

She didn't want to complain, but she was cursing internally with every step. Her room didn't even have a bathtub—not that she would want to use it if there was one, but it would have been nice to have the option for a soak after all this.

She tried to tune out the pain, focusing on the environment, which was just as pretty as it had been the day before, except muted now under dark clouds. That was all this day needed. Mood suitably darkened by the weather, Margot turned her annoyance towards Greg and Sydney, who were chatting merrily and keeping pace with Spencer as if they were both seasoned distance hikers.

No, they were just still in their early thirties, which was even more insulting.

Spencer was no longer giving them tidbits about the environment, but he did periodically shout back warnings about what to do if it started to rain, and suggestions that they keep up the pace.

Margot caught Alana's eye briefly, and thought that though her friend didn't seem to be in as much pain today, there was a chance she was just getting better at hiding it. There was no way she didn't have blisters all over her feet. Margot offered her a sympathetic wince.

"I'm going to throw these boots off the Bay Bridge when this is over," Alana whispered conspiratorially.

"Well, that's a silly idea," Margot said. "The pedestrian part of that bridge doesn't go all the way to San Fran. You'd be better throwing them off the Golden Gate."

"Smart."

Once they reached the campsite, things took on a more somber tone that felt more in line with the weather and the job ahead. Dr. Ava was waiting for them, though none of the students were with her. They must all be at the grave, working to unearth the remains so another team could come take them back down the trail.

Margot tried to look at the scene before her with the eyes of a hunter. The camping area was set a little off the trail, and regulations in the national park meant that any hikers taking the trail through the protected area needed to have a permit to camp there.

Of course, that didn't mean people didn't cheat the system, or perhaps have a bad hiking day and need to camp somewhere other than their registered site. Margot needed to determine, first, how someone might know that campers would be at the site on any given evening, and second, how no one noticed that at least seven different hikers had vanished from this exact same area.

It was wild enough that Holmes had been able to hunt the trail for thirty years before anyone caught on to it being one killer. It seemed almost beyond comprehension that no one noticed such a localized hotbed of activity until the bones had all been unearthed.

Margot peered into the thick brush, wondering how difficult it would be to tell someone was lurking just on the other side of those trees, someone intent on making those campers his prey.

In the waning light of day, with their only motivation being to get a tent set up before darkness fell, with the exhaustion of hours of hard hiking weighing them down... Margot didn't doubt for a moment that Holmes could have gone unnoticed here.

Whatever was to be said for his intelligence in terms of book smarts—testing suggested it was below average—he was a gifted and merciless hunter. He could move quietly through the trees and underbrush. Quiet enough to take deer and other animals by surprise. With predatory skills like that, what hope did weary hikers have?

Ava greeted their crew with a nod and a stiff smile. She looked well put-together despite having no access to a shower for at least the last four days, and having spent much of that time doing back-breaking work inside an open grave. She didn't appear to be a woman prone to complaining.

"Welcome back, FBI people," she said generally. "If you'll follow me, we have managed to get all four of the bodies loosened enough to be removed safely, and wherever possible we believe the remains are as complete as can be hoped."

"As can be hoped?" Sydney asked.

Ava gave her a quick look. "Yes, well. In the wild there are elements beyond our control. Animals, weather, environmental wear and tear. Finding a truly complete skeleton in these conditions is beyond realistic expectation. We've done our best." She didn't wait for any additional comments or questions, clearly not interested in hearing what any non-expert opinions were on the matter.

Margot had googled Dr. Ava Langstrom back at the motel the previous night. Ava was a noted forensic anthropologist, and this burial site was practically in her backyard. She was a professor and working researcher at the University of Tennessee in Knoxville, home to the Body Farm, an active research facility where forensic anthropologists worked to study human decay in almost any conceivable scenario. How did burial depth impact the rate of decomposition? Did bodies succumb to decay faster or slower if they were dressed? These were the questions that scientists like Ava set out to learn the answers to.

It was a fascinating if macabre job and Margot was impressed by Ava's credentials. Margot had met other forensic anthropologists in her day, but Ava was one of the preeminent minds in her field. When other experts made their findings with certainty, they were only certain because of the work Ava had done.

Yesterday she had just been another local expert to Margot, someone worthy of respect, but perhaps not awe. Now that Margot knew better, though, she felt awe aplenty.

Ava led them through the thick brush, but this time Margot managed to avoid living up to her Skid Mark non-trail name, and was extra careful to stay on her feet. When they got to the grave site, it looked remarkably different from yesterday.

The four bodies were now free from the soil and had been laid out on four blue plastic tarps, all covered again by another tent to protect them from a probable incoming storm. The skeletons had been arranged in what appeared to be their correct anatomical order.

It seemed like a lot of effort to Margot.

The truth was that, no matter how careful the doctors were in their sorting, unless they did DNA testing on every single piece of bone there was a very good chance that some of the body parts would be mixed up, and, in that sense, remain buried with each other for eternity.

Still, she appreciated that the anthropologists wanted to be thorough, and also give their victims as much of a sense of completeness as possible.

Margot pulled out her phone, noting there was no signal. She didn't need a connection, she just wanted her camera, but it was interesting to know that out here, even if someone sensed there was something awry, that they were in danger, there was no way they could have called for help.

And even if they could, there was no way anyone could get to them in time.

A light rain began to sweep over them, creating a smoky effect with the rolling hilltops around them dense with mist. Margot wondered if this was how the Smoky Mountains had come by their name. The rain was a dampening annoyance, but for the moment not enough to risk damaging the scene, and the skeletons were all carefully covered. The three students, Beckett, Lieberman, and Jones, were diligently working in the soil, each situated in a square of the grid, gently moving earth or sifting soil through a tray with mesh on it.

They were looking for missing bones.

Ava had seemed certain there were no more bodies to be found, at least not where this current grave was located. Margot could see why she was so convinced. The existing pit was already more than six feet deep in places, but beyond that the rocky hillside meant there weren't a lot of additional places more bodies could have been buried.

There would very likely be a need to have cadaver dogs do a full sweep of the Appalachian Trail, but that would be an undertaking that could take months if not years to complete. Cadaver dogs weren't as common as tracking dogs. Not just any bloodhound could do that kind of work, and they were in high demand. And going along the trail looking for old bodies would require overnights in the woods and a lot of strenuous hiking, even if the trail was broken into multiple sections.

It did seem like it would become a necessity, though. The seven new bodies were already getting a *lot* of media attention, and Margot had no doubt that any family who had someone go missing on the trail was calling up the local police right now.

It was only a matter of time before there was a lot of attention back on Holmes—who had long ago been dubbed the Hillbilly Wolfman, a name that didn't engender fear as much as derision— and people would certainly be talking about his crimes.

The pressure was going to be hot and heavy, not just on the local cops but on the FBI, since their presence had already been so widely noted. The public seemed to suffer from a general delusion that simply by being involved the FBI would be able to magically solve everything. While Margot sincerely wished that was true—

and had even suffered from that same misunderstanding to a degree when she was a cop—the truth was that the FBI faced most of the same obstacles as local police.

Sure, they had excellent databases and some of the most skilled agents, but there were still limitations that made everything they did exceedingly difficult, just with higher expectations and even more of a caseload.

There was a reason that the agents in most demand for violent crimes—the team at the BSU, the Behavioral Science Unit—were so backlogged they rarely had more than a day to give their feedback on a single case. If quizzed, most of them wouldn't know if their feedback had helped lead to an arrest or conviction. They simply never had the time to revisit those cases.

Margot and her team had a little more breathing room. They weren't generally up against the clock trying to lock someone away, and they had the bonus hindsight of being able to look at file upon file of evidence of crimes that they knew had been committed by their killer. It wasn't a magic wand, but it was a leg-up, certainly.

Margot pushed her damp bangs back from her forehead. "Were there any belongings or items that might be considered evidence that you've found in the excavation?" she asked.

Ava looked towards the students, all three huddled together in matching khaki-colored Tilley hats.

"Jones," Ava said, nodding a chin towards the most surly of the group, who looked up at his name. If Margot hadn't spent her entire professional life watching people's faces for micro-expressions, she might have missed the minuscule glimmer of delight that momentarily passed over his face.

These three obviously respected the hell out of Ava and were dying for any little morsel of approval they could get. The fact that she had brought the three of them out here instead of any of her other students suggested they were already the favorites, but they still seemed very eager to please.

Margot wondered if it had something to do with the environment and sleeping conditions being more of a punishment than a reward. Field anthropologists must be used to sleeping in tents, but Margot suspected that most modern forensic anthropologists didn't spend a ton of time in the field on overnight visits.

None of them looked like they were going to complain though.

Chip Jones cleared his throat and got to his feet. He seemed perfectly comfortable as he moved over the uneven terrain. It was like watching a mountain goat scale the vertical face of a cliff. Margot wasn't sure she could have been remotely so smooth even if she had been here four days in a row.

Jones guided them towards another tarp, this one a darker green that looked more like part of a tent than a traditional plastic tarp, which explained why Margot hadn't noted its presence yet.

Jones crouched down beside it and then, as if pausing for dramatic effect, he turned his head over his shoulder and asked sharply, "Grace, where is the umbrella? I don't want this stuff getting wet."

If Grace Lieberman was tuned in to the snark in his tone, it didn't seem to bother her. She bounded out of the grave with the same ease he had displayed and returned holding a massive black umbrella. Rather than hand it to him, she stood beside the tarp with the umbrella open, covering anything that might be hiding within.

Grace's expression was stoic as she waited for Jones to lift the tarp. She seemed to be steeling herself for it, not wanting to show any visible reaction.

Jones pulled back the top of the tarp to reveal a small collection of items inside. Margot peered at them. At first, they all just looked dirty and unimportant, but the longer she looked at them the more their individual features started to show themselves, like an image hidden in a magic eye print.

Margot crouched down to mirror Jones, pulling out her phone as she did.

"We can't really determine who all the items belonged to, but in any instance where we noted that an item was located close to a particular individual, we've added a tag with the identifier of the remains. The bodies have been labelled A through G. A was the first body we found at the top, B and C were buried together, the bones were intermingled. It looks like they might have been right on top of one another. D and E were both individual burials, their bodies were found a few inches lower than B and C, but in distinct positions and we believe their own graves, possibly several months or years apart. F and G are another grouping. Based on the placement of the remains we have reason to believe at least one of them might have still been alive when the burial commenced, just due to how the body was positioned in the soil layers."

Margot stared at him, the words making sense but her brain refusing to process them.

"You mean..." Alana began, but couldn't find the right words to go on, leaving the statement hanging.

"It looks like she tried to dig her way up, yes," Jones said, his tone grim, face impassive.

Grace was staring at her boots.

What a horrific thing to have to discover and piece together.

Margot considered the items on the tarp in front of her. It didn't seem like enough. The last remembrances of seven people and it was all contained in five square feet.

Other things might have been taken away by the killer—their packs, most likely, or anything of real value—or there was a chance that errant items left behind might have been picked up by other hikers. While no one on a multistate hike like the Appalachian Trail wanted to add any extra weight to their packs, Margot knew there was a sense of obligation among many hikers to help keep the trail clear of human interference. People would certainly have collected items they felt had been lost or abandoned on the trail to keep them from becoming litter.

The same was likely true of any evidence their killer might have left behind. Holmes had been a notorious tobacco fiend in his day, but sometimes when the chaw wasn't available, he would turn to chewing gum. Any gum left behind thirty years ago would be long gone, and even the wrappers would have been collected by rangers or hikers, or been worn away by time and the elements.

All they had left was whatever had been on or near the victims when they went into the ground. Margot could see one set of tattered clothing, mostly blackened from its time in the soil, which was more hole than it was clothing, but looked to be everything from boots to pants, to a pair of women's underwear and a bra. None of the other hikers appeared to have clothing that had remained intact, so either they had been buried naked or they had been lying in a position in the grave more conducive to the destruction of fabric.

There were two pairs of eyeglasses, both with broken lenses. One was plastic tortoiseshell with a cat-eye frame. Women's most likely. The other were a simple silver wire frame that would have suited either gender. Margot noted that there were two wedding rings, marked F and G: the couple in the bottom grave.

A missing married couple had to have raised some flags.

There were a few metal hiking accessories that had survived. A metal whistle, a compass, the buckle of a belt. There was another ring—this one looked like it might be a school ring, which would probably prove to be very useful helping them figure out who it had belonged to. There were two pairs of earrings, simple diamond studs and gold hoops. A necklace with a cross on it.

And there was a wallet.

Margot stared at the wallet for a full minute, unable to accept either that such a valuable piece of evidence had been left behind, or that it had miraculously survived this long. It was tagged E. One of the middle burial sites. If there were documents inside with dates, it would go a long way to helping them determine when all these people had gone into the ground.

These items would go back down the mountain with Margot and the rest of the team, where they would better be able to look at them without ruining them or damaging any potential evidence left behind. While there was little hope of fingerprints or DNA after all this time, it wasn't an impossibility, and no one wanted to be the person to mess up potential evidence.

Greg took off his backpack, which contained evidence bags of various sizes, and in the cool dampness of the afternoon they began the painstaking process of bagging and labelling all the items the anthropologists had unearthed.

The air smelled of damp soil and pine, and Margot couldn't help but think that, under any other circumstances, this would be a beautiful day to be outside.

SIX

MANY YEARS AGO

Wyatt Holmes always liked the way nature smelled.

Whenever he was stuck indoors for long periods of time, the scent of it suffocated him. Dusty, airless, too many fake human fragrances like perfume, soap, shampoo. Nothing natural in those nature-inspired scents. They cloyed at him, made him feel nauseous, made him long to be back outside.

School had always felt like a chore to Wyatt for that reason. He was forced to be still, to listen, to obey. He liked to imagine these were all things he was very good at in different environments.

He could sit for an hour watching a doe move across a field. He could listen endlessly to the chatter of birds, whose calls changed from day to night, and knew many of their names just based on what songs they sang. He could obey, but only a master who was greater than him, and that was not the case with his schoolteachers.

Wyatt learned very little in school. Nothing there was able to hold his attention, and even when he did catch fractured pieces of the curriculum none of it felt necessary. Why should he learn to multiply numbers? Why did he need to be told his grammar was incorrect? If the teachers and other students understood what he was saying, then why did it need to be *saw* and not *seen*?

No one was learning to set snares for rabbits or how to kill a squirrel with a homemade slingshot. These were lessons Wyatt had taught himself, and, considering he was helping feed his ma and sisters, well, it seemed to make a lot more sense than knowing what nine times whatever was.

He was also keenly aware of the gap that existed between himself and other students. He wasn't the only poor boy in school, wasn't the only one whose ma used food stamps and worked two or three jobs at a time. He certainly wasn't the only one whose daddy had up and left. But the kids like him felt the divide just as much as he did.

He saw the way they looked at his clothes, a bit too big, a bit out of style. Ma didn't pay attention to those things. These were donations from the local church, and she took bigger sizes because the kids would be able to wear them longer.

Wyatt knew she did the best she could. He knew how frustrated she got when he was unruly in class, when he spoke back or didn't speak at all. She finally stopped fighting with the teachers and told them to let him sit after school and think about what he had done.

This, it turned out, was the precise right punishment, because it forced him to be indoors longer. Recesses or lunch breaks forced to sit at his desk instead of playing outside. After-school detentions rather than sitting in ditches looking for frogs, or going hunting in the woods with only his pocketknife—the last thing he had left of his father other than his eyes and his name—and the shoddy homemade slingshot.

He would have fought the devil himself to be outdoors, even if it meant forcing himself to do better at school so they'd stop keeping him.

This was also how he learned not to trust his mother.

Ma didn't understand. She was raised in a nice house, a place where there was always food on the table, and always someone to kiss her goodnight.

Then Ma married Wyatt's daddy and everything kind of went to shit after that for all of them. Ma's parents wouldn't help her because they'd told her not to marry such a no-account hillbilly. But love was often stupid and blind, and, in the case of Ma and her kids, it was also a giant letdown.

Four kids in seven years turned out to be the breaking point for Wyatt's daddy, and they didn't see him again after Ellie was born. He left behind his knife and a note to his only son that just said, *Take care of them, you're the man of the house now*, and split.

Wyatt didn't miss him. He'd been loud and cruel when he was around, and Ma hadn't been all that warm even then. Now she was cold and distant still, but at least she wasn't around a lot to take things out on them.

The bills mostly got paid. They usually had food, even if it was peanut butter sandwiches for a whole week at a time. And she clothed them, even if it was from the stuff that the richer kids in town threw into donation bins.

Meanwhile, Wyatt learned about the woods.

He knew there was no place for him inside a school, inside an office, even inside a house. The only place he ever felt at home was in the woods, his shoes left behind on some rock, the soles of his feet as tough as leather, as dirty as pitch. He could only breathe when the smell of pine was in the air. Could only see when there were trees around him.

It was in those woods, surrounded by the only things that made him feel alive and present, that Wyatt heard for the first time.

He heard their voice crystal clear in his mind, the rough and commanding way they spoke to him. They knew his name, knew what uncertainties lurked in his heart. They understood his wants, the desires that drove him.

They told him he needed to learn to hunt if he could ever be called a member of the pack.

He needed to prove his fearlessness if he was ever going to

belong to them, which was the only place he'd ever wanted to belong.

They wouldn't even let him see them until he had shown that he was ready to do what it took to be a wolf.

And a wolf wasn't afraid to kill one of their own if they needed to.

SEVEN

Margot was the kind of exhausted where she was too tired to actually sleep, even if it was the one thing her body truly needed.

There was a diner in town, and at eight o'clock, after everyone had had time to shower and change, she and the other exhausted members of her team sat in a booth together to peruse the menu.

Andrew was the only one who didn't join them, having begged off to take a conference call, which Margot was sure was a lie. She knew he wanted the team to learn to gel without him, since he would soon be gone.

It was a bit like an overbearing parent hoping his teenagers would learn to do laundry and cook for themselves before college, except his children were all fully grown adults with mood disorders who didn't know how to hold conversations that weren't about serial killers.

At least among themselves they could be at ease, though they had learned over time that what was normal for them was not normal to regular folk, so when they all gathered together in public spaces, they did their best to *not* discuss work.

Margot had changed into her favorite pair of jeans and an over-sized green fisherman's sweater, the long sleeves rolled up to her elbows. Summer was inching closer and the daytime temperatures could get sticky and too warm, but the evenings were quite cool still and the diner's air conditioning had been going full tilt the last few nights Margot had come in to get dinner. She had learned her lesson.

Greg's red hair was well suited to the navy blue henley top he'd opted for. Sydney was sporting a Depeche Mode T-shirt over ripped jeans, her braids twisted into a bun on top of her head. Alana, who joined them last, wore pristine, wrinkle-free eggplant-purple trousers and a cream-colored silk blouse that tied in a bow at her neck. The only allowance she seemed to have made to comfort over fashion were the Oxford-style flats she wore in place of heels. Margot had to imagine her feet were absolutely killing her if she had forgone heels.

The four of them found a booth at the back of the diner, and as a middle-aged waitress with a nametag that read *Layla* brought them their laminated menus, they fell into a contemplative silence. Margot was starving and the food was typical American diner, with twenty-four-hour breakfast options, burgers, fries, and even the overlooked senior favorite of liver and onions. After they'd ordered and Layla had brought their drinks—ill-advised coffees and colas all around—Margot and her team all did the same wary glance over the place, seeing who might be within earshot.

Despite the diner being one of the only games in town in terms of eating out, the place was fairly empty for a Wednesday evening, with most of the other patrons sitting on the other side of the restaurant. They all seemed to universally decide that it was safe to talk shop for the time being.

Margot took the lead. "We have to figure out the best approach to bring these to Holmes," she said, mixing some sugar and cream into her coffee and taking a moment to appreciate the way the cream bloomed across the dark liquid. "He's been notoriously cagey talking to anyone, so I don't want to waste what little time we're going to get with him by sticking my foot right in my mouth."

Sydney sat up straighter and set her Coke down. "I've been reading some transcripts of previous visitations he's had. He's an unusual subject. You can't appeal to his ego, he's just not that kind of killer. He doesn't have a grand sense of self, doesn't need to be fawned over or told he's the smartest man in the room. From everything I've read, I think what Holmes wants most is to be *believed*."

"About the wolf thing?" Alana asked, the only one at the table healthy enough to have ordered plain water, although she did mix in a little packet of electrolyte powder she pulled out of her purse.

"He doesn't fit a lot of the profile," Greg interjected. "No history of abuse, though he did come from a broken home. It seems like he didn't have a close relationship with his mother or sisters, though he has given indication in some previous interviews that he felt obligated to care for them after his father left."

"That can create a sense of animosity," Alana offered, sipping her now pale blue water. "He might not have been abused, but being forced into a caregiver role could have given him residual trauma. It also could have made him specifically angry towards women, since he felt obligated to his mother and sisters. All women."

"His victims weren't all women though," Greg noted.

They paused their conversation as Layla returned with their meals. If she had overheard what they were talking about, she didn't make any show of it. It had to be fairly obvious who they were. The town was small and the news of their arrival had provided fairly big gossip, from what Margot could ascertain. When they had contacted Spencer to help guide them up the trail, it had seemed as if he was already waiting for their call.

They weren't wearing their FBI gear at the moment, but from the glances that kept drifting in their direction, they didn't need to be.

Margot dipped a fry into her ketchup and chewed it thoughtfully. She was sorely missing Wes's home cooking on this trip, but the food here was wonderful, the fries crispy on the outside, pillowy inside, the smash burgers so juicy and flavorful. There weren't a lot of benefits to being on the road as much as the team was, but one of them was certainly coming across good local food.

She couldn't eat like this all the time, but with all the hiking they'd been doing the past two days it wasn't like she needed to worry about it.

"Holmes was an opportunistic killer," Sydney said. "He hunted what prey was available."

Alana wobbled her hand side to side. "Yes and no. While he didn't have a particularly strong victim preference, I wouldn't say he's a traditional opportunist. An opportunist most of the time is someone who will take any victim they come across. If he was a true opportunist, he would have just hung out at a single spot on the trail and waited for whoever happened to come along. But based on what we've seen, and even what he's admitted to in the past, that's not how he would usually work. He would stalk specific victims, often for dozens of miles, more than a day or two at a time, just to wait for the right moment to strike. That's really focused work."

Sydney's expression was briefly annoyed; she seemed to take Alana's correction personally, and Margot could sense the mild beginnings of an animosity forming there. It wasn't something that they could allow to ferment in their environment. Alana was a profiler; she had worked directly with the BSU. Sydney had worked in Cyber Crime before moving to their team. It wasn't that Sydney was *wrong* about Holmes, because she wasn't—it was just a matter of finding the language that worked for both of them.

Margot felt like she needed to be a peacekeeper, lest Sydney harbor ill will towards Alana going forward. That would be especially dicey if Alana was chosen as the new team lead.

"You're not wrong," Margot said to Sydney. "He's a subject who bucks the trends we typically look at for killers. He's purpose-motivated, even though we might not psychologically understand that purpose. What it means is that he believes someone else is guiding his selections. So in that sense you're both right. He is able to stalk victims over long distances, but as to who becomes a victim it is really all a matter of chance. Do the wolves speak to him or don't they?"

"But that's all still him," Greg said earnestly, as if they weren't aware of the difference between reality and schizophrenia.

"I know," Margot said, smiling softly. "But he doesn't."

Alana pointed at Margot, picking up the argument like it was just a fun thought exercise they were working through. "That presumes that his auditory hallucinations are legitimate, and not something he's using as a cover." She was apparently not picking up on any of the tension she had caused; Alana was very frequently unaware of the emotional damage she left in a wake behind her.

"I don't think he's Son of Sam-ing this, Alana," Margot countered.

"We won't know until we talk to him, and even then, who knows? He's been pretty convincing up to this point."

"What makes you so sure he's faking it?" Margot darted a quick look over at Sydney and was relieved to see her posture had changed. It was no longer so rigid, so uncomfortably stiff. The annoyance that might have become anger had faded into something else as well, more of a curious interest in the debate Alana was engaging Margot in.

They'd been a team for a long time, but sometimes it took even longer for people to learn not to take everything so personally.

Greg had learned that lesson early in his FBI career when his penchant to get obsessive about his areas of study got him slapped with "Gory." But since moving to this team he had become a deeply respected agent, and even though his awkwardness hadn't faded at all, he was much more confident in himself, and didn't seem to worry about any barbs he might get from anyone else.

Sydney, who had only been joining them in the field for six months despite her years working in the unit, still seemed to feel like she didn't fit in. She was making strides, but she was going to need to learn to be a little less serious when the situation called for it.

Alana didn't argue just for the sake of argument, it seemed to be one of the ways she worked on her thoughts, the way some people spoke out loud. It wasn't uncommon for her to seem passionately committed to an idea one moment, only to change her thinking entirely after a brief and heated discussion.

Margot wasn't sure if this was one of those situations or if Alana believed that Holmes was faking.

"I think," Alana said, a speared piece of chicken-fried steak balanced on her fork as she poked it in the air to make her point, "that people with secrets are very good at doing whatever it is they need to do to protect those secrets. Berkowitz had a lot of people convinced he was talking to a dog. I don't see how this is different. Hell, it's not even that original. Wolves. Dogs. Same difference. Holmes saw what worked and realized that if he just laid out his story and stuck to it, no one would doubt him, he'd just be one more crazy motherfucker behind bars." She popped the piece of steak into her mouth and gave a little *I said what I said* shrug.

"I think someone who worked four years in the BSU knows better than to pigeonhole anyone as a *crazy motherfucker*," Margot countered patiently.

"Are you kidding me?" Alana said with a laugh. "That job made me an expert on the topic, and that's largely because almost everyone who works there is probably a crazy motherfucker, too."

"If you're the rule and not the exception, I would believe that wholeheartedly. But I don't like to make generalizations." Margot ate another fry, then looked at Sydney. "You've been reading all the interviews, what do you think? Is he genuine or is he faking it?"

Sydney seemed surprised to be brought into the discussion. Sometimes, as the older agents on the team, people deferred to Margot and Alana, but the truth was Sydney had been with the FBI longer than Margot. So had Greg. While Margot was a big fish in their very small pond, she wasn't all that important in the grand scheme of the FBI. She wanted to remind Sydney and Greg that their contributions mattered just as much as hers or Alana's did.

"He's steadfast in how he talks about the wolves and their influence on them. I had a forensic linguist look at some of his phrasing from over the years to see if there might be something that would indicate a changing story or a lie he might get caught in, but there's nothing there. His language hasn't changed since the day he was arrested." She pushed a heavily breaded chicken finger around her plate, seemingly lost to her own thoughts as she explained her position. "All the evidence seems to suggest he's genuine in his belief."

"It is interesting," Greg added, like the thought had just come to him, "that he doesn't seem to show any other signs of schizophrenia. Even the way he stalked his victims was organized and methodical, not something you'd usually see from someone with the condition. And his memory is *excellent*—he had almost perfect recall of his entire childhood."

"According to him," Alana said. "We have little to go on from his family, since they haven't been the most forthcoming."

"Hard to blame them," Margot said quietly.

This seemed to bring a temporary lull to the conversation as everyone realized the weight of her words. She was the only one at the table who knew why a family might not want to get involved with cutting open old wounds just for the sake of a little more insight into a killer. She knew all too well how hard it was to be someone who loved a monster, and how that shaped how the world looked at you.

Had they known?

Why didn't they stop him?

Were they monsters, too?

These were the questions that haunted the families of killers. And while certainly cases existed where the family were involved, intentionally helping to hide the crimes or even participating in them in some capacity, Margot knew that most of the time the revelation of who their loved one truly was, was an even harder blow for those who knew him best.

Because it made them realize they hadn't known him at all.

Margot felt guilty for the silence, but she couldn't help her history. There'd been a time she'd hidden the truth of who she was from almost everyone. She'd changed her name so she could leave

Megan Finch, daughter of Ed Finch, behind her. She'd lost weight, gotten a nose job, moved with her family to a place no one knew her. But the truth was, no matter what changes a person made, there was no way to leave who you were completely in the past.

Margot had learned that hiding who she had been was actually harder than accepting it. A lot had changed for her over the past six years, and she was grateful that, even though the conversations could be awkward, she didn't have to lie to anyone.

She was about to give the conversation a nudge when the little bell over the diner door jingled. A police officer, his dark coat slick with rain, glanced around the room, then spotted them. He gave a quick nod to Layla behind the counter before he headed right in the direction of their table.

"Evening, folks," he said with a nod, taking his hat off, water droplets falling to the tile floor.

"Hello, officer," Margot greeted him, since she was one of the people closest to him. This wasn't one of the police officers they had met while they were doing their initial information gathering when they'd arrived. It wasn't a very big town, but it was evidently big enough for more police than they might have thought.

"I'm really sorry to interrupt your dinner. I know you folks have an awful lot going on right now, but I was hoping I might be able to bend your ears for just a moment."

Margot exchanged a quick glance with the rest of the table, but none of them seemed inclined to say no, so the ball was left in her court.

"Of course," she said. "What can we help you with?"

"Well, see, I'm from Browning, just one town over, and the police chief here said you folks specialized in cold case homicides?"

"We do," Margot said calmly. This would hardly be the first time a local police officer had asked for their help when they were visiting somewhere. The BSU, when available, had a massive backlog of cases, and not every small-town jurisdiction knew how to ask for that kind of help, or indeed thought they were justified in asking.

It was a lot easier to seek out help from a real person who you could explain your troubles to face to face.

"See, about a year ago we had this homicide, real ugly business, all the local leads dried up real quick. Then it was the darndest thing, and we don't know if it's connected, but about a month ago some hunters came across a bucket buried in the woods, and it was filled right up with some pretty bone-chilling things."

The rest of her colleagues showed only passive interest, but Margot pivoted in her seat so she was facing the officer. She pulled out her phone and scrolled back several months until a shock of orange on the screen told her she'd found what she was looking for. She turned the phone towards the officer.

"Did that bucket look anything like this?" she asked.

He took the phone gently, looking at the photo on the screen, then his eyes widened and he looked back at her, more stunned than a deer in the path of a Mack truck.

"Yes, ma'am. I reckon it looked almost exactly like that, right down to the bucket itself."

They stared at each other for a moment, then Margot said, "I'll help you."

EIGHT
MARCH 2025

Northeast Tennessee

The man didn't like to come this far east all that often, though it was funny how places like Kentucky and Tennessee didn't feel like they were east. There was a general slowness to life in those states that reminded him of his early days in Missouri. Sticky-sweet summers, friendly people, a general sense of warmth that you didn't frequently find other places.

People were kind to a fault.

Trusting to the point of lunacy.

It was places like that he could still find unlocked doors at night, and people might flag a passing car down for a ride if it was too hot or rainy. That kind of openness was delicious to him, but it was a double-edged sword.

The reason people were so willing to trust was because of the sense that they knew everyone around them. Because of that, outsiders were far more likely to stand out and be noticed, which were two of the last things he wanted for his purposes.

In the cities, people were harder, but the hunting was easier. It was a trade-off, so he never did the same thing twice back to back. Once he finished in a city, he'd find one of his treasure troves, leave behind anything that wouldn't serve him, and take what he would need for the next trip.

There were long breaks in between, as well. A necessary evil.

He'd been home for close to two months after his last stay on the road, making sure everyone saw what a good and doting family man he was. He was attentive to his wife, showering her with his time and energy in a way that exhausted him to his core, but it would also go a long way towards ensuring she never asked too many questions when he was gone.

As long as she knew he was coming home, and he would take care of her, the rest was largely incidental. She'd be mad at him in the future, he knew. He'd overstay his time away, and she would feel forgotten, abandoned, and the cycle would start over where he would stay home, dote, fawn, and build up the trust again so that he could start planning where he'd make his move next.

He'd thought about Nashville, a city he'd never worked in before. It seemed like a fine place for a man to get lost, and an ideal place to find people who weren't paying enough attention. But that was where an idea could end up becoming a problem. Because he couldn't just nab a drunk girl off the streets. That sort of thing drew a lot of focus. People panicked when a person went missing from a busy tourist area. They looked at security cameras, they asked witnesses if they'd seen anything.

While the hunting was fertile, it was also dangerous.

Likewise, hunting in a small town had its risks.

The thing about doing what he did was that there was never a safe or easy way to do it. There were risks. And part of what he enjoyed the most about it was that he consistently outsmarted those risks. Maybe that was a cocky thing to think, but he hadn't been caught yet. No one had ever asked him a single question about any of the work he'd done.

Back at home, people thought he was a pillar of the community. Loving husband and father. His job allowed him the flexibility to work from anywhere, while his wife believed his job was the *reason* he had to work from anywhere. It all worked exactly as he needed it to.

The town he'd picked tonight was a little blip on the map called Browning. Somewhere he—and most other Americans—had never heard of. He'd be willing to bet that even most Tennessee residents wouldn't have been able to find the place on a map.

It was in an interesting position, just a stone's throw off the I81, with proximity to the North Carolina border, but not all that close. The kind of town that used to be right on an old main highway before the interstate was built, so that it had slowly started to dwindle from being a hot spot for travelers to stop, to a place people needed a reason to visit.

Amazing what shifting infrastructure could do to an entire community.

What it meant was Browning was a big enough place that not everyone knew everyone's names, and they had people coming in from the interstate to get meals or stretch their legs with a little shopping, but it also wasn't *too* big.

In the eternal wisdom of the Three Bears, it was just right.

If he was careful enough, smart enough, he could wait for a solo traveler to come in, someone who was unknown to the town, but also unlikely to raise alarms right away if they went missing.

Someone he could take a credit card from to use for a few days.

Someone to take the edge off.

It was a good place for it, plenty of folks heading to hike parts of the Appalachian Trail, or coming to or from more interesting parts of the state like Pigeon Forge, home of Dollywood.

He rented a motel room, paid cash and used a fake name. Places like this, they didn't care. A night's room payment mattered more than whoever was staying in the room. He could understand why they wouldn't lean too heavily on rules, because the room was a piece of shit. There was old wood paneling on the walls, and art that had probably been picked up at a thrift store and had already been outdated in the 1970s. There was a faintly musty smell to the space, and the ceiling tiles were stained. But the room was clean—

as clean as a space like that could be—the sheets, while yellowed with age, smelled of laundry soap, and the shower had been wiped down recently.

He could appreciate that there was a difference between old and disgusting, and this place was more toward the former. He'd slept in worse places for sure, though, so this would be a suitable option to rest his head when he did his work.

He decided to walk from the motel to a nearby gas station with a restaurant attached, a good place to scout for people who were born to just pass through. The night was cool, late summer, and though the bugs were bad during the day, at night they seemed to vanish almost entirely. He actually liked the feel of the breeze on his skin, the sounds of light night traffic and a lone owl somewhere.

It was at night he felt his most free, at ease to be what it was he was meant to be. He liked the way he blended into his surroundings at night and became something no one was looking for or expecting. Something no one would ever see again.

He felt especially suited to this place on the cusp of the Appalachians. This was a place steeped in folklore, something so many parts of the country had forgotten. This place, they told you not to whistle at night, and not to look too deeply into the trees. People here still believed in skinwalkers—otherworldly monsters who could mimic any form, albeit in a way that felt just a little wrong—and they were careful of them.

And what was he if not a little bit wrong? Something that should be avoided at night. This was a good place for him, he could feel it in his bones.

The motel was a short walk from the town's largest gas station. There were a few semis in the lot, an RV, and a handful of cars with out-of-state license plates.

He headed to the restaurant and ordered a burger, then started to watch.

Because of its habitual use as a place for truckers to stop, the gas station had an area at the back where they and other weary travelers could pay a few bucks for a private shower stall to get themselves cleaned off. From where he was sitting in the restaurant, he could see people come in from outside, and could watch those heading down the hall to the shower.

That was how he knew the girl was alone.

She was probably in her early twenties, plump, tired-looking, and after she went to the shower, he scanned the lot, looking for a likely car. There was a little Honda parked on its own, and even from where he was sitting he could see how loaded it was with items.

So she was either homeless, or doing some sort of coming-of-age road trip across the country in her car.

He tried to gauge how visible the car was from where the trucks were. It was also visible from the restaurant.

Risky.

But he did love a challenge.

NINE

A trip to Browning, Tennessee, hadn't been on their agenda, but as there had been no new discoveries on the trail, and their next stop would be Nashville in two days, Margot felt like the detour was warranted.

And once she explained what she'd found in her own town only six months earlier, her colleagues agreed.

In the fall, after the murder in her hometown, people had been looking everywhere for someone to blame, and that blame had fallen on Wes. While Margot—and almost everyone else—now knew without question that Wes wasn't guilty, the question of who *had* killed that girl still hung over the town like a dark cloud.

Six months and they were no closer to learning who had really done it.

There were, Margot knew, still people who thought it might have been Wes, but it was a minority small enough to keep them from being run out of the county. And evidently small enough that Wes no longer needed to worry about his job.

But Margot had made a frightening discovery; one that seemed to point to their killer being someone much scarier, and likely more prolific.

What Margot had found in the woods between her home in

Elk Creek and the nearby town of Willows had been—to put it lightly—harrowing. She had never seen anything like it before, and never expected to see anything like it again, except now she was looking at a nearly item-for-item identical piece of evidence, and she felt so nauseous she thought she might throw up.

She and the officer, whose name was Ryan Gibson, were in the Browning Police Department's largest meeting room, which she guessed was where they had their full squad meetings. A folding table had been brought in, and Margot was standing beside Gibson at one side, while the rest of her team, as well as Gibson's boss, Captain Donnie Adducci, were clustered around the opposite side, looking on as spectators.

Captain Adducci didn't seem too thrilled by the FBI's arrival, but Gibson had spoken to him privately, their tones hushed and serious, and by the time the conversation was over the captain seemed to have grudgingly accepted their presence. It was surprising to see someone that far below him on the totem pole exerting so much influence, but Margot assumed that Gibson was no stranger to pushing to get what he needed. In a case like this one, in a *place* like this one, things could get messy fast if the officer in charge wasn't willing to advocate for themselves and their victim.

Adducci and Gibson were a study in opposites. The elder was pale, balding, and looked like he had been cut from an old postcard depicting Wild West sheriffs, with his large belt buckle—surely not uniform standard—and paunch that rested just over it. He had piercing blue eyes that cut right through Margot whenever he happened to look in her direction.

Gibson, on the other hand, was young, handsome, and Black. His hair was in a close-cropped Afro, his brown eyes were warm and imploring. He was probably thirty at most and, while both men sported wedding bands, there was something about the way that Gibson touched his from time to time that gave Margot an idea that he was more happily married than his boss.

After long enough on the job, a person couldn't stop profiling others, even if they didn't intend to.

Gibson made Margot feel welcome, needed. He wasn't afraid of women. With Adducci, Margot wasn't sure if it was her gender or her employer that bothered him more, but he hadn't cracked even a hint of a smile since they'd arrived, and he seemed far more inclined to speak to Andrew than to Margot, even though she was the subject matter expert in this scenario.

Margot was wearing blue latex gloves, but even so she hesitated to touch any of the objects before her. The notion of a kill kit was nothing new in her line of work. During one of his brief moments of talkativeness before he came back into her life, her father had told prison officials about the kit that he used to take in his car with him from scene to scene. It contained at least one knife, but usually more, because his whims and favorites were constantly changing depending on what new items he'd collected from garage sales and pawn shops. He also had rope, duct tape, and in his later years an Exacto knife to help him cut through window screens without dulling his beloved knives.

Ed Finch kept his kit light, not a lot of bells and whistles. Whoever had made the one in front of Margot was an entirely different kind of monster. *Too showy*, Ed's voice said at the back of her mind. *What is this asshole trying to prove?*

What, indeed?

The kit, contained in an orange Home Depot plastic pail with a latching lid to match, was unlike anything Margot had ever seen in her years as a homicide detective, and now her time as an FBI investigator.

A standard kit was to help a murderer prepare for one specific event, usually even a specific victim. This, though, this was like someone had created a one-stop shop for anything they might ever need to commit a homicide.

The empty ski mask staring back at her from the table was a taunt.

"I assume you've checked the mask for hair? DNA?" She lifted it gingerly, looking into the empty eyeholes as if they might offer her answers, but instead they just left her feeling uneasy, like she was being watched by someone she couldn't see.

As if the mask's owner was able to look at her even now.

"Nothing there," Gibson said. "As best we could tell it has never been worn, it's just... there."

"Just in case he needed it," Margot said.

Or maybe he wants you to think he's the kind of person who hides away, when really he's not. Maybe a smile is a much deadlier mask than any cheap black knit could ever be.

She wished she could tamp Ed down, keep him out of her thoughts, but there were times she had to admit he had a point.

"What if he's hoping we find this?" she asked, looking over all the items before her.

Handcuffs, zip ties, a vibrator—also so clean she figured it was right out of the box—gloves, tape, several knives, two boxes of bullets, one for a shotgun, one for a handgun. Several empty plastic zipper bags, the larger ones. There was absolutely nothing about the bucket or its contents that gave away any personal details about whoever owned it or had buried it. They'd been careful; Gibson had already confirmed that not a single fingerprint had been found on the bucket or any of the objects inside.

So whoever buried it had known there was a chance someone would uncover it. But if it was anything like the one Margot had found, it wasn't placed in a way that invited discovery.

He didn't want them to find these, but he wanted to be prepared in case they did. This was a meticulous man, a man who planned.

And they had now found these buckets on opposite sides of the country.

Of course, there was the possibility it was more than one killer, organizing, mimicking each other. But Margot knew killers, and paired or grouped ones were exceedingly rare. The fact that the kits were so identical, it went beyond just checking items off a list, it was someone collecting things unique to them. Each kill kit was as unique to its user as fingerprints.

Margot tried to imagine the effort that went into creating and stashing these kits, and it defied reason. The amount of planning, the sick, twisted obsession to build and bury identical kits across the country. That spoke of the mind of a methodical and terrifying man. How many more of these were out there? And what purpose did they serve? Was he just putting them in the ground in the hopes of one day having a reason to use them? Or were they all evidence, only evidence he had cleaned too well to be useful to them?

The answer, she suspected, was somewhere in the middle.

"You have a victim that you think goes with this?" Margot asked.

"We do," Gibson said. He turned to the counter behind him and grabbed a large beige and brown banker's box. He managed to find room on the table and opened the box, then handed Margot a blue binder that was sitting on top.

Below that she could see bits of clothing, other bagged items of evidence, but she wanted to look at the meat of the case before she started to pick at the bones.

She stepped away from the table, giving her team members a chance to look at the unpleasant diorama on the table and start discussing among themselves what they thought it meant. Margot heard Alana say *coordinated killer*, which was a generally outdated term within the Bureau but certainly fit here better than just about anything else the DSM might try to pin on this guy. Because he *was* coordinated.

Freakishly coordinated.

Her father's MO was to stalk an individual woman for days, even weeks. He knew they were single, typically, because they had placed personal ads with the paper where he worked. That was how he got the name The Classified Killer. That level of planning was not atypical for most serial killers. Some were more chaotic—they would just go out with an intent to kill and hope someone suitable would come along. Men who waited for someone to just be the victim they needed in that moment.

She sat down in one of the hard, plastic chairs facing the front of the room and flipped open the binder.

The victim's name was Ariel Van Wick, and, as Margot looked through the file for a picture of her, she wondered: did she look like Whitney?

She wasn't sure where the question came from, but as soon as it entered her brain it made perfect sense. Why else would that kit be so close to Willows, if not because the person who buried it had made use of it?

Was Whitney his first?

Was Ariel?

No, Margot assumed his first kill had happened before he'd become organized. Something happened with that one, something that almost got him caught, or brought the police too close for comfort, and it spooked him. It didn't make him give up what he was doing—very little short of death or prison could stop a serial killer—but it was something he had learned from.

Be careful or they're going to get you.

Be careful or you'll have to stop.

So, he had created a way to keep doing what he loved, what he craved, but in a safer, more controlled capacity. She had no doubt that Alana was going to have a field day dissecting what that kit said about him as a person, but to Margot it wasn't the contents that told the story, it was that it existed at all.

He couldn't take what he needed with him. Why? Did he have someone in his life he needed to hide things from? A wife, a husband? While statistically speaking it was unlikely a gay man would target female victims, there were always exceptions to every rule. Serial killers didn't read the checklists about how they were defined. They didn't care.

Still, Margot felt confident this killer was unlikely to have a husband. A wife, though, that wasn't out of the question. She knew all about how those relationships worked. But her father had felt confident enough to often leave his kill kit in the trunk of the family car.

Her mother had never noticed.

It's funny, the way those things sound in retrospect, but it *was* possible for a family to have no idea they were living in the same house as a killer. Because if there was one thing psychopaths were skilled at, it was learning to lie, to blend in, to make sure no one saw them as abnormal.

Margot flipped through the pages of the Van Wick file, looking at the autopsy report, the crime scene photos, with the detached lens of someone who saw this carnage on a daily basis.

The girl didn't look like Whitney, at least not superficially. Whitney had been slim, blonde, and pretty in a high school cheerleader way. Ariel was on the chubby side, round cheeks and belly, her hair was brown, and while in Margot's eye she was definitely a pretty girl—especially in the file photos where she had been alive— she wasn't the cultural beauty standard.

The wounds on her, however, felt like a visit from a familiar but unwelcome relative. The slash across her lower abdomen, the cut all the way up between her ribs. Bits of intestine loosed from their comfortable housing, spilling out onto the grass.

The exact same wounds she'd seen when she'd gotten a look at Whitney's file. This man was looking for something, but Margot still didn't know what that was. He was... exploring? Was that even the right word?

"She wasn't assaulted?" Margot said, phrasing it like a question even though she suspected she knew the answer.

"No, we were surprised by that."

Margot wasn't. She knew the thrill for a lot of these guys *was* sexual, but by the time they were this good at what they did they no longer found that gratification in penetrating their victims. At least not that way. Oftentimes they actually couldn't. It wasn't uncommon for a sexual sadist killer to be triggered by actual sexual acts because of performance impotence, something they would blame on their victims or women in general.

Margot wasn't sure if this guy was a sexual sadist though.

She didn't know him well enough yet.

She continued to flip through the file, but all it told her was what she had seen. They had evidence they suspected was related to the homicide, but couldn't tie to it directly. And they had a young woman in her early twenties who had been on a road trip following the death of her father—her only close relative—when she had made the wrong stop, talked to the wrong man, done one thing that led to her life ending.

No one had reported her missing until she failed to contact her pet-sitter at the end of the month when she had been scheduled to return.

She had paid all her bills through summer so she didn't have to think about it while she was away.

Margot tried to imagine her, a young woman grieving, trying to find herself after a loss. Those were shoes that Margot herself had walked in. After her father's arrest, it had felt in a lot of ways like he had died. The idea of him that she'd had for fifteen years *was* dead. Now he was dead for real. The grief of that first loss had been much harder than when his physical body was gone.

Though perhaps one of the reasons for that was that she had been the one to kill him.

But Ariel, she had lost a real father, someone she probably cared a great deal about. She had been on a trip of discovery, of moving on, and had paused her whole life at home to decide what would happen next.

What had happened was the wrong place. The wrong time. The wrong man.

Margot tried her best not to get attached to victims on a personal level, but something about this girl tugged at her heartstrings.

She shut the binder with a *snap*, drawing the attention of everyone at the table. When she stood, she found it hard not to keep touching the blue book, her fingers nervously tracing patterns on the cover.

"There's no hard evidence connecting your victim to this bucket, so what makes you think they're part of the same case?"

Gibson gave her a stoic look that said nothing at all. "Ma'am, with all due respect, we get about twelve homicides a year in Browning, and that's a bad year. Most of that is related to brawls at the one bar in town. Otherwise, it's domestic. Now, I don't mean to offend you, but we just aren't used to seeing death the way you are. And when I see something like *that*"—he pointed to the binder— "and *this*"—he nodded at the bucket—"well, it don't exactly take a genius to figure out there has to be a connection. Especially when they're found one month apart."

"How far apart?" Sydney asked. When everyone looked at her she cleared her throat and clarified. "How far between the crime scene and where the bucket was found?"

"Twenty miles, give or take."

This brought silence to the whole table. It wasn't an ideal scenario. One was not a smoking gun for the other, and it also wasn't a good blueprint to help find other cases that might match the MO.

Still, without thinking or consulting anyone else, Margot tapped the blue binder with her nails and said, "We'll take the case."

TEN

They had come to Browning in two cars, one driven by Margot, the other by Andrew, so on the way back to their motel the only person whose sharp focus Margot needed to deal with was Alana.

In retrospect, she wished it was anyone else. Alana was too smart, she saw too much. It made her brilliant at her job, but impossible to keep things on lockdown with. Profiler brains never quit.

"You think it's the same guy from that case last year, the one with Wes."

She already knew this much. Margot had needed to explain her hunch to get them to tag along to Browning in the first place.

"I do."

"Were the connections as slim there?"

Margot pursed her lips. There was nothing accusatory in Alana's tone, but it was still a hard truth about this case. The threads were so flimsy they might not have existed at all. But Margot's gut told her this was the same man. That they had a serial killer who had worked in both California and Tennessee; and she wanted to chase those spiderweb-thin threads as far as she could.

"If anything, there was probably even less connecting the case in California. Just a body and a hunch. But it's the same as it is here, it's just not a place you see violent crime like that."

"And the evidence in your case, it was just as clean?"

The case in Willows had never been hers. Because of her connection to Wes, any direct involvement she might have had in the investigation would have been viewed as a huge conflict of interest, so she had stayed away. Well, she had stayed away to the extent she was capable. But after the FBI did get involved, she'd been given an opportunity to look at the files. She knew exactly how similar their victims were.

"The evidence was clean, there was nothing we could find to point to someone who had done this. But Alana, before you think I'm crazy, those victims were killed in the exact same way. Down to the slice mark. I wouldn't be chasing this if I thought it was just the buckets. That alone is weird, but it's just... buckets. Their victim and the one in California, I know the same man killed them both. I don't have even a sliver of doubt."

Alana was quiet for a moment, looking out the window at the dark shapes of trees passing by. The road back to the motel was mostly backroads. They could have taken the interstate, but it would involve backtracking, and even now Margot still got anxious on busy highways. She would go out of her way to avoid interstates wherever possible. The part of her brain that looked for negative outcomes everywhere just went into hyperdrive on a highway.

Plus, she had seen *Final Destination* 2 when she was in her twenties. She had the same healthy fear of log trucks that all millennials did.

After a long pause, Alana spoke again. "Tell me why."

Margot glanced over at the other woman, whose white-blonde hair looked almost blue in the reflected light off the dash. "Why I think they're the same killer?"

"Yes."

"Is this a test?" Margot's brow creased. They'd worked together for six years. Before that, Margot had worked SFPD Homicide for over a decade. She'd solved the Redwood Killer case, for crying out loud. She'd recognized those murders were connected long before anyone else wanted to believe it.

Alana smiled softly. "No, Margot, it's not a test. I believe that *you* believe the cases are connected. I have no doubt that your instincts are good. But there's also a personal connection to one of these murders, and I just want to talk it through with you so we're both a hundred percent sure that this is something we should be working on and not something in which you want there to be a connection so that we can further prove Wes is innocent."

Margot shot her another quick look. She felt like she'd just been punched in the gut and wanted to retaliate, but that wouldn't have made her a popular person for the rest of the drive. Instead, she tried to look at things from Alana's perspective. It was something her therapist had told her to work on whenever she felt defensive, rather than retaliating in anger, or her other forte, sarcasm.

Being an emotionally well-balanced human being was fucking hard work and she didn't always want to put in the effort. But she also didn't want to be harsh with Alana. Especially, she thought after she considered it for a moment, because the other woman was right.

It wouldn't be out of the question for Margot to see a connection where there wasn't one simply because she wanted to be able to point somewhere else—anywhere else—and to say to the people in Elk Creek and Willows, "Look over there! The real monster!"

Wes was, as far as Margot could tell, totally fine. He had his job back, people at the school were still friends with him, still invited him to social events, still talked to him outside school hours. The kids, for the most part, still felt the same way about him as they had beforehand. The other girls on Whitney's softball team had been steadfast in their support that Coach Fox would never and could never have hurt any of them.

A few other kids seemed to take an opposite approach and double down on the rumors, but there were going to be dickhead kids in any school environment. That was the thing about human beings. Shitty adults had to come from somewhere.

She took a deep, calming breath before she replied, and was

proud of how steady her voice sounded when she did. "I know my personal connection to one of the cases might cast some doubt on my credibility, but do I need to remind you that the entire reason I got this job in the first place was because of my ability to compartmentalize my personal and professional lives?"

"Margot..." Alana reached over and squeezed her hand where it was placed on the wheel. Her skin was so soft and smooth it should have been a tactile ad for whatever hand cream she used. She pulled away after a second. "I don't doubt your ability to compartmentalize. But not everyone knows you. Other people are going to ask questions. They're going to ask Andrew questions about why FBI resources are going to this case. We will have to have answers, and that's going to fall to you. So just think of me as the friendlier version of some future prosecutor who is going to have these same questions."

Margot's jaw developed a tic.

Dealing with lawyers was something she didn't miss from her police days, and it was something they only handled rarely in their current line of work, since it was usually local law enforcement handling those things after their investigations were over. But sometimes she still got called to be an expert witness, and she had never learned to like it.

She wasn't sure Alana was being entirely truthful with her, but she decided to swallow back whatever retort she might have made and answer the question like it was coming from a place of genuine care. Maybe it was.

At times like this she missed working alongside Wes. Wes would have just accepted her bad mood barbs and rolled right along with them. Perhaps that was the reason they were still together six years later.

"I think we can both agree," Margot began stiffly, "that if we looked at these things separately, we wouldn't be in a rush to connect everything. The two buckets—yes, that's a connection, no doubt—but they aren't immediately obvious as being connected to the crimes. I can completely agree with that from an outside point of view."

Alana nodded but did not interrupt, for which Margot was grateful.

"Then we look at the murders. The victim profiles are somewhat similar, but not identical. I'm sure if we were to dig into the specifics of each victim, we'd find that, beyond their physical appearance, they likely have very little in common to connect them. Age and gender are not typically enough for us to call something a thread."

She could feel Alana's gaze where it was aimed at the side of her cheek, but she didn't look over. She would rather finish this as if she were performing the speech to an empty room.

"But the manner of death is remarkably specific and almost identical in these two young women. And I think if you couple that with the buckets both being found in such close proximity, the smart profiler would find the same connection I did. Because we either have two killers working the exact same regions across the country, or these cases are connected. And I think it takes a lot more of a mental stretch to turn this into two killers than to make the much shorter leap to these murders both being done by the same man, the same man who buried those buckets."

Alana was quiet for a while, either considering Margot's words or just letting there be a silent moment between them. Car headlights drifted by, but the road was relatively empty, for which Margot was grateful. She didn't like driving at night—it forced her to admit that her eyesight wasn't what it once was, which forced her to admit she was older than she once was. All of it wound into an interesting uneasiness about mortality that she hadn't really considered before.

For a long time, she had spent all her energy worrying that she might lead a killer right to her door, but now she spent her time thinking about aging. For some reason it had never occurred to her until then that it would be something she would need to worry about.

After a few beats, Alana said, "I think you're right, and I think you've got the right reasons for believing it."

"You know, despite the fact that I have a little bit invested in this personally, I am capable of being objective."

"I know."

"Then why push me?" Margot darted a quick glance at Alana, who was no longer looking at her.

"Because I wanted to make sure *you* knew."

ELEVEN

While the new case in Browning was nagging at Margot for her attention—it was certainly where she would prefer to spend her time—the reason they had made the trip to Tennessee was so they could speak to Wyatt Holmes.

It was time to pay him a visit.

Although Margot's entire job was predicated on her ability to speak to serial killers, it was easily the thing she hated the most about her work.

People she worked with or spoke to about her career often assumed that because the first serial killer cold case she had worked in this way, via interview, had been her father's, anything after that would be a walk in the park.

That wasn't how it worked in practice. Yes, on one hand it was a lot easier to talk to killers she wasn't personally related to. But on the flip side, she didn't have a pre-established connection with these killers either. For all the complexities there had been in working with Ed Finch, at the end of the day he was her father, and she knew how to push his buttons.

With new killers, it was a learning curve each and every time. She had to find ways to get through their barriers, to get them to talk to her, and sometimes it felt like running a marathon, only with her mind.

She knew Holmes was going to be an especially difficult egg to crack, as well. Sometimes killers wanted to talk, even if it was to spout bullshit, or plead a case for innocence, or try to barter for some kind of benefit. The latter, Margot found, was usually an easy in to get them to start opening up. A few extra hours outside, maybe more time in the library, or whatever might appeal to someone who had to stare at the same four walls for the rest of their lives. They wouldn't give any kind of financial incentive. No gifts, no money applied to a commissary account, nothing like that. But the FBI could sometimes negotiate little incentives for the killers to get them to chat.

Holmes wasn't going to be that kind of killer. He didn't want to talk to anyone, and had been notoriously tight-lipped over the last several years. He felt he'd been burned in the past when some of what he'd said had been used against him to make him look foolish. Margot suspected he didn't appreciate that no one seemed to believe him.

So that was going to be the first thing she tried.

Believing him.

She'd reviewed her notes on Holmes thoroughly before coming, so everything about him felt fresh in her mind, including all the details of how he had finally been caught. At the time of his arrest, there were twenty-eight suspected murders linked to him. When he'd been arrested, the FBI and local law enforcement had felt there was a very real risk that he might choose to take himself out as well as anyone coming to arrest him.

FBI's SWAT team had been mobilized, flanking that little cabin in the woods as the arresting officers moved in.

Holmes found the SWAT team first. He had crept up behind one of the sharpshooters and lain down next to him, a freshly killed and skinned rabbit nestled in the grass between them. He'd said, "I suppose y'all were going to find me sooner or later."

While the sharpshooter had damn near shit his pants, Wyatt

had turned out to be unexpectedly docile. The only thing that unnerved the arresting team more than his calm demeanor was the ear-splitting howl he let out before they were able to tuck him into the back of a squad car.

He said, later, that he'd been letting the pack know he was leaving.

In the ten years that Holmes had been in prison he had been a model citizen, but he was also a confusing case study. Those with delusions like his were often making them up as a way to make their crimes look like a by-product of insanity, but psychopathy didn't mean a person was insane. For an insanity plea to actually work—which they rarely did—the onus was on the defense to prove that their client didn't know the difference between right and wrong.

Holmes had very nearly done it, because almost every single therapist he'd spoken to since the time of his arrest was adamant that his delusions were very real to him.

He believed he was chosen by the wolves that roamed the hills near his home.

He believed those wolves told him to kill people, even going as far as to tell him who to kill and when, and how to leave their bodies.

What ultimately put Holmes in a prison cell instead of a permanent padded room was that he did know it was wrong to kill other humans. This was another consistent fact that had come up through interviews with his therapists. They all asked if he knew what he'd done was wrong and his words, exactly, were, "It's wrong in your world, I'll admit that. But it's not wrong in my world, because it's what they want me to do."

It seemed clear that Holmes worshipped the wolves like gods, and believed he was proving himself as an honorary member of their pack—as wild as that story was, he never strayed from it.

Of course, there was one major problem with Holmes's story, no matter how staunchly he stuck to it: there were no grey wolves in Tennessee.

There were red wolves, but the population was so sparse that the species was among one of the most endangered in the world. There was no evidence from wildlife experts in the area that a red wolf population had ever lived within any reasonable distance of Holmes's cabin.

This just further emphasized the defense's point that he was mentally unwell, but it was a lingering question mark that had never allowed the case to sit quite right with those who had picked it up after the sentencing had been handed down.

Was Holmes crazy enough to believe he'd been speaking with wolves who didn't exist? Or was he just an incredibly convincing and gifted liar?

Both options seemed equally plausible.

Today she was hoping to find out which was true.

Riverbend Maximum Security Institution had a lovely name, which was about the only thing it had going for it. It was a squat collection of grey two-story buildings in an expanse of land so boring that even those who got to look out a window every day probably wished they couldn't see it. Tucked into a bend of the Cumberland River, it was ostensibly in Nashville, but the way a stray cat was in a house when it was sitting on the porch looking in forlornly from the outside.

It wasn't a part of anything, really; with the John C. Tune aviation airport cutting it off from any easy access to anywhere, it was a little blight in the land, as hidden from the glitz of Nashville as possible.

Margot's only note of praise for the place, aside from the name, was that it was much easier to get to than a prison like San Quentin. When she was finished with Holmes, she'd be a stone's throw from Nashville hot chicken and a bed in a real hotel for at least the next two nights.

The latter was definitely what was getting her through this interview.

The prison on the inside was about what she expected. Antiseptic cleaning supply scents that barely managed to cover the odors associated with hundreds of men pissing and shitting and sweating inside the same concrete box.

Most of the interviews Margot did were face to face in a segregated room, where guards could look out for her safety and she was able to get a better connection with the killers. But Riverbend was different. They wouldn't let her use one of the family rooms to meet with Holmes, and insisted the best she was going to get would be a standard guest meeting space where she and Holmes would have to speak by phone and look at each other through glass.

Margot had only had to do this once or twice before, and it usually indicated either a staff shortage of guards, or that something had happened recently in one of their in-person meeting spaces and they were worried about an incident involving a federal agent.

Margot didn't love doing her job through barriers, but she also didn't mind having the peace of mind associated with there being a thick sheet of plexiglass between her and a known serial killer.

And given the situation, it meant she would be doing all this by herself. There was nowhere for the rest of the team to set up and observe, and adding too many unnecessary eyes to the discussion would probably make Holmes balk immediately.

Now it would just be her, her words, her memory. And that would need to be enough to get them what they needed.

The fluorescent bulbs overhead managed to be both too bright and too yellow, giving the entire prison a headache-inducing sallow tint, like in movies when a lazy cinematographer wanted to indicate the action was happening in some random third-world country.

The combination of the smells and the light was enough to make Margot feel the pinch of a migraine blooming behind her eyes. She hoped she'd be out of here before it started to really sink its teeth into her. She had some decent medication for migraines, but she hadn't been allowed to take her bag into the prison.

A guard showed her into a narrow room lined with individual beige booths, each with an old phone on the wall, and a long sheet of plexiglass lining one wall. Margot thought most prisons had phased these kinds of meeting spaces out for more high-tech options, but it seemed Riverbend was a bit behind the curve on that. The whole place felt like it was trapped in the sixties, so she probably shouldn't have been surprised.

The room smelled mostly of Windex, which of all the cleaning options she'd gotten a whiff of so far was probably the least offensive. She let the guard show her to a cubicle, and then he left her. The cubicle was meant to make her feel more secure, protected from Holmes, but instead it gave her an uneasy, nervous feeling. Normally she'd be seated at a table with her subject, guards nearby to act if anything went wrong, but in this scenario, she felt as if the distance made Holmes scarier than if he was sitting with her.

To date, she'd never had an issue with physical violence. Sometimes the killers would say things to her, intimate a certain level of threat, but they were locked away for life. Margot was good at not reacting when a serial killer tried to suggest he was going to gut her in her sleep one night. It wasn't a real worry, just... one of those things.

She glanced up as a guard opened the door on the other side of the glass with a muffled buzzing sound, and in walked Wyatt Holmes.

Margot had seen photos of him, she'd watched footage of his trial, she'd seen previous interviews that had been recorded—interviews that didn't take place behind a glass partition—yet somehow, there was no real way to prepare herself for the Wyatt Holmes experience.

He was a monster of a man, not just metaphorically. He towered over the guard, which might have been why, despite the partition, he was still shackled at the wrists and ankles. Even through the glass Margot could hear the rattle of his chains. She was surprised they hadn't put the Hannibal Lecter mask on him with all the precautions they were taking. There was nothing in his file to suggest he had ever injured a guard in the past, so she wasn't sure what to make of it beyond the guards just being intimidated by the sheer magnitude of Holmes.

He was at least six foot eight, which really didn't register in photos or video clips. The guard, who was probably a very normal height, looked almost like a child beside him. His hands were absolutely massive. The cuffs, Margot mused, must have been ordered specially for him, because she doubted the standard size would latch around his wrists.

He had long brown hair, a little on the frizzy side and greying at the temples. It was pulled back into a low ponytail. He had a beard now, something she hadn't seen on him in the past, a salt-and-pepper number across his lower face. He looked as if he had just traded biker leathers for an orange prison jumpsuit.

Or, more accurately, he looked as if he had just wandered out of the wilderness, having never seen the modern world.

He sat across from her, chains jangling, and fixed her with a cold stare.

Killers didn't all have dead eyes. She'd met a few who might even convincingly be considered charming, whose expressions were warm and inviting. People who seemed normal. But then there were guys like Holmes, who she took one look at and knew there had never been anything even remotely normal about them. Their eyes lacked any kind of warmth or humanity.

Her stomach churned uneasily and she resisted the urge to look away.

Holmes stared at her for what felt like a full minute before he lifted the phone from its cradle—it looked like a child's toy in his hand—and jerked his chin towards Margot to indicate she should do the same on her side.

She did as she was meant to, lifting the receiver to her ear and cradling the phone against her shoulder as if she was in junior high school and about to settle in for a good long discussion with her best friend about the newest episode of *Friends*.

It was too intimate a gesture. She, like most of her generation, hated making phone calls. Being seated across from the person she wanted to speak to, but also forced to use a phone, felt like a personal affront to her.

"Good morning, Mr. Holmes," she said.

"You can call me Wyatt if you want to," he replied, and the deep rumble of his voice was astonishing, even if she should have expected it from a man his size. The pitch was so low, she worried she might not be able to understand it because her ears simply didn't work at that frequency.

"Wyatt, my name is Margot Phalen, I'm a special agent with the FBI."

He grunted. He would have already known who she was, since he had to agree to the interview ahead of time. Her title didn't impress him. She was hardly the first FBI agent to ever sit across from him.

"Do you know why I'm here?" she asked.

"Don't like to guess. Gotta be about the murders though."

She suppressed the urge to laugh. She found it interesting he would call them murders. Given his committed stance to the killings being a ritual he had done to appease the wolves, it seemed like a strange way for him to phrase it.

We always know what we did, her father's voice said in the back of her mind. *Just because we don't see it the same way you do, doesn't mean we don't know what it is.*

Margot shoved that nagging voice down. She knew it was just something her brain did to cope, perhaps a way for her to make peace with what she had done to Ed. At the end of the day, whether or not he had it coming, even she had to admit it was emotionally damaging to have killed her father. She knew it wasn't really him, but that didn't make the voice any less his.

It was uncanny, really, what the subconscious was capable of doing.

Wyatt Holmes was the monster she needed to focus on at the moment, the man sitting in front of her, looking stoic and as immovable as the mountains where he had hunted.

She needed to get him to talk, but the setup was frustrating.

The glass wall and the phone gave Holmes more opportunities to create distance between them. If they'd been able to sit down face to face, she would have been better able to get him to see her as a person, someone he could open up to.

Instead, she was half a body framed by grey walls, and with the phone pressed to her ear she probably looked like she could have been talking to anyone. This was no way to form a connection. She was going to need to plead her case to the warden before they came back tomorrow, because she knew other people had met with Holmes without these precautions. She was worried that they had done this because she was a woman, which was ludicrous.

She put the thought out of her mind, because even if it was true, she couldn't do anything to change that in this moment.

Margot locked eyes with Holmes. "I went for a hike earlier this week," she said. He didn't look away, but his face betrayed no emotion whatsoever. He didn't answer her. "Out on the Appalachian Trail."

Again, he remained quiet. She hadn't asked him a question, after all, and it seemed like he wouldn't be inclined to give her anything until she pried it out of him.

Fair. She wasn't much of a giver herself, conversationally. People had learned to draw talk out of her, so she had a firsthand awareness of what might work for him. But it would be a slow and steady marathon to get anywhere, not a sprint.

"I thought about you when I was in the woods," she told him. "It was hard not to. There were so many places a person could hide unseen. It would be so easy to be there and watch, wait, without anyone knowing you were there. That has to have an element of power to it, doesn't it, Wyatt? Knowing that you can see them when they can't see you?"

He mulled this over for a moment, but the question was there, something waiting for an answer. For all his other faults, Wyatt Holmes had been raised to be polite, especially to women. Margot knew that from the very few interviews with his family, of the people who'd known him when he was young.

Such a polite young man.

As if *pleases* and *thank yous* and *yes, ma'ams* could stave off a killer instinct written in his blood.

He scratched his beard and considered his answer for long enough it almost felt like he wasn't going to say anything at all. Finally, he cleared his throat, his grip tightening on the phone for a fraction of a second in a way that made Margot's mouth go dry.

"It's not about power," he said gruffly. His voice was rough, raw, like he rarely had an opportunity to use it. "That makes it seem like a game."

"But it is a hunt, isn't it? And what is a hunt if not exerting your power over someone else? Or the thrill of the chase?"

A thin smile crossed his lips, and it would almost have gone unseen amid the thick hair of his beard if Margot hadn't been watching him carefully. It wasn't a happy smile. There was almost something pitying about it.

"You don't understand. Most people don't, it's okay, it is what it is. I've tried my best to explain it, but no one listens."

"I want to listen, Wyatt. Tell me what I've got so wrong."

"I didn't do what I did for fun. Wolves don't hunt for fun, they hunt to survive. That's what I did all of this for, survival."

Margot wanted to call him out on the absurdity of that statement, but reminded herself that Wyatt Holmes wanted the world to believe that wolves had told him who he was meant to hunt. That his actions were meant to connect him to the pack.

"Lone wolves rarely survive in the wild," she said, watching his face carefully.

There it was, just a momentary glint, something alive and eager that flashed over him, and she saw the way it made him soften into his chair, like he was no longer primed to walk out of the room.

He nodded.

"That's right."

Margot knew this was what she had needed to get an in with him. That by speaking to him like she believed him, he would open up more. It wasn't hard, she realized, to take this approach.

Because she got the feeling even in a few short minutes with him that this was a man who was sick of people talking to him like he was crazy.

And that didn't mean he *wasn't* crazy, because if he had killed those people for the reasons he had indicated, then he was likely a raging schizophrenic or something along those lines—Margot was not a psychologist and could not diagnose him after a five-minute conversation—but it gave her a good place to start. If his belief was genuine, it didn't matter if the wolves were real, because they were real to him, and that was what mattered the most in this discussion.

If he believed it, then Margot needed to know, not why Holmes had killed the people they'd discovered, but the answer to a more interesting question: why had the wolves told him to hide them? All his other victims had been found either at their campsites or not far off the trail. There had been no efforts made to bury them, and rarely any efforts made to cover them at all.

They were, effectively, gifts, left out for the wolves.

It didn't matter that the wolves were never the ones to find them, but rather horrified hikers, exhausted from a day of trekking.

"Tell me," Margot said. "Tell me how they spoke to you." Her voice was filled with earnest curiosity. She imagined when most people asked him this question there was an air of disbelief or mocking. *Oh, the wolves spoke to you? Tell me how, then?* That wasn't what she was aiming for here. She truly wanted to know how this worked for him.

Holmes regarded her carefully for a moment, his dark, empty eyes boring into hers like he might ferret out any ill intentions just by staring at her. It might have worked on someone else, but Margot had looked into eyes like those across a dinner table, then across a prison dining table, for most of her life. She wasn't easily intimidated. And from the contemplative way he looked at her he seemed to realize that her question wasn't a patronizing or mocking one. He scratched his beard with one hand, and his silence stretched on so long Margot began to wonder if he was going to answer her at all, but then he cleared his throat.

His voice when he spoke again was rough, and Margot got the sense he was a man of few words given the option.

"It's not a voice, so much," he began. "It's a *feeling*. I can feel them, in my heart, in my bowels, in my blood. They're just a presence that is always there with me." He smiled, mostly to himself, as if this was something that brought him immense comfort. The same way some people talked about Jesus.

Margot could honestly say she'd never been comforted by anything in her bowels. Either they went unnoticed, or they bothered her, there was no in between. She wondered, vaguely, if that was just his unusual way of saying he could feel it in his gut, the way people often spoke of innate feelings that defied logic.

If so, he was a more unusual man than she had previously estimated.

"How did you know it was wolves?" she asked.

Holmes closed his eyes, his chin lifting towards the ceiling and that same faint self-satisfied smile on his face. He looked for all the world like a man on a beach vacation, basking in the glow of tropical sunlight on his skin.

"You ever hear things in your head, Special Agent?" he asked, his eyes still closed.

"Sure." She wasn't going to elaborate on this. "I think everyone does."

"And you know that voice you hear, it's yours, right? Even when there are no words, you implicitly understand who is steering the ship."

"Most days," she said.

He opened his eyes to look at her, making sure she wasn't making fun of him. When he saw her smile, he smiled back, in on the joke. "Most days." He gave a soft chuckle. "I like that."

"I think I understand what you're trying to say," she urged. "The way I go around knowing that I'm the one making my decisions, you understand that what's guiding you isn't you, it's them."

He straightened up and Margot was reminded of just how huge a man he was. Intimidating and overwhelming, even with the plexiglass between them. She fought the urge to push her chair back. She needed to stick with this. She couldn't afford to show him that he made her at all uneasy.

It wasn't that she was afraid. There was nothing for her to be scared of. But the same way Wyatt Holmes believed wild animals guided him through his daily life, there was a part of Margot that wanted to keep herself safe, and that part—almost as animal as Holmes's wolves—didn't like this one bit.

Fight or flight was very real, even when the circumstances didn't call for it.

Margot had read somewhere that the human body was still wired for self-preservation in the way it had been when people were still hunter-gatherers. The inner workings of the human psyche understood stress as a threat; they hadn't gotten the memo that things like car payments and arguments with co-workers were not the same as being chased by a lion.

The body simply wanted to get away.

It was the reason people who ran and exercised when they had been in a stressful situation felt so much better. They had tricked their body into thinking they had escaped the threat.

Margot's body and animal brain were doing their own inaccurate threat analysis right then, and they were telling her she was awfully stupid for staying in the chair.

She wiped one sweaty palm on her pants.

"Wyatt." She had to clear her throat and try again. "Wyatt, I want to ask you something very specific, and I'm hoping you can help me."

"Okay," he said, cautiously, but at least he was still speaking.

"I need to ask you about a grave we found."

He was silent, staring at her again. She worried she might have moved to this topic too soon, but after a moment he issued a grunt.

"Which one?"

TWELVE

Margot's mouth went dry. Of all the things Holmes could have said to her in that moment, of all the revelations, confessions, denials, of any words he could have uttered, those were the two she hadn't prepared herself to hear.

"Which one?" she said aloud, before realizing she should have just kept her mouth shut. She'd given away her own ignorance, which was never a good foot to start these interviews off on, because it let him know that there were things she didn't know.

But if he was willing to admit there were more graves than she knew about, then that meant he might be willing to share details.

All was not lost.

She pushed past the lump in the back of her throat and kept her expression as relaxed as possible. She'd come here to find answers, and it looked like she might get more than she bargained for.

"How many are there?"

She'd been around so many killers at this point that she half-expected a sinister smile to cross his lips, like the smugness of him knowing something she didn't was too much for him to keep in check. But she was slowly starting to realize that Wyatt Holmes was not always going to fit the mold established by other killers.

He considered her question, his expression stoic and thoughtful. He was unlike any other killer she'd known. They all had their own unique quirks, but typically they fit into certain patterns. Those patterns were what allowed her to get a read on them quickly, and give her the best approach to talking to them.

She was having a hard time figuring out what Holmes's patterns were. They didn't make sense to her, at least not in the context of his killings. Margot was going to need to let go of all her preconceived notions about the makeup and demeanor of a serial killer when it came to this man. She was going to have to start from scratch.

"I didn't do it often," he admitted. "It didn't seem right, to hide them. That wasn't the point, after all. I wanted to make sure their scent carried on the wind so the rest of the pack could find them."

"But sometimes you buried them."

"Sometimes."

"Why, what was different about those ones?" This wasn't necessarily relevant. Mostly, she just needed to know if these new bodies they'd discovered were connected to Holmes, but part of what made her good at this job was digging deeper, asking more, being curious. That curiosity could often pay dividends.

Even when it didn't, it saved her asking herself those *why* questions down the line and kicking herself for not voicing them when she had the chance.

He might not even have a reason, but at least she would have asked.

"Some of them were spoiled," he said, his nose wrinkling in response, like he had just smelled something disgusting. Margot's own nose itched in response to the gesture, like a silently transmitted yawn. She rubbed her nose without thinking.

"What do you mean by spoiled?" Surely he couldn't have meant they were already rotting. There was no way he was revisiting the bodies that frequently. And leaving an unburied corpse out on a well-traveled hiking path was a pretty quick way for it to be discovered before he could come back and bury it. So he meant something else. Even the way he'd said the word *spoiled* seemed like it had a loaded meaning.

He regarded her again, and she knew she would never get accustomed to those long, silent stare-downs. He was looking right through her, right to the meat of her, like he was trying to figure out the easiest way to get flesh from her bones. To eat her alive.

There had never been any indication of cannibalism in Holmes's case, but that didn't change how he was making Margot feel.

It took everything in her power to hold his gaze and not squirm. She typically felt more confident in an interview room, and wondered if, perversely, the security of the glass was making her lose her edge. Maybe she *needed* to feel a little bit afraid of these men if she was going to do her job right.

If that was the case, the look he was giving her now should only help.

"Have you ever opened a carton of milk, and before you even taste a drop of it, you know the whole carton has gone bad?"

"Sure," she replied, though groceries never went bad in her house anymore thanks to Wes. The man didn't know how to waste food. She hadn't always had her life together, though.

"Same thing is true of people. Sometimes, you take one whiff, you know they're rotten to the core."

Margot could relate to this idea. She did know how it felt to recognize that someone was no good almost immediately, though for her it was a prickling sensation under the skin rather than a smell. She figured it was her gut telling her to watch her back, and her gut was rarely wrong. It used to try a bit too hard to tell her she was in danger, but if caution was safety, she'd been the safest person she knew.

"Why didn't you just leave those people alone, then?" she asked. "If they were no good to be food?"

"It's not just about food. When a lone wolf threatens a pack, that wolf must die. If there are people out there who are rotten, why would I leave them to spoil the earth with their presence?"

Margot mulled this over for a moment. It was an interesting concept, but teetered a bit too close to playing God for her taste. Of course, in a sense that was what all killers did. They took who lived and who died into their own hands, often gleefully. She didn't expect that a man like Wyatt Holmes would recognize the difference between playing wolf and playing God. Especially not when the wolves mattered more to him than any religion ever would.

Margot had been able to bring in with her a few photos that had been taken at the grave site. They had been approved by the prison, so no one would freak out at her for sharing them.

Some killers loved to see their old work, while others reacted quite poorly to the reminder. So far, Holmes had seemed generally ambivalent to reminders of what he'd done outside. After speaking with him today, Margot had a better idea of why that was.

He didn't seem to view his killings as murders; he looked at them more as an offering. A means to an end with his chosen—albeit imaginary—pack. Margot had been suspicious of this alibi before, but, even in such a short time with him, his sincerity was evident to her. He believed what he believed and didn't care if anyone else bought into it.

She held up one of the photos of the grave, showing all the skeletons still in place. There were bits of gear from the anthropology students littering the edges of the dig site, but it mostly just looked like an open hole in the middle of the woods.

She was hoping the arrangement of the bodies, rather than the grave itself, might help jog his memory, since the woods were the woods and it would be hard for anyone to see exactly where these bodies were from just one photo.

Somehow, though, she thought he would know.

He scooted closer, leaning forward in a way that made her want to move back, but she chided herself for being silly and held her ground. Holmes squinted, taking in the scene.

"You have more?" he asked, his tone flat.

Margot set the photo down and pulled up two more. One was a closer shot of how two of the victims had been stacked. The other was a photo of the items that had remained on the bodies. Even if he didn't recognize the scene, he might at least see something there that sparked recognition.

His expression gave nothing away. He sat back, scratched his face.

"Not sure," he said finally. "I think I'd need to see it for myself."

Margot snorted. This was a classic move, something she'd heard before. They wanted to show the FBI additional sites, but could only do it in person. They could lead them to a body, but only with a hall pass. Margot was almost disappointed—she had thought Holmes was better than that.

"Sure, we could do a video call." She held back her smirk, because this was usually where the backpedaling started.

Only once had Margot seen a convict successfully argue for their temporary release to help take the police and FBI to hidden bodies.

That man had been her father, and that excursion had ended in his death.

Since then, no one on their team had determined any case to be worth the hassle it caused to get a guy out of prison for the day. They'd started offering video calls instead, and when they heard that suggestion guys stopped asking. Sometimes they would shut down completely, while other times they would find new things to ask for.

She wondered what Holmes would choose.

"That could work."

Margot was surprised. He didn't fight, didn't huff, just shrugged it off. It threw her for a loop.

"Did anything in the photos look familiar? That was an awful lot of bodies in one place," she said, hoping to urge him towards an admission.

"It was. Not really something I did. But maybe I was lazy. Maybe I was in a hurry."

"Some of them were partners. Two people together."

His lips pursed into a thin line. "No, that doesn't sound like me."

This wasn't entirely true, as he had killed at least one couple that they were aware of. But it wasn't his standard MO, that was true.

"You're saying you don't think this is your grave site?" she asked, barely able to keep the incredulity out of her tone.

Holmes shrugged. "Been a long time. Anything is possible. Doesn't look right, though. Not for me."

Margot pushed the photos into a small stack, staring at them as if they might give her the answers that he wasn't. Some kind of sign that he was lying, that this was his work.

Unfortunately, much like with his conviction that the wolves spoke to him, she found she believed him in this, too.

"Well, fuck," she said, unable to stop herself.

"You'll find them," Holmes said, scuffling his chair back loudly, which brought the guards back in to collect him. Before he unfurled to his full standing height, he looked her dead in the eyes and said, "I know another hunter when I see one."

THIRTEEN

Margot usually felt better when she left a prison, but today she brought the heavy, ugly feeling of the place with her back to her rental car.

I know another hunter when I see one.

It was a little too close to things her father used to say to her, intimations that there was more of him in her than she wanted to believe. Ed's voice in the back of her mind was silent at that moment, letting her stew on Holmes's words all on her own.

He'd give her a smug *I told you so* later, she had no doubt. He always broke through when she needed to hear him the least.

She sat in the car for a long time, keys clutched in her hand, her phone still secured in the glove compartment. What had Holmes meant by that? She'd watched other interviews with him, read other transcripts. He'd never said anything like that to anyone else. If it was a ploy to make his story more convincing, he would certainly have tried it on someone else long before Margot. He had nothing to gain from her by fucking with her head like this.

What was worse, as she played it over and over in her head, she realized he'd meant it as a compliment.

She gagged and opened up the water bottle she'd left in the car. She took a long gulp of warm water. Even in the depths of fall,

Nashville was surprisingly hot. Sweat beaded on her forehead and she finally yielded to discomfort and started the car, letting the air conditioning cool her down and help her focus.

The words had rattled her, but the implication of them was much worse. Holmes was suggesting that this burial site wasn't his at all, which meant—if true—that there was an entirely different killer who had frequented that section of the trail, one who either had never been caught, or had never been tied to those murders.

Which meant Margot and her team were going to need to start from square one and treat this crime scene with different eyes. Instead of looking at how it could be Holmes's work, they would need to look at it and profile an UNSUB—unknown subject in BSU-speak—they didn't know.

Square one wasn't a place they were used to starting from, since most of them weren't in the habit of exploring unknown killers anymore. They might need to loop in the BSU on this one. She was getting ahead of herself, though. The first thing she needed to do was get back to the hotel and debrief the team on what she had learned during her interview with Holmes. Once she got through that, deciding what came next would no longer be in her hands. She was more than happy to hand it over to Andrew.

Before she could drive, though, she needed something.

She pulled out her phone and dialled Wes. It was during the school day, and she wasn't entirely sure when his free periods were, but he answered on the third ring.

"Hey, you," he said warmly, though she could sense the caution in his tone. He was worried about her. She didn't usually call him in the middle of the day.

"Hey. I just wanted to hear your voice."

"How'd the interview go?" he asked.

"About as good as they all go," she said, though this wasn't true. Some interviews were such successes she felt like she was high when she walked out of the prison. Today, she felt like someone had driven into her with a semitruck.

She had trouble explaining the good days to Wes, though. The euphoria that came from a job well done. It was equally hard in this moment to put into words just how deflated her interview with Holmes had left her.

"You get what you went in for?" he asked, seeming to understand how to ask the perfect question without prying.

"No. Maybe. He says it might not even be him. Implies there could be another killer out there."

"Do you believe him?" Wes's voice was hushed and she could hear kids laughing in the background, a pop song blaring.

"You're busy, I'm sorry."

"Nah, they're running laps for the next fifteen minutes, you're golden, kid. I always have time for you. So answer me. Do you believe him?"

"I think I do."

"Well then, there's your answer. Your instincts are unlike anyone else's I've ever known, Margot. Trust yourself. I know whatever this guy said to you put you on edge, but you're the smartest person I know when it comes to understanding how these guys think. If you think he's being honest, then see where that takes you. He's not going anywhere, you'll have other chances to talk to him if it turns out he's full of shit. See where your instincts lead."

"And what if that means looking for another killer?" she asked.

There was a pause. She knew he was thinking of the unsolved homicide that had happened practically in their own backyard. The one she now believed might be tied to the murder in Browning. God, she hadn't even had a chance to tell Wes any of that yet. It could wait, she decided. She wanted to share that in person.

"Margot," Wes said quietly, his voice firm. "I can't think of a better person on this goddamn planet to find a killer than you. Go do what you're best at."

She breathed in sharply through her nose, as if she could inhale his confidence in her. He believed so unequivocally in her skills, and if she just let herself feel that, she almost thought she could get a grasp on this case.

"Thank you," she said after a long pause. "I don't know what I'd do without you."

He chuckled. "You'd be just fine without me. You're a tough bitch."

She snort-laughed. "A tough bitch who couldn't eat at restaurants on her own for twenty years."

His voice took on a more soothing quality when he spoke again. "But look at you now. I didn't do that. You did that."

Margot felt her flash of confidence wane. She wasn't sure if he was right, not this time. She knew that a lot of what she'd overcome *was* something she had done on her own, and she had been helped a lot by the death of her father. With Ed Finch no longer walking the earth, it suddenly felt like a safer place to be.

But Wes had been the one who taught her that it was okay to trust someone else. That it was okay to love someone and believe they wouldn't hurt you.

"All right," she said finally. "You convinced me. I'll go solve a murder. Or seven."

"Attagirl. And when you're done could you bring home some Nashville hot sauce?"

Margot let out a laugh, one that shook her ribs and made the dark cloud lingering over her head vanish, at least for the time being.

"Yeah. I can do that."

FOURTEEN

Talking to Wes helped Margot's mood immensely, but it also made her wish he could be there with her. The team she had was wonderful and smart, but she often missed her detective days, when she and Wes could bounce ideas off each other and find the bad guy together.

She still bounced ideas off him, even if it wasn't exactly allowed, but it wasn't the same thing as having him by her side, poring over case notes or playing good cop, bad cop in interview rooms.

Her bad-cop surliness didn't work the same with Andrew sitting next to her in interview rooms. Or when she was on her own. She missed the gentleness Wes's presence offered that tempered her own volatility.

She got back to the hotel and immediately headed to Andrew's room, which was on the same floor as her own. She wanted him to know what she had learned, but also, she just couldn't stomach the idea of being alone with her thoughts another minute longer.

He answered immediately and let her in without questioning her presence. Since it was meant to be a quiet day for them—everyone was reviewing notes or checking emails while she was at the interview—he was wearing a pair of jeans and a soft-looking gray sweater.

She noticed that his salt-and-pepper hair and beard were significantly more salt than pepper these days, something she had barely even noticed as it happened. When did they all start getting old?

He looked as put-together as ever, though. His beard was neatly trimmed, his tortoiseshell glasses sitting low on his nose like she had interrupted him in the middle of reading something.

In his room there were two double beds. Both were made, and one had an assortment of papers spread out on it, including print-outs of new photos from the burial site, and old burial sites of Holmes's for comparison. The small desk built into the wall had his laptop open and the caddy under the TV where the small coffee maker was hidden had been pulled out. The only sign of a mess in the whole room was a room service tray shoved to one side of the desk, which held the remnants of his lunch.

He pushed his glasses up and gestured for her to take the desk chair, while he sat on the end of the bed. It was a subtly considerate gesture, rather than have her sit on his bed and feel awkward.

"So, how did it go? I was expecting you to call when it was wrapped up."

She nodded. "I needed to sit with it a bit on my way back."

Andrew said nothing. He had a way of just quietly observing that often felt as assertive as an interrogation. She'd seen people crack under the weight of his stare without him having to ask a single question. When she had been fifteen, that stare had been a mighty thing.

But Margot no longer cracked under pressure. Pressure had molded her into something stronger.

"I hope that means he gave you something useful."

"Him personally? That's hard to say. He isn't a particularly chatty man. And he wanted to come see the site in person."

Andrew rolled his eyes. "Of course he did."

"But the funny thing about that is that, when I shot him down and offered the video link, he didn't seem to mind. He didn't argue or insist."

"That's certainly different. Do you think there would be any value in trying to get him a temporary release?"

Neither of them wanted to do this. It was rarely worth the effort and cost, especially going into such a remote environment where Holmes knew his way around so effortlessly. It seemed like a recipe for disaster.

It also wasn't necessary, as far as Margot could tell.

"I don't think he did it," she said at last.

Andrew absorbed this information slowly, sitting back slightly on the bed. Another person might start to fidget or pick up the papers from the other bed just to have something to do with their hands. But not Andrew. He crossed his arms and pushed his glasses back up his nose, as they seemed insistent on slipping down.

"What makes you say that?"

Margot tried to find the words that would explain the feeling that lived inside her. It wasn't a simple thing, boiling down gut instinct into a single sentence. "He was almost too curious about it, like going out to see the grave site wasn't about visiting something he had done, but more like it was wanting to see how another hunter—another wolf—went about it." She didn't mention what Holmes had said, about seeing a hunter in her. It didn't feel relevant, and she was still embarrassed by it.

Andrew considered her words and nodded.

"All right. Let's have the team work both angles. I don't want to drop the Holmes possibility entirely, not just because the MO doesn't match perfectly. Killers can change. But let's start working some alternative angles, and let's revisit the crime scene photos and video with the eye to it being an UNSUB rather than assuming it's Holmes."

Going back to the studs with this case was going to be a unique experience for the team, as they were more accustomed to working with *known* killers.

Margot was grateful that Andrew hadn't pushed any further,

that he'd trusted her enough to believe her instincts. It would take more time and resources to approach this from two angles, but at least they would know they weren't missing anything.

She didn't want there to be another killer, but she also didn't want them to be so blindsided by the devil they knew that they overlooked someone who was still walking free.

FIFTEEN

TWO YEARS AGO

The man liked to be aware of his surroundings.

Always know your exits, always know who might be watching.

If a building had security cameras, there were easy ways to tell if they were real or fake. He never let himself be immediately turned off by a camera, because it wasn't always a sure thing that it would be trouble. It often was, but he'd found that recently a lot of places just used fake ones hoping that would be enough.

He preferred to perfect his hunting ground rather than looking for ideal victims. In his experience, the victims would find their way to him once he figured out an ideal location. He had spent years finding places that worked, leaving behind what he needed, and then coming back when the time was right.

Truck stops with no cameras and low weekday traffic.

Motels in the middle of nowhere where they still took cash and didn't care if you filled out a guest card.

Towns where things were half-abandoned and an air of decay about them, places where people up and left without anyone noticing.

Those were the kinds of places he loved.

But he was also no stranger to picking heavily populated, busy places, which created natural blind spots.

He knew places where bus depots only had stick-on cameras from Amazon. He checked out local halfway homes, shelters, and the in-between places people went when they left prison but before they started their attempts at a new life.

College campuses were getting harder, but the sports bars near them were as easy as ever.

The problem with cities was that he had to come prepared rather than rely on a stash, which meant more planning, more frustration if a victim didn't pan out.

He hated wasting his time.

He sat in a car outside a women's shelter, one eye on the clock, the other on the front door. He knew from past observation that this place had a set nine o'clock closure, and if the women weren't in by nine, they would be locked out for the night, a gate rolled into place. It didn't matter if their things were inside or not, didn't matter what excuses they made—he'd heard a fair bit of hollering on past visits—there were no exceptions to the rule.

His gaze scanned the street. No one seemed to be heading in the direction of the shelter. He was parked in a dark lot, no cameras nearby, only a few cars brave enough to take the risk. No businesses nearby to wonder why someone was willing to sit in a car for over an hour just watching a building.

This was the kind of place people minded their business.

He liked places like that.

The clock on his dash switched to nine o'clock and he watched as the shelter attendant came out the front door. She looked up and down the sidewalk, a generous allowance to see if anyone was on their way, and, when she saw only empty streets, she pulled the heavy gate closed and locked it.

The gate gave him pause. Was it connected to an alarm system that would automatically open it in case of a fire or emergency? There had to be at least two exit routes, otherwise the women inside were sitting ducks.

It was, admittedly, an idea that appealed to him, but also one that didn't make much sense. There certainly had to be other ways out of the building.

This was just musing, though, because he had no interest in going inside the shelter.

He waited about five more minutes, then he spotted her, a woman running down the sidewalk, her open jacket flying, having slipped off her shoulders, her hair in a messy, dark ponytail, a grocery bag dangling from one arm. Her desperation was evident.

He knew there was a bus that was supposed to stop up the street about two minutes before the shelter closed. If he was a betting man, he would guess that bus had been running about seven minutes behind schedule.

He rolled down his window so he could hear the frantic slap of her shoes on the sidewalk, the rattle of the gate when she came to it and realized it was already locked.

He listened for her plaintive cry, or her swear of disbelief, but neither came. Instead, she kicked the gate once before sliding down to the ground, her grocery bag slumped over beside her. With her jacket slipped down to her elbows, her bare shoulders were exposed. She would start to feel the cold soon, and from there she would begin to wonder what kind of options she had for tonight.

He started the car, headed away from the shelter, then rounded the block and approached it from a different direction. When he pulled up beside her on the curb, she initially didn't acknowledge him, and when she did it was with a wary glare. This was a woman who had been hurt before and didn't trust easily.

"You get locked out?" he asked, his voice warm and friendly.

"Yeah," she said, swiping at the tears that had slipped down her cheeks. This close, she was younger than he had expected. Maybe nineteen, barely twenty if she was. Her cheeks were still round, and even with her world-weary glare she carried that youthful air of innocence. She wasn't very pretty, but that didn't matter to him.

They looked much better when he was finished with them.

"Look," he said, leaning across the seat so she could see him better. *Look how clean-cut I am, look how non-threatening.*

Look at my white collar.

"I'm a priest," he said, gesturing to his collar, like it wouldn't be obvious enough. He chided himself to reel it back a little.

"So?" she said, tucking her legs into her chest and wrapping her arms around them. She was shivering. Perfect.

"Well, I know they lock this place down awfully early. And we have a few places open at Holy Trinity tonight. I thought I'd swing by a few of the other shelters to see if anyone was unlucky enough to get stuck out in this bitter cold, and it seems like the good Lord wanted our paths to cross tonight."

He had only tried this approach a handful of times before, but he found that, no matter what someone's religious leanings were, when they were in a bad situation they tended to trust someone who looked like they believed in God.

He could do that, if it meant getting her into the car.

If there *was* a God up there, it wasn't a particularly kind one. Not if He could look down at what was happening and say there was a just reason for it. That this was how this young woman was meant to go.

Because of that, he didn't really fear any kind of repercussions in his afterlife. If there was a hell, it was coming for him, but in the meantime, he was on Earth, and he had work to do.

"I've never heard of Holy Trinity before," the girl said uncertainly.

"It's a big city, my dear. Lots of churches. He needs space to oversee his flock." He smiled softly at her. "We have beds, warm food. A place you can feel safe for the night." He looked up and down the block meaningfully. A homeless man tottered by, pushing a shopping cart with a squeaky wheel. This punctuated the man's point so perfectly he almost thought the Almighty might be on his side with this.

"It's for women?" the girl asked, pushing herself to her feet.

She was already gathering up her shopping bag. He knew he had her.

"Yes, my dear. You have nothing to worry about. We'll take very good care of you."

She looked back at the locked gate. He felt certain she had things in there, the small tethers of a life.

"If you'd like, when we get back to the church, I can call this shelter and let them know you'll be back tomorrow, that you missed the lockdown time by accident." He almost said *because of the bus*, but caught himself. That would spook her, would tell her he'd been watching her.

Or maybe she wouldn't notice.

She brightened at this, the last of her hesitation fading away. "You'd do that?"

"Of course. We have to look out for each other in this life, don't we? That's what He would want." The man pointed upwards, as if to help capitalize the H in He.

"Thank you so much," she said, letting out a sigh of relief. "It's my third time being late, and I don't want them to throw out my things. They do that sometimes, to make room for other people. But it's not my fault the bus never runs on time out here."

She pulled her jacket tightly around her and opened up the passenger door, then slid into the seat beside him. She let out a small sigh of relief when she felt how warm the car was.

"My name is Cassidy," she said, smiling at him.

"You can call me Father Randall, if you'd like."

She smiled, completely sold on the lie.

He smiled back, pulling away from the curb and into the night.

SIXTEEN

An hour after Margot met with Andrew, the team were gathered in a small conference room. This one was much more generously outfitted than the spaces they often got to use at backwoods motor lodges or Best Westerns outside small prison towns.

Realistically the whole team hadn't needed to come to Nashville when only Margot was interviewing Holmes, but Andrew was a boss who appreciated fairness, and he knew it might sow discontent if only two members of the group got to spend a few nights in a nice hotel in Nashville, near amenities and civilization, while the others were forced to stay in a place that most cross-country hikers wouldn't be thrilled about.

The hotel had left them bottles of sparkling water on the counter, and Margot imagined they would be charged by the bottle, much like with an overly tempting minibar, but that didn't stop Greg from taking two and putting them in front of his seat.

Margot followed his lead, because the FBI certainly wouldn't go broke if she was hydrated. Meanwhile Alana had her own fancy bottled water in front of her, and Sydney was drinking from a trendy reusable water bottle. They'd also been provided with coffee, which each team member was genetically predisposed to taking, even if they were already too caffeinated for their own good.

Margot snapped a photo of hers and sent it to Wes. She did this almost every time she had coffee in a new location, because sharing coffee at work had been their thing when they were with SFPD. A moment later she got a picture back of a Willows High School Track and Field mug, almost empty, with his thumb up next to it.

Andrew cleared his throat to get the attention of the room, and Margot obligingly set her phone face down on the table. Alana was still scrolling on hers, but they had all learned over the years that Alana was always listening even if it seemed her attention appeared to be somewhere else.

Especially if it seemed her attention was somewhere else, actually.

Sydney had an eager look on her face, a notepad at the ready. Greg was fumbling to get his laptop connected to the conference table's selection of projection cables. A moment later, one of their crime scene photos was up on the massive screen on the far wall, and Margot suddenly felt perfectly at home, like they were right back at their offices in San Francisco.

"Margot, I'd like you to brief the team on what you learned today in your meeting with Wyatt Holmes."

Alana darted a quick, unreadable glance in her direction, then looked back at her phone.

Margot stood, but didn't bother to go to the front of the room. The small team could all see her from where they were.

"Holmes was, as expected, not a terribly forthcoming interview suspect, but I didn't find him to be dishonest, at least in my personal interpretation. He didn't really speak up unless direct questions were asked, and didn't come across as boastful or like he was trying to get attention or rewards. When I asked him about the crime scene, he indicated an interest in getting to visit in person."

Alana scoffed but never looked up from her phone.

"However, when I suggested we could do video instead of in-person he didn't balk. I think he's more curious about seeing the scene than revisiting a place he knowingly buried a body."

Sydney looked downcast; she seemed almost disappointed that they wouldn't be taking a serial killer on a field trip. But she also hadn't been with them when they'd taken Ed Finch to find his final victims. She didn't know how badly it could go.

Margot gave the team the same rundown of her conversation with Wyatt she had given Andrew, before wrapping up with her theory that she believed he might be interested in seeing the scene because he wanted to see the work of another killer. That they might have to look for some other person to pin this to.

For a long moment after she was done, everyone sat in silence, absorbing the news she had dropped on them. This changed everything; it changed the entire approach to not only this case, but also the Holmes case, because they had spent months trying to find people who had gone missing on the Appalachian Trail who might be unknown Holmes victims, but this new grave site might mean they had two serial killers working the same trail.

What a grim thought that was.

It wasn't unheard of, though. In areas with certain kinds of human traffic, there were better places to find prey than others. That was why there were so many serial killers who hunted along interstates. That was why there were so many still unknown serial killers hunting in places in the United States where homelessness and drug addiction were highest.

If a predator knew where to look, there was easily accessible prey everywhere.

Hunting on a major cross-country hiking route was a risk. The people who made those treks were typically from families, and often from money. It wasn't cheap to drop out of daily life for several months just to go for a hike, and planning for that hike took time and money. All that meant was that the victim pool for a location like the Appalachian Trail was going to be a lot different from the types of victims found along the interstate, or in crumbling Ohio industrial areas.

"So, what are the next steps then?" Sydney asked, setting her pen down on her notebook. Her braided hair was pulled back into a low ponytail, and her expression was that of someone desperate to get to work. "Do we turn this over to BSU?" Her tone suggested she didn't want to, but was afraid to suggest anything else.

Margot looked quickly to Andrew for an assist. Her gut instinct was to push ahead and make her own suggestions, but she remembered she wasn't in charge here, and didn't want to be in charge here.

Alana met her gaze briefly, and Margot wished she knew what the other woman was trying to get across. Was she annoyed that Margot had been given the spotlight? Margot knew Alana wanted to take over the leadership role, and she was welcome to it, but perhaps that wasn't clear enough. Or maybe it wasn't that at all. Maybe she was trying to gauge how Margot was feeling after her meeting.

Margot reminded herself that they were both grown adults, and she could just ask Alana later if there was something on her mind. Of course, that sounded frighteningly close to confrontation, something Margot had never been very good at, at the best of times.

She pushed her concerns about Alana aside for the moment. She was probably just making something out of nothing, projecting doom where none existed. Her therapist, Dr. Singh, would have a lot to say about it if she remembered to bring it up later. He called it catastrophizing. He had told her in the past that, because one time in her life the worst-case scenario had been true, she was inclined to believe it could happen at any given time.

See, she barely even needed therapy anymore, she already knew everything her doctor would tell her.

She also needed to remind herself that Alana was not the type of woman to go about things in a passive-aggressive way. Alana was not shy about sharing her feelings with Margot and never had been; it just wasn't the kind of person she was. If something was bothering her, she would come right out and say it.

That alone helped Margot feel more at peace. At least enough to focus her attention back on Andrew.

Andrew went on. "We won't be involving the BSU in this right now. I have three agents at this table who have spent multiple years working inside the BSU, I have one seasoned homicide detective, and I believe that I was more than capable of solving a crime back in my day. The BSU might get involved to give us some independent insight down the road, but you know how it works there. They look at a file for maybe a day, and then they move on to the next. They're too backlogged for this, and we're already in the thick of it, so I don't see any reason we can't work alongside local agencies to see what we can figure out. I know fresh cases aren't our standard fare, but I also think we're completely capable of working one."

Margot glanced around the table to see if anyone else reacted to this. It was very different from what they typically worked on, and she wondered if that made any of the others nervous.

Personally, like Sydney, she found herself unexpectedly excited about getting to work on this case She hadn't worked an active homicide since she'd left the police department, and getting to tackle one with the expansive resources available to the FBI sounded thrilling. This was something she was good at, something that none of the others on the team had the same hands-on, in-the-trenches experience as she did. She felt unusually confident.

"Alana," Andrew said, finally getting her to look up from her phone. "I want you and Sydney to head back to Trumbull, see if you can get their local PD to talk to you about any missing persons cases. Let's also start to dig into any cases we had potentially tied to Holmes and see if the MO more closely matches this new site. We need to look at it fresh. Greg, I want you to search through any open cases in all the states along the trail, see if any deaths or missing persons cases show up in the states where Holmes didn't operate that we might have overlooked."

Margot waited expectantly for her assignment. Everyone else had taken notes and Greg had disconnected his laptop, though she could still see the outline of an image of the grave site on the screen.

"Margot, you and I are going to go to Knoxville to visit Dr. Langstrom at the Body Farm."

An unexpected rush of excitement tingled in Margot's toes. She knew this was macabre, and that the goal of all this was to find a killer. Still, that voice in the back of her head that never quite shut up had only one thing to say about this development.

Cool.

SEVENTEEN

The hotel bar was the only part of their accommodation that gave away the fact that they were staying in Nashville. While the rest of the place was polished and posh, with luxury finishes and only a few scattered portraits of the city in days gone by, the bar leaned fully into *yee-haw country*. And while it was one of the more high-end honky-tonks Margot had seen, that was likely only because it did not have a mechanical bull anywhere in sight.

And also, perhaps, because Margot had never been to any other honky-tonks.

She wasn't even entirely sure what made the difference between a bar and a honky-tonk, she just liked the phrasing of the latter, and, when in Rome...

Margot also knew that this was exactly where she would find Alana, and her instinct was proven accurate as she spotted the blonde perched up at the bar, a lowball glass in front of her and a dazzled bartender spending far too much time cleaning the area near where she was seated.

Alana had switched from her day ensemble to a pair of tight black pants and a soft lilac sweater that hung off one shoulder. The shade of the sweater brought out the natural gray that streaked her bob and gave her already platinum hair an almost violet hue.

Margot took the stool next to her, and, since the bartender had been so keen to keep vigil in front of Alana's spot, was soon able to order a gin and lime.

Alana waited until Margot had been served before she spoke. "What did you really think about Holmes?" she asked, not looking in Margot's direction, but still somehow giving her complete attention to the question.

Margot sipped her drink thoughtfully, wondering how to answer the question honestly but not *too* honestly. Alana was her friend, but Margot didn't have a lot of deep connections, the kind where she could truly open up about what was going on in her head. Most people didn't want to know.

"I believed him," she said simply.

"About?" Alana prodded.

"I think that he genuinely believes that what he was doing was for the good of some unknown wolf pack. I don't think he's making that up. And I think it gives him an unusual respect for others who he considers to be hunters."

She swallowed more of her drink to push down the memory of his final words to her.

Alana was thoughtful, swishing her whiskey around in the glass, a large globe of ice rattling the interior. An orange twist was on the napkin beside her. Old Fashioned, then.

"Why is it, do you think, you're so good at getting them to open up?" Alana asked, changing the subject slightly, but not in the direction Margot had anticipated.

Margot shrugged. There was a bowl of mixed nuts on the bar between them, and she picked out a handful, set them down on a spare napkin, and started to pick out her least favorite ones to eat first. Start with peanuts, then almonds, end on cashews always.

"I don't think it's like a weird superpower or anything. I mean, you were a profiler for a long time, you know that a big part of finding these guys is getting inside their heads. I don't think what I'm doing is all that different. I have a rough idea of what makes them tick, I've seen what they're capable of. I have those tools with me when I talk to them."

"It's different though, I think. When I was with BSU, we just made outlines of people. Suggestions based on what we'd seen. You sit across from real people and you pick them open like they're pistachios."

Margot had to smile at the simile. "Have you ever done an interrogation?" she asked.

Alana shook her head. "No, there was never a situation where it came up before."

This wasn't surprising. While it wasn't uncommon for agents to come from law enforcement backgrounds, some joined much earlier, if their academic prowess was enough to help them find a place in the Bureau.

"I was really good at interrogations," Margot said, hoping it didn't sound too boastful. It was just the truth. She knew how to talk to people. "The important thing to remember, I find, is that no matter how innocent or guilty a person is, they all have something to hide. And to get to that little nugget of truth in them, you just need to take the time to understand them. Find a weakness. Find that thin hairline crack everyone has and exploit it. There's no difference with the guys we work with. If anything, they're even more eager to talk than the guys I used to sit across from." She shrugged and popped a peanut in her mouth, surprised by how good the seasoning was.

Alana was quiet, then took an almond from Margot's napkin and said, "Most people wouldn't think it was easy, Margot."

"I've never been most people."

"You sit in tiny rooms with people who have done unspeakable things. You just... talk to them. You can look them in the eyes and carry on a conversation like it's nothing. I don't know how you do it, and how you can divorce yourself from the reality of who they are enough to get what you need from them."

"Well. I guess I'm kind of uniquely capable of knowing that

most of the time, especially when they want to be, they're just acting like people."

"Acting is the important word there," Alana said.

"We all act. All of us, every day. We're putting on a performance for whoever we're with. It's not necessarily a dishonest thing, don't get me wrong, but the way we show ourselves to friends is different from how we show ourselves at work. How I act around Wes's parents is different from how I act around Wes, and even that is different from how I am alone. It's all acting, in a sense. I think the skill I bring to the table is that I learn how to act *with* them, to craft the performance they want to see. That's how I'm able to get things done."

"Is it any different, with them, than it was with Finch?"

Margot appreciated that Alana didn't say *your father*.

She nodded. "Yeah. With Ed, I had already been studying that play my whole life. I didn't need to learn the lines." She gave a soft smile. "Why do you want to know?"

"I guess I'm just trying to figure out what Andrew is thinking. In terms of what comes next. I want to believe he trusts me, because he's letting me lead things back in Trumbull, but then a part of me looks at how much he trusts you, the way he leans on you, and I start to doubt that he sees anyone on this team aside from you. I mean, we can't do what we do without you."

This was the first time Margot had witnessed this kind of open uncertainty from Alana. The other woman was usually so confident, so self-assured; this kind of nervous energy was almost unheard of for her.

Margot set down her drink and pivoted in her seat until she was facing her friend. She waited until Alana finally looked at her before speaking again. "Alana, I'm just a cog. Andrew is the machine. I do what I do, and I'm pretty decent at it, but that doesn't mean I am the right person to be the machine. In fact, given my psychological background and my very stubborn resistance to working in the actual office, I think you'll find I might be the worst person to be the machine."

"You don't want to be the machine?" Alana asked, her voice low.

Margot had to snort. "I would rather be drawn and quartered than be anyone's boss. The last thing on this planet I want to do is run this division. I want to sit across from shitty serial killers three days a month, then go home and feed my chickens."

Alana let out an unexpected bark of laughter, and Margot couldn't help but notice her eyes were slightly red, like she might have been on the cusp of crying. That was certainly something she had never expected to see from Alana.

"I want *you* to have this job," Margot insisted. "Because you're the right person for it. And if Andrew offered it to me, I would tell him he was a goddamn fool for not seeing what was right in front of his face."

Alana clinked her glass against Margot's.

"You're a weird fucking lady," she said. "But I'm glad I know you."

EIGHTEEN

Knoxville, Tennessee

The official name of the Body Farm was the Forensic Anthropology Center. It came by its unfortunate but accurate nickname when it became the national epicenter for forensic anthropologists to study human decomposition up close and personal.

Using donated bodies, the anthropologists studied how the body broke down in a variety of different environments. What was the difference in decomposition for a body left lying in the sun, compared to one buried in woodland? Was there a difference if the body was wrapped in plastic sheets versus burlap tarp versus nothing at all?

Here, science was working to help understand everything that could impact a body after it died, and as a result, that information was making it easier to assess bodies found in the field. It was helping to solve real-world cases more accurately.

Inside the building, active cases were being worked by a team of highly trained forensic anthropologists, and chief among those was Dr. Ava Langstrom. She met them at a locked gate, so unassumingly placed at the back of a parking lot that Margot initially thought they had arrived at a groundskeeper's building. Google Maps had kept insisting they needed to go to the Anthropology building in the middle of campus, and they'd tried their luck once at the modest brick William M. Bass III Forensic Anthropology building a few hundred yards down the road from where they were now before a very polite assistant director sent them to the adjacent parking lot.

The lot held dozens of student and faculty cars, and just on the other side of it was a condo complex. Margot wondered if it had been disclosed to the condo owners that their view of forest and river was also quietly a view of about fifty bodies in various states of decay.

The entrance was behind two locked gates and a double fence, one of which was topped with barbed wire, not unlike a prison—though this wire was to keep people from coming into the farm, rather than getting out.

Margot hoped.

Dr. Langstrom had rightly assumed that, aside from their purely professional reason for being there—to find a killer—Margot and Andrew would want the once-in-a-lifetime opportunity to see the Body Farm in action. It was not accessible to outsiders, except those on law enforcement or research duties, meaning that most people didn't get a chance to visit it.

If Ava found the work she did here to be strange or off-putting in any way, it didn't show in her manner as she welcomed them into the wooded lot where her team's research took place.

"Once we're done here, I'll take you back to the Bass building," she said, "but I thought you might like to see what our team has going on right now."

Ava handed Margot and Andrew white booties to slip over their shoes, which took Margot back to her crime scene days.

"Now I hope I don't sound like the stern teacher my students claim I am, but I have to be clear that this is a visual-only tour. No touching, no interfering with the bodies." She smiled. "You'd think it would go without saying, but sometimes people can't seem to help their curiosity." She ushered for them to follow her.

Margot hadn't expected to be shaken by the place, but she couldn't help but feel a sense of alarm when they passed the main open lot and headed into the trees, and suddenly there were bodies everywhere. Her eyes seized on them, years of homicide training wanting to yank her from the path to get closer, to investigate. But she remembered Ava's warning, and she didn't want to overstep, no matter how badly her instincts demanded she go take a closer look.

There were bodies in states of decomposition Margot had never seen in person before. Bodies where the skin had practically mummified, turned black, almost like someone had vacuum-sealed a skeleton in a plastic garbage bag. It was both grisly and fascinating. Some bodies were clothed, others were nude; many were shrouded in some kind of plastic or cloth, shielding them from view.

It was incredible to see just how many bodies there were in the three-acre lot. Everywhere Margot looked, there was another unmistakably human lump. After a while they almost stopped seeming real, if it hadn't been for the scent of decomposition lingering in the air. She had actually imagined it would smell worse than it did, but it seemed to depend a great deal on where they were standing.

Margot pointed out an old car among the trees. "What's going on there?"

"We're researching how a body will decompose inside a car trunk," Ava said matter-of-factly. She pointed towards a white pop-up tent where a busy crowd of people in head-to-toe white protective jumpsuits were working. Margot had seen similar outfits on crime scene investigators. "We have a group here from Canada this week learning new techniques for uncovering mass graves." Her mouth formed a thin line, the first time she'd shown any kind of emotion about her work. "The work is important, but knowing how it's being used can be very sobering sometimes."

Ava continued to lead them through the wooded area, and

while something about Farm's very existence was unsettling, Margot found that the longer the anthropologist talked about the Farm and the work being done there, the more Margot was impressed with the place. It would probably never be somewhere she would want to go for a sleepover, but there was a reverence and respect in Ava's voice as she talked about those who had donated their bodies to the program, and all the good they'd been able to do with the research and training done on site.

After an hour, Margot felt a new sense of appreciation for Ava Langstrom and the work her team were doing. She was even more appreciative of them being the ones who had helped unearth the graves on the trail.

They made the short walk from the parking lot to the William Bass building, which felt somehow quieter than the environment they had just left. "We typically use the labs here to do extended research from what we learn in the field." Ava gestured vaguely in the direction of the Body Farm. "But it seemed like the best place to bring our friends from the trail. We have an additional anthropology unit right on campus, but I wanted to be sure these weren't the center of too much attention. Everyone who works in this building is among the most highly trained and trustworthy in the program. They have to be, to get access to the Farm."

This made sense. Margot had to imagine that cellphone-toting social media users weren't a big concern when Bill Bass was running the program, but with things being the way they were now, the Body Farm could only risk granting access to certain students.

Ava led them to a lab where a note on the door said *Authorized Personnel Only—Ongoing Investigation*. There was a badge lock on the door that beeped as she entered. Before they approached the table, Ava gave them both blue latex gloves, and once again Margot felt that surge of comfortable familiarity remembering her homicide days.

If she were to swap Ava with the San Francisco chief medical examiner Evelyn Yao—who would certainly have hit on Andrew with cheerful inappropriateness—this would be just like the good old days in the trenches.

But Ava Langstrom was about as far from Evelyn Yao's sunny disposition as one could imagine. She was professional and warm, but there was nothing particularly cuddly about her demeanor. This was work for her, and while it was clearly something she was very passionate about—you would have to be to traipse through the Farm every day—she was not interested in making them more comfortable in her world.

Margot had expected the lab to feel like Evelyn's morgue, with cool air and lockers for the bodies, but instead she found that each one of their victims was laid out on the same kind of tables that Margot had used during chemistry class in high school. Waist-high lab tables, ten of them, evenly spaced around the room.

In another time, Margot imagined, students of the forensic anthropology program had gathered around these tables to look at skeletons pulled from the nearby field and to learn from them.

She realized then that the sign outside wasn't meant to keep out snoops, it was meant to prevent overeager students from thinking this was a lesson, and potentially contaminating evidence.

Margot wondered if the students who had been with Ava out on the trail would be helping her work on this, or if it was going to be primarily left to her and the associate directors of the program. The students had seemed eager yet professional out in the field, but still Margot had some reservations about them being the ones to help find answers that might pin down their killer.

It felt strange to even think that. *Their killer.*

Coming into this, they had firmly believed they were only in Tennessee to help close some cold cases tied to Wyatt Holmes. In a million years Margot could never have predicted that it would turn into a hunt for a potential new killer.

And all of this was in addition to the kill kit they had found in Browning. She didn't think that was connected to this case, but she believed to her very core it was connected to the Whitney Eflin murder that had taken place in Willow. So there was a personal element to this for her.

She wanted very badly to find the man who had left that kit buried, but for the time being their focus needed to be in this room, looking at seven skeletons and trying to figure out where they belonged.

Ava's expression shifted and she went into full professional teaching mode. "We'll start with the positive. All seven of the victims had well-preserved skulls, with almost all their teeth present. One skull was missing the mandible, likely taken by local predators at some point—all the bodies were missing some bones— but with the maxillary teeth we will still be able to do dental comparison once we narrow down our options for victims. We're in the process of submitting the results we have to compare those that already exist in missing persons odontology archives, but that could take some time, and would of course require that the victims were at some point added to that database, which is unfortunately never a sure thing."

Margot nodded. Using dental comparison was a helpful tool, but always meant they had to have some idea of who their victim was. In this case, they were going in a bit blind until they could start to narrow down some of the missing persons cases in the area.

"Do you know more about how or when they died?" Andrew prodded. He had drifted over to one of the skeletons, the bones a grey-brown and still dirty from the field.

Margot wasn't sure why she thought they would be clean and white. It wasn't like they had been sitting out in the sun to bleach.

"Well, in a sense you're lucky we found them where we did. Of all potential environments, our team happens to be best versed in the soil of Tennessee." She gave a small smile, indicating this was an attempt at levity. Gallows humor tended to run deep in communities that frequently worked alongside death.

"So what can you tell us?" Andrew asked.

Ava and her staff had only had the bodies back at their lab for two days, so Margot wouldn't have been surprised if the answer to

Andrew's question was *nothing*, but instead Ava, on the opposite side of the skeleton from him, looked down at the bones like they might speak for her.

They probably did speak *to* her, in a sense. Crime scenes often spoke to Margot, giving her a sense of what had happened there that was so clear it might as well have been a movie in her mind. She wondered if that was what it was like for Ava when she looked down at decomposing or skeletal remains.

Margot had worked alongside forensic anthropologists before, in a limited capacity, but she'd never seen one quite so much in her element before. The way Ava spoke and toured them around the remains, she was more comfortable like this than she had been making polite small talk with them.

"From our initial lab assessments, we've been able to narrow the window for each level of burial. This is not going to be as precise as a time of death would be for a fresh victim—these remains are all skeletal, of course, which creates broader time frames for when they could have been put into the ground. Based on what we know about the acidity of that soil, and local soils in general, as well as an understanding of how shifting seasonal temperatures could have slowed or hastened decomposition, plus the general wear on the bones, here's what I can tell you."

Margot fell in beside Andrew, waiting eagerly to hear what Ava was going to say. Ava seemed to enjoy the brief pause for dramatic effect, but then began speaking hurriedly, with excitement. "Victim A, the first that was uncovered, had been there about twelve to eighteen months. That's our most recent burial. She is a female, late teens to early twenties, and she does not appear to have ever given birth. Victims B and C, you'll recall, were buried together, and we were able to determine they were both female, in their twenties. One had previously broken her femur, which will further help with identification later, and neither had ever given birth. These victims we can say with good certainty were buried about five years ago. Victims D and E: one was male, in his late teens, early twenties, and the other was another female, thirties—she *had* given birth at some point. Victim D was about seven years in the ground, Victim E, we suspect, closer to ten. Then our deepest-buried pair were a male and female victim, in their twenties. He showed signs of several broken bones that were healed, and she had never given birth. They've been there about fifteen to eighteen years. Because of some degradation of their bones, and the position of victim F, the female, who we believed had been buried alive and attempted to dig out, we can't be more certain there, but they've been in the ground a decent length of time."

Ava took a half step back from the table and waited for Margot or Andrew to speak. Margot had been busy taking notes, though she was sure Ava would give them a report.

"That's tremendous work, Dr. Langstrom." Andrew pushed his glasses up on his nose.

"Well, we're just getting started. We might be able to help narrow down more specifics as we get into it further."

"Do you have any indication of how they died, yet?" he asked, his gaze trailing over the skeleton in front of him, as if the cause of death might become obvious if he stared at it long enough.

Margot wondered how long it had been since Andrew had worked an active investigation. She had no doubts about his ability—the man had literally written the book on hunting serial killers—but it was an adjustment, to be sure. He'd need to remember skills he hadn't used in a long time.

"That's going to require a little more work to be absolutely certain. We want to do full 3D scans of each skeleton, which will better help us find any nicks or knife marks left behind if the victims were stabbed. Often, we find that wear from animal teeth can present in a similar fashion, so the modeling helps eliminate any errors. Unfortunately, there were very few hyoid bones found among the debris. A broken hyoid is the best way to accurately determine if someone may have been strangled, but it's also a very small and delicate bone that can often be difficult to locate as a body deteriorates. Of the bones we were able to locate, seeming to belong to Victims A and C, they were intact. That doesn't necessarily rule out strangulation for all the victims, but it would be very unlikely in those two cases. We found no bullets or bullet casing at the grave site, so shooting is very unlikely." She gave a half-hearted shrug, as if apologizing for the lack of evidence. "We did find some substantial skeletal damage to three of the seven skulls, though we'll need more time to determine if it's consistent with blunt force trauma, or if it might have been a result of a physical struggle. There are a lot of rocks out there, and someone fighting for their life could get hurt a lot of different ways. We should know more when we complete the scans and have a bit more time with our subjects."

"Do you think they were all killed by the same person?" Margot asked.

Ava gave her a serious look. "If the other option is that multiple people were using the same mass grave, I suppose I have to say I hope they were all done by one person."

Margot nodded. She was looking at seven murders over the course of almost twenty years. She hoped they were done by one person, too. And she hoped this guy was still alive for them to catch.

NINETEEN

The drive from Knoxville to Nashville was about three hours. It was also only an hour and a half from Knoxville to Trumbull, home of the unofficial worst motel in America. Alana and Sydney would already be there, working alongside local law enforcement to see what they could dig up.

Greg had stayed behind in Nashville, which meant Margot and Andrew had two options. They could return to Nashville to check in with him, or they could join Alana and Sydney in Trumbull, with its limited police department and more limited resources, to see if they'd come up with anything useful.

The decision was entirely up to Andrew, but he paused at a Knoxville gas station and looked to Margot.

"What do you want to do?" he asked.

She regarded him uncertainly, wondering if this was a test. "I don't want to take over from you," she blurted before she realized it was what she was going to say. Once the words were out, she felt her cheeks flush, but she also felt an immense sense of relief.

Andrew sat back in his seat, blinking slowly as he absorbed what she'd said, then, once it finally sank in, let out a soft chuckle. "Well, I knew if I asked you it would be an uphill battle, but I didn't expect you to be quite so adamant. If anything, this was kind of the response I expected from you when I originally asked you to be in the FBI." His expression was soft, voice full of humor instead of insult. She found herself unexpectedly at ease. "Can you tell me why you don't want the position?"

"I'm not a leader, Andrew."

He made a small scoffing noise, then reached over to open the water bottle he had sitting in the cup holder. After taking a sip, he held the bottle on his thigh. "I understand why you might tell yourself that, but I don't think it's true. I think you're actually a very natural leader, especially in situations like this. I see it on your face sometimes, especially if I take too long to answer something. You want to jump in, you want to steer the ship."

Margot started to shake her head, but he held up a finger to stop her.

"But like I said, I understand why you think you're not a leader. I'm just telling you I think you're wrong, and I think you'd be a good person to keep this little island of misfit toys together when I'm gone."

She hated to hear him talking about things that way, as if he was dying and tying up the loose ends of his will. Not only could she not imagine herself in charge, she couldn't imagine the department running without him. She assumed the Bureau had felt the same way, which was how he'd managed to escape his mandatory retirement all these years.

"It's not just that I don't think I'd be a good leader. I don't want the responsibility. I couldn't do what I have to do if I was also worrying about every other little thing the team needs to do."

Andrew glanced out the car window. It had begun to rain, little droplets splattering on the windshield. Margot couldn't help but think of the bodies at the Body Farm. Of course, their exposure to the elements was all part of the research, but it was still sad to her, the idea that they were out there with no one to protect them.

"I think you would have made a good leader for the team, Margot, I really do. But I'm not going to force the subject. I respect you for being honest with me, and I'm glad I won't have to make a fool of myself advocating for your promotion to the higher-ups only to have you turn it down." He smiled, mostly to himself.

"You've done enough advocating for me at this point, I think," she replied.

"You were and are worth the effort. I've always believed that."

Her cheeks flushed involuntarily. She was glad he thought so highly of her, and flattered, even, that he thought she was capable of filling his shoes.

"I think you should pick Alana," she said. She wasn't sure if there would ever come a day where she would need to defend this conversation to her friend, but if that day came, she wanted to be sure she left it all on the table. No doubts, no questions.

Andrew nodded. "She makes the most sense. On paper, she is a better candidate than you." He darted a quick glance in her direction, likely to see if this would make her rise to some kind of challenge.

Margot just smiled to herself. "She *is* the better person for the job. I think you just feel like I'm not living up to my potential."

"I suppose." He sipped his water again, looking out the window at the rain. "I hate to admit it, Margot, but sometimes I look at you and I still see you as a fifteen-year-old girl. Scared, uncertain—and I guess I just want what's best for you."

Margot would be lying if she didn't sometimes look at Andrew and feel like he filled the father figure role she had lost when her own father was hauled off to prison in handcuffs.

"I appreciate it," she said honestly. "I wasn't sure, even when I joined the FBI, what your motivations were, but I think it all comes from a good place."

"It does."

"Even if I want to kill you sometimes."

They both grinned.

"You think the rest of the team would be okay working under Alana?" he asked.

Margot nodded. "I can't imagine anyone else coming in and getting the same level of respect, especially from the outside. The team knows her, they understand how she works, and she'll make you proud."

"I'd be prouder if I could get her to put her goddamn phone down during meetings."

Margot laughed. "Well, lucky for you then. Because when she starts leading those meetings she won't have much of a choice, will she?"

TWENTY

Trumbull, Tennessee, was not a town people went to for fun.

There was nothing there that would make someone pick it from a list of other Tennessee small towns as a place to visit. There were no museums, no local Largest Dinner Roll in Tennessee type attractions. Just a welcome proximity to a popular hiking trail.

It hadn't always been a forgotten place, though. In the fifties the town had been a bustling mining community, but in the decades that followed much of what had once made it one of those small, wonderful industrial towns had disappeared. Because of its proximity to the Appalachian Trail, it now focused all its energy on what little regular revenue that brought along with it.

So many of the buildings in town were shuttered, and looked to have been that way since the eighties based on the design choices. The local elementary school was still going, but the high school had been shut down, and the kids were bussed to a school in a town nearby. Margot had learned a lot about the town's history from a chatty waitress at the diner.

There was a single grocery store, and a post office that appeared to have been recently renovated. It was now a parcel drop location for those hiking the trail, so they could pick up packages they had sent themselves prior to the trip, or collect cards and gifts en route.

There was also a small supply shop running from the post office building, stocked with anything campers and hikers might need, from dehydrated food to fresh socks.

The town had a motel—where the FBI crew were staying—that proudly offered discounted rates to hikers who wanted a night off their feet and off the ground. The local gas station offered upgraded shower facilities to hikers and truckers, though Trumbull was no longer on any major trucking routes.

What it did have was at least three restaurants, which would have been impressive if they weren't all some variation on the same thing: diners.

Margot could have crushed some Chinese food after the day they'd had, but unfortunately the most exotic thing served on any menu in town was French toast.

One of the few things she missed immensely about living in San Francisco was the ready availability of so much delicious takeout food. She'd lived in North Beach, only a stone's throw from Chinatown, and there wasn't a week that had passed since she left that she didn't crave pad see ew from her favorite Thai restaurant.

Privacy and contentment were great, but she missed soup dumplings.

She had texted Alana ahead of their arrival to meet them at a place called Jenny's Diner, which was about a block from Jim's Diner, which was a block from the Smoky Mountain Bar and Grill.

Jenny's seemed to be the nicest of the three, leaning hard into the fifties aesthetic, with lots of old photos on the walls from the town's heyday and the waitresses in cute pink uniforms that they probably hated.

Margot spotted Alana and Sydney in a booth in one corner. There was another table where a young man, obviously a solo hiker going by the overstuffed backpack on the floor beside him, was so intensely focused on eating his burger Margot had to imagine it was the best meal of his life.

A few other tables were filled with people who were likely locals—a lot of silver-haired heads among them, but at least the place had guests.

Margot and Andrew settled into the booth with the others.

This would have been much better done over takeout food in a private meeting room, but their motel didn't have anything like that, and after all the driving—and despite the forest of dead bodies —Margot was completely famished. So they would need to keep their discussion as private as possible, which would be a challenge given that everyone in the restaurant—with the exception of the hiker perhaps—knew precisely who they were and why they were here.

Not a lot of FBI coming through a town like Trumbull, especially not these days.

Margot was hoping the town had an equally long memory for people who had gone missing, but given the unfixed nature of hikers taking on the trail, that was going to be a challenge.

Margot hoped Sydney and Alana had something interesting to share with them. She almost felt like they should conference-call Greg in, but the reception in the area was questionable at best, and she reminded herself Greg was sleeping in plush Nashville bedding tonight, while she would be sleeping on a motel mattress most frequently used by smelly hikers or local kids desperate to find somewhere to lose their virginity after prom.

Sydney had a stack of files sitting beside her in the booth, which she hugged tightly to her side like someone might slide in and grab them. With Andrew next to her, her posture seemed to be more relaxed. Margot took the outside spot at the table, because even though she wasn't a neurotic shut-in anymore she still liked to know where her exits were at any given moment.

They ordered and, while they waited for their food, Alana cast a careful glance around the room.

"I don't love discussing this here," she said.

Andrew nodded and dumped a sugar packet into his coffee mug. "I know, but let's do it anyway. We don't have a lot of options, and I'm willing to bet that a lot of what you guys dug up is old news to some of this crowd." His gaze cut over to the tables where the more elderly residents were gathered.

Alana nodded to Sydney, who placed the stack of folders on the table. She did a quick scan of the restaurant to make sure no one was immediately headed to their table, then handed the first on the stack to Andrew, who opened it enough that Margot could peer over the ledge of the folder, but no one would see the contents if they happened to come up with a food order.

Margot scanned the paperwork and was surprised to find this was not a missing persons case, but another murder. She looked over to Alana and Sydney for some confirmation of what she was seeing. For some reason she hadn't expected them to unearth any additional killings.

Sydney began. "We found a few interesting things in our digging. It seems that, against all the odds, we have a local cop who's been working in Trumbull about twenty-five years, and he *isn't* phoning it in. When we came in to talk to him about other cases in the area, he had it ready to go, like he was just waiting for the moment to give us all this." She waved her hand over the folder and the files.

"And what exactly are we looking at here?"

They paused long enough for their waitress, her curious gaze absorbed by the folder like she was hoping to be able to see through it, to drop their orders off and scuttle away again, no doubt ready to gossip with the line cook about what they were up to.

"That first case is Teddi Baxter. Thea, legally." Alana gestured for Sydney to pick up the thread from there and Margot glanced at Andrew, hoping he was seeing her step into the leadership role.

He was too busy flipping through the file.

"Teddi Baxter was thirty-two when she went missing. She was just day-hiking part of the trail, and someone reported that her car had been at the trailhead with no permits on it for over two weeks, which was unusual. She'd been doing a cross-country road trip living out of her van, her and her dog."

Margot's hand stilled as she lifted a French fry to her mouth, and she set it back down again. She could keep up her appetite after seeing decaying bodies. But the implication that something might have happened to a dog was sour enough to curdle milk.

Sydney seemed to register what had changed in Margot's demeanor and nodded towards the file. "The dog was fine. A little skinny, but he's actually the reason they knew something must have happened to Teddi, in combination with her car. The dog, Ambrose, was licensed, and the number on his tag was for Teddi's parents in Virginia. They hadn't heard from her in over two weeks, which was a little unusual for her, but she had mentioned she would be doing some hiking and, since this was the nineties, she wasn't exactly toting along a phone. Anyway, between the dog and the van, local PD realized there was something hinky, they sent a search party out to see what they could find, and what they found was what was left of Teddi."

Margot ate her fry and considered this carefully. "Was she buried?"

"Hastily, and not very well. Mostly some brush was pulled over the top of her. She was a fair distance off the trail, though, so that was why no one seemed to find her."

"What about her belongings?" Andrew asked. "No one reported finding anything before she was uncovered? Even on a short day hike a seasoned hiker would have the ten essentials with them. Especially on a trail as difficult as the AT."

"Ten essentials?" Margot snorted, dipping her fry in ketchup. "Sorry, who are you? When was the last time you went camping, seasoned outdoor adventure guy?"

Andrew shot her a look. "I hike."

She nodded sarcastically. "Okay, buddy."

"Margot's lack of belief in my abilities aside, my question stands."

Alana was having a hard time hiding her own smirk. "Her bag was still with her."

"Was anything taken?"

"No, it seems like everything she went in with, she still had. The only exception being that it looked as if the bag was disturbed by wildlife to get to some food she probably took with her."

"And was the body also disturbed by wildlife?" Margot asked.

Sydney nodded, taking back control of the narrative. "Yes, though she remained mostly intact."

"Were they able to get a cause of death?" Margot asked. "Or whether or not she was assaulted prior to death?"

"She was still fully clothed when they found her, though there was too much decomp at that point to do any kind of swabbing."

"Looks like the coroner ruled that they didn't think she was sexually assaulted," Andrew said.

If he was reading the coroner's report then he already knew what the suspected cause of death was, but he let Sydney go on with her presentation.

"Cause of death was blunt force trauma. They believe she was hit in the head with an axe or hatchet, or something similar with a cleaving edge."

Margot winced. There was something unpleasant about the phrase *cleaving edge* that made her mouth dry. Getting hit in the head with an axe would be an awful way to go, but also awfully distinctive.

"Ava—Dr. Langstrom—she suggested with the recent burial there were some signs of blunt trauma, but she didn't seem to indicate anything quite as obvious as an axe."

"She also didn't have any conclusive answers on cause of death yet." Andrew handed the file back to Sydney. "Any suspects? I'm surprised this one didn't show up during our investigation into Holmes."

"Probably because of the axe," Alana interjected. "Definitely not Holmes's MO."

"Could also be that Teddi was a first effort by this guy, and he changed his MO later. If she is one of the same victims she predates the ones in the grave by a few years," Margot offered.

"No strong suspects were found," Sydney said, pulling them back on task. "It looks like they worked through everyone who had a trail pass and was in the area at that time, they checked around town to see if anyone stuck out, but there was no physical evidence, no DNA, and no one ever found the murder weapon."

Margot continued to eat her burger, though she was distracted thinking about the hundreds of thousands of cases every year that just dried up and faded out of memory. She'd never heard of Teddi Baxter on a podcast or true crime special—though she tended to avoid those thanks to her father being such a popular topic—and it seemed crazy that so many people going missing or dying on the same stretch of the trail wasn't a much bigger story.

But she had to wonder what the statistics were on people who did long-distance hiking and whether or not they were more likely to have no strong family ties, or tended to spend a lot of their time alone. People who could go missing and no one would notice for a long stretch of time, or people they did know might just assume they packed up their lives and started fresh somewhere else, just failing to report back to those they'd left behind.

Margot had done something similar herself twice. Once, when she and her family changed their names and moved to St. Louis, leaving behind anything connected with Ed Finch and the memories that went along with his name. The memories, as it turned out, were much harder to leave behind. She'd done it again when she had moved back to California after college. Her mother was dead, her brother was proving to be beyond her help, and she had a stirring inside her that insisted she needed to go back to Northern California. She didn't have any close friends in St. Louis, so when she packed up, she'd just left that whole life behind. Her brother, David, was the only one she had given her new address and phone number to. So, in a sense, she understood that there were plenty of people out there who could fit their lives into a suitcase or a converted van and just leave it all behind.

She also suspected those people might be the type who would

want to do something as insane as hiking through several states just to say they did it.

That was a kind of insanity Margot did not subscribe to.

Of course, none of that aligned with Teddi, but Sydney had moved on from Teddi's case by the time Margot tuned back into the conversation. Andrew was holding a new folder, this one showing a dead woman who had been found inside her tent along the trail. From what Margot could gather, she had been strangled and sexually assaulted, and left where anyone could find her. The only effort to conceal what had been done was that she had been securely zipped into her sleeping bag.

Despite her location at a common overnight camping spot and no efforts being made to hide her body, she still hadn't been discovered for almost a week.

"Evidently, there's a trail etiquette that you just don't bother someone in a tent, even if you share the same campsite. The only reason she ended up being found at that point, was that an overnight hiker came in and returned the same way, and found it unusual that the same tent was still there a day later, and the campsite was unchanged from when they had passed it the previous afternoon. Because she had been concealed within the tent and sleeping bag, and because it was still early spring and the temperatures were so low, her decomposition was slowed enough that she was still recognizable when they managed to get her off the trail."

Margot couldn't help but think of their trip to the Body Farm that day, and all the little scenarios that had been laid out to be studied. She wondered if any of the bodies had ever been left in a sleeping bag. In a tent.

Still, she didn't think the MO fit their UNSUB.

"We're still waiting for more on the method used to kill our folks, but we do know we can rule out strangulation on at least two of them," Margot reminded Sydney and the others.

"Methods can change. This case is ten years old," Alana said, playing devil's advocate. "There's a chance he moved through several different methods during his time, trying to determine what he liked best."

"But we know he was burying his bodies as long ago as fifteen years, maybe longer. Why would he suddenly leave someone exposed like this?"

"He could have run out of time," Sydney suggested. She could sometimes come across contrarian in their discussions, but this time Margot didn't think she was arguing for the sake of it.

Although she didn't want to shoot the idea down or to deter her from becoming more assertive on the team, Margot still wanted to point out the potential issues with this theory. "He had enough time to zip her back into her sleeping bag," she said.

"Sure, but we've also seen from the length of time she was left in her tent that people will ignore what's going on out of politeness. If there was a potential witness, and our guy played it cool, they might have just assumed it was a couple, or someone alone in the tent, and left them alone out of privacy. The guy just needed to wait until the other camper was asleep or had moved down the trail, and then he could leave. But I could see that spooking him enough to not stick around to bury the body."

Margot couldn't remember the last time Sydney had said so much during a debrief. She also made a good point.

Margot nodded. "All right, we leave it in the pile for now. I think we may need to wait to weed any of these out until we've heard back from Ava with a better idea of how all our mass grave bodies died. The more she can tell us, the better chance we have of figuring out this guy's method, if he has any consistencies over the years beyond just liking this one grave site. The timeline of the victims really gives us a broad cross-section of his kills, so that should help us, provided they're able to get anything useful from the bones." Margot pushed away her half-eaten burger. She was suddenly very tired, and even a lumpy motel bed sounded like a good idea right now.

Andrew seemed to pick up on the flagging energy around the table. It had been a long day for all of them.

"Okay, tomorrow we regroup. We'll get Greg down here, see what he's come up with, and we'll go over the rest of the cases." He took a look around the diner, giving his head a little shake. "And maybe I can find us somewhere a little more private to work from."

TWENTY-ONE

Margot stopped outside the diner as the others headed to the rental cars. She had walked over from the motel, and didn't need a ride back. She checked her phone and saw a few texts waiting, so she sat on a bench in front of the diner, enjoying the cool night air.

This town, despite its grubby exterior and terrible lodgings, felt quiet and safe. Margot didn't think there was anywhere on the planet she would feel one hundred percent comfortable to be on her own at night, but it was something she was working on. As exposure therapy went, sitting in front of a diner in a little Podunk town was probably as safe as she would find herself away from the ranch.

There was a message from Wes, just checking in to see how her day had gone. She sent back the yawning face emoji. She might call him when she got back to the motel, but she also didn't want to become one of those partners who was desperate for his attention all the time. They were independent people; she could survive a few hours without talking to him.

There was a text from Officer Gibson in Browning, reeling her right back into that case again. It wasn't that she'd forgotten it, but there had been other pressing things on her mind. Working with a serial killer and trying to find the identity of seven unknown homicide victims was the kind of thing that could get distracting.

Gibson's message brought her right back to the task, though. She'd been honest with them when they left Browning, that the case would have to wait. She wanted to give it her full attention, and she couldn't do that until they were back in California.

Honestly, she hadn't thought she would hear from him again until they had a chance to check in after returning to San Francisco. His text was simple, direct.

> We did some digging and found something you might be interested in. Sent you an email.

Margot pulled up her email, her pulse pounding. Suddenly she was very glad to be sitting outside, because the cool night air was helping to keep her grounded and not get too woozy from the anticipation. There was an email from Gibson waiting for her with attachments.

Hello, Special Agent Phalen, we had some time to look into a few of the items in the bucket and thought you might find the information useful. I've attached what we were able to track down.

There were three pictures, one with the bucket, which it didn't take a genius to know came from Home Depot, but there was a close-up shot of the bottom of the pail, showing a lot number. Margot hadn't noticed or looked for that when she had found the previous bucket. Perhaps they could pinpoint where those lot numbers were originally shipped to and narrow down where their killer had bought them.

The second photo was of the sheath and knife from inside the bucket. The blade was lying next to a nearly identical model, its sheath slightly more worn down, with a receipt from a store called Reid's Hunting and Fishing. Under this photo the officer had added a note.

One of our volunteers is an avid hunter, recognized the knife and sheath as similar to one he owns. Reid's is available all over the east coast, but it might be a good place to start.

This was useful. She'd need to compare the knife in the kit from Browning to the one they'd recovered in California, but if they were the same it meant their killer was building these kits with items not available on one side of the country, so the advance planning was monumental.

The final picture made her heart leap into her throat. It was a close-up of the metal handle of the bucket, and popping out was the slightest fragment of a fingerprint that had been recently dusted.

Incredible.

It wouldn't be enough to run through a database, but if they ever managed to find this guy it *might* be enough to tie him to the kit. That kind of evidence could be the difference between reasonable doubt and a death sentence.

She let out a little huff of relief. While nothing the Browning police had found was going to crack this case wide open, at least they had the next steps.

She typed out a quick thanks to Officer Gibson, promised she would be in touch soon to continue the investigation, and applauded him for the good work.

As soon as she finished with that, there was one final text on her phone, the one she had intentionally avoided to the very end.

Her brother, David.

Sometimes he was good, and those times it was nice to hear from him. But more often than not, the only reason David texted her these days was because he wanted something.

Hey, can you give me a call when you have a minute?

No how are you? No how's the ranch? He wanted something. And from such a vague message, she knew that what he wanted was money. Margot had learned a long time ago that, when dealing with an addict, the things they wanted were rarely the things that would help them.

She didn't want to call him, because she knew the conversation would just result in her trying to offer more substantial help, and him calling her a meddling bitch for not just forking over however many thousands of dollars would get him out of trouble.

Instead of calling, she texted him.

> Busy with work, everything good?

Once upon a time she might have asked what he needed, but now she knew better. That would only make him defensive.

She put her phone back in her pocket, not wanting to wait for his reply. She hoped she wouldn't get one, and that whatever it was he was angling for, he would have smartened up and realized it wasn't good for him.

There wasn't much of a chance of that, though.

When she looked up, she noticed Sydney coming back across the parking lot. Her hair was down, and as she got closer Margot realized she was wearing makeup, which she definitely hadn't been when they parted ways after dinner.

Sydney paused, looking startled to see her. "You're still here? We left like twenty minutes ago." She glanced around the parking lot as if there might be someone waiting to pop out and surprise her, like perhaps this was a test.

Margot offered her a smile. "I just wanted some fresh air while I checked my texts, guess I got a bit distracted."

"Phones," Sydney said in a huff. "I think if I wouldn't literally die without mine, I would just throw it in a lake or something."

"You look cute, what's the deal?" Margot gestured in Sydney's general direction, noting that she had also changed her outfit.

The other agent flushed, then sat down next to Margot on the bench. Margot knew Sydney was in her early thirties now, but she looked especially young in that moment.

"I'm meeting Spencer here, we're going to head over to some dive bar." She shrugged like it was no big deal, but Margot caught the uneasy expression on her face and the way she kept looking back at Margot herself. Like she was waiting to get in trouble.

"Spencer, the hiking guide?" She raised an eyebrow, immediately uncertain about whether this was a good idea.

Sydney nodded. "We exchanged numbers after the last hike, he invited me out."

Once again there was that lingering pause after she finished, her gaze darting to Margot before she looked down at her hands. Margot had noticed with Sydney an intense desire for approval. It was usually directed at Andrew, making Margot think she just wanted the attention of her mentor, but now that same earnest appeal was in her eyes as she looked at Margot.

She obviously wanted so badly to fit in with the team that she was worried about Margot's opinion on this impromptu date. Margot wondered, if she told Sydney it was a bad idea, would she cancel?

There was something nagging at her, telling her that she *should* try to stop Sydney from going. She thought back to the time she'd spent with Spencer, the few brief interactions she'd had with him one on one. There was no disputing that he was a bit of an unusual guy, but Margot figured part of her opinion was shaped by a generational gap, of her just no longer being twenty or understanding people that age as well as she once had.

"I'm not going to tell Andrew, if that's what you're worried about. But I just want you to think about this for a minute. I know he's cute, and you're as entitled to a personal life as any of us. But just make sure you're being smart about it."

She didn't know a better way to say that the prospect of the date made her uneasy, because anything else felt like it was overstepping her boundaries.

It also felt like she was being a touch paranoid.

Some of the tension seemed to uncoil, and Sydney sat back on the bench, though her knee was bouncing, controlled by nervous energy. "I don't get out a lot. At home. It's... well, it can be really hard to meet people when you spend all this time doing what we do."

"I can imagine it makes for some awkward getting-to-know-you conversations."

Sydney snorted. "Your husband was a homicide detective, right?"

She'd met Wes, but only in passing. It wasn't like there was a holiday party they brought their partners to every year.

Margot didn't bother to correct her on the *husband* thing. It was close enough to the truth. "Yeah. We were partners at the SFPD before we got involved."

"You're lucky, in a way. He gets it. A lot of guys don't. There are so many who just dismiss you if you're in the Bureau. I think they worry I'm going to run background checks or something. And then if they don't get scared off by that, you tell them you work with serial killers and it just becomes a *thing*."

Margot nodded. She had never bothered dating when she was a homicide detective, but even the few one-night stands she found herself involved with, the conversation could get awkward once they learned what she did.

"And you don't get that vibe from Spencer?" Margot asked.

"He has barely asked any questions about the case at all. He seems way more interested in telling me about the forest," Sydney said with a laugh. "I'll gladly listen to a guy tell me about trees if it means he doesn't think I'm a freak for the work I do. Or worse still, gets *too* interested."

Margot made a face, and Sydney chuckled. "Exactly."

She found it strange, though, that Spencer wasn't at least a little curious about the case. Maybe he was and he was just trying to play it cool so as not to spook Sydney.

"Well, I guess enjoy a good evening of learning the difference between pines and spruce?" Margot said.

Sydney smiled, more of the nervousness sloughing off her. "You don't think it's a bad idea?"

"Sydney, you do good work. I know you might still feel like the odd one out, or the new kid, or whatever, but you need to let go of that. You're a part of this team. You have nothing to prove to us, and especially not to Andrew, okay? He wouldn't have brought you on if he didn't think you were a damn good agent. And you are. You're also young and need to have a life. If you think he's a good guy, I trust your judgement. Just make sure he's alert enough in case we need to go back up there at some point, okay?"

Sydney took a moment to process all of this, then bumped a shoulder against her. Margot sensed that what the other agent really wanted to do was hug her, but she appreciated the restraint.

"That... that means a lot," Sydney said finally. "Thank you."

Margot spotted Spencer crossing the parking lot, his gaze locked forward. His expression was blank until he spotted Sydney and smiled brightly. Margot felt like she was looking at something private, and her gaze reflexively drifted towards the trees that were thick behind the diner, which made her think about his Appalachian warnings. A little shiver went through her.

"Have fun, and be safe. Don't whistle at night." She was trying to be funny, but her mouth felt dry as she said it.

Sydney gave her a perplexed look before getting up to join Spencer, her smile wide, Margot completely forgotten. Evidently, he hadn't shared his creepy forest stories with her just yet.

As they left, she looked back into the trees, and, just for a moment, wondered if she heard someone whisper her name.

TWENTY-TWO

Indiana

Getting married had been a mistake.

He knew that, but at the time, it was the only thing to do. Being with someone—especially someone he had known as long as Marianne—helped make him look more stable, more rooted. They'd been together since high school, largely because he couldn't be bothered to look for anyone else, and because she didn't ask any questions. She never seemed to find anything about him strange.

Maybe it was because she'd never known any different, but she simply never seemed to mind that he was gone for long stretches of time, or that sometimes he would choke her during sex. He toed that line very carefully, because he knew that one wrong thing whispered between girlfriends and soon someone would be putting poison in her ear about him.

But Marianne didn't really have any friends, which was a blessing and a curse. They lived in a small town where she knew just about everyone by sight, but she didn't go out, didn't participate, at least not beyond the usual town events that everyone felt obligated to attend.

And for a long time that had been a blessing, because she had no one to talk to about his comings and goings, his foibles. His kinks.

But lately, she seemed to care a great deal when he was away. She needed constant communication and reassurance. He had to coddle her. And then when he got home, he needed to make sure she got all the attention she was so desperately craving.

The turning point had been the baby.

The baby had been a real bummer for him, if he was being honest.

They'd been married straight out of high school because he'd needed her normalcy to tether him to their community, and if he'd let her leave town she might have realized there was a better life out there for her. It was a risk he couldn't take, so he'd proposed, they'd gotten married, and she'd moved into his mother's house with him, the one he had inherited when she had died.

If the house belonging to someone else bothered Marianne, she had never voiced that out loud to him. She hadn't really had much to bring with her; it had all fit in the back of her father's truck. All of it had seemed so normal, and just how things were done. They moved in together, among all the furniture and decorations of his childhood, and neither of them ever did anything to make it more their own except putting up their wedding picture on the dusty mantel, next to the one of his own parents.

For ten years, that had been enough for both of them. She cooked and cleaned and kept up the little vegetable garden his mother had started decades earlier. He worked his job that kept him on the road for weeks at a time. He didn't know what she did while he was gone, and she rarely told him. He just knew some of his money went to craft supplies, some of it went to booze, some to books, and in the middle of all those vices she seemed content enough.

And then, one night when he'd been away for two weeks, right after he'd found a girl hitchhiking on her way home from a party somewhere in Ohio, Marianne had said the words that made him rethink everything.

"Babe, I'm pregnant."

Even she hadn't seemed thrilled about it. She had basically whispered it, rather than announcing it with enthusiasm. Like she was afraid that saying it out loud was what might make it true. He wasn't happy, but her response to the news was still surprising to him somehow. He'd never forbidden children, they'd just never really talked about it. Not since they were still in high school and she'd said that one day she wanted three kids. She'd even told him the silly names she'd picked out, something he had long since forgotten. But since they'd been married, it had never come up. She wasn't the kind of person to coo over babies. She didn't demand to hold other people's children. It honestly hadn't seemed like something she wanted.

Yet, when she had told him she was pregnant, he couldn't bring himself to ask her if she was happy about it. In his mind, he wanted to tell her to just get rid of it, but he suspected that happy or not, that wouldn't be the thing to do, and he didn't want to make waves where they'd had a calm pond before. He'd hugged her, said it would all be okay, and then immediately stopped thinking about it at all until the baby arrived six months later.

She was a little girl and she looked like his mother. Marianne wanted to name her Evie, and, since he had no better suggestions, he let her.

He thought the baby might ultimately be a good thing. It would give her something to focus on, something to do while he was gone. But this hope had been dashed very early on when he had to make his first trip since she was born. Right away, he noticed the difference. The calls. The whining. The pleading.

She was not happier. If anything, she seemed to feel his absences more acutely.

Which meant she was paying attention more.

This was the antithesis of what worked so well between them. In the past, he'd been able to get by with one evening text or call to let her know she was in his thoughts and he would see her soon. Once Evie was born, she would send constant texts through the day. These were typically presented as updates on the baby and the milestones she was reaching—first smile, first laugh, first time rolling over—but he saw them for what they were. Desperate cries for attention. Marianne needed them more and more. He was no longer able to travel for more than two weeks at a time; she simply couldn't stomach it, and demanded he come home more frequently.

She'd asked him once to look for a more local job, but he had shot this down immediately, reminding her of the financial freedom his job allowed them, the health plan that had kept them from bankrupting themselves when she'd had Evie. Those kinds of jobs didn't grow on trees, he'd reminded her. Especially not in this economy.

She had dropped the subject, but hadn't quite let go of the nagging.

So when she called him and he was in Boise, cleaning blood from his hands in a rest stop bathroom close to where he had buried a kit, he answered reluctantly, tucking the phone against his shoulder while he used rough brown paper towel to scrub the stubborn stains under his fingernails.

"Babe," she said, her tone sounding tired, a bit slurred, like she might have had one glass of wine too many tonight. "When are you coming home?"

He rested his knife between the back of the old sink and the already stained wall. He wasn't worried about anyone coming in at this hour, and, even if someone did, they would likely be too focused on their own business to pay any attention to his.

"I'll be home in three days," he reminded her, not for the first time this trip.

"I miss you," she said.

"I miss you, too," he lied easily. "How is Evie?"

A hiccup, a sniff. She could be even more temperamental than their one-year-old. "She had some trouble getting to sleep tonight. I think I'm just a bit worn down."

"Well, I'll be back soon. It's all going to be all right," he said.

He had memorized these lines over the years, the lines that would smooth her ruffled feathers.

"Okay."

She didn't sound placated though. She sounded worried. Fraught. She sounded like she would be thinking about this a lot after he hung up, and that was the last thing he needed. Too much scrutiny from anyone was no good.

He was going to need to figure out a way to take care of her before she became a real problem.

TWENTY-THREE

There was something comforting to Margot about being back in a police station, even if it was a small local PD. Although Trumbull was no longer bustling, the PD had stuck around.

They now serviced three small towns in the same area, and Margot felt certain that this mass grave discovery was one of the wildest things to happen to their department in a good five to ten years.

This just didn't seem like the kind of place where horrible things happened regularly. She would have bet money that their usual fare consisted of some domestic disturbances, bar fights, and whatever it was that local teenagers did to blow off steam these days. When Margot had been young in Petaluma, that generally consisted of prank-calling friends whose parents didn't have caller ID, or pestering local radio stations to play songs with swears in them.

She had no idea what kids did now, and felt like she wouldn't understand it even if she asked.

The police station was a decent-sized building that had likely been built in the fifties. It was well maintained, though, with tidy-looking landscaping out front and paint that couldn't have been more than a year old both inside and out. Someone clearly cared very much about the building and what it represented, and Margot had a strong suspicion that person was Captain Darryl Barnett.

Barnett had that same air of competent cleanliness about him. His silver mustache was carefully trimmed, and, though he had to be over sixty, he didn't have the prominent beer belly she'd noticed on so many other aging lawmen. If anything, he looked as if someone had told Sam Elliott to go deep undercover in rural Tennessee to prepare for the role of a beleaguered lawman, and now he just didn't know how to tell everyone he was only an actor.

He even wore a cowboy hat, which he took off whenever a woman entered the room. It was kind of endearing.

Barnett approached his new FBI colleagues with two opposing feelings, both of which he wore plainly on his face. He didn't want them to be there, because he knew this town and its people, and they did not. And, in conflict with that, he seemed truly grateful to not have to handle this case on his own.

So he managed to be both gruff and polite at the same time, like a cat who wants to be petted but can't stop swatting at the hand that's doing the petting.

He'd given them access to a conference room, something Margot was grateful existed. It was a holdover from the past life of the station, and was now primarily used to house boxes with extra uniforms, which Andrew's team had carefully stacked against one wall so they could better use the room.

Margot felt transported. The shabby little space, with bits and pieces of former cases left behind, whether in old arrest reports or the faded black marks on the whiteboard from something that was likely last looked at twenty years earlier, this place *felt* like a police station. The whiff of burnt coffee, the old, unmistakable scent of cigarettes smoked in this same room decades earlier, this place took her right back to San Francisco.

She would never claim the FBI was posh and polished—their own shabby office was a testament to that—but it was still miles of difference from her time with the SFPD. She wished she could capture the smell of this room and send it to Wes, because a photo simply wouldn't work the same.

It also made her miss her old friend Leon Telly with a sharp pang. Though she and Wes had left San Francisco, they had remained in contact with Leon, who had worked alongside them in the homicide unit. The three of them had all left together at the end of the Redwood Killer case, but after a short retirement Leon, missing the thrill of the case, had started to take on private investigator work.

They'd seen him a handful of times in the intervening years, but Margot suddenly wished he was there with her to lend thoughtful insight or just listen to her work through the case. He had been a huge influence on her during her time with the police, and she hadn't realized how much she had missed that until she was so strongly reminded of it.

Once they were settled into the space—including Greg, who had arrived early that morning, making Margot wonder what time he must have left to get there—they invited Barnett and his second-in-command, Sergeant Calvin Widdicombe to join them. There were no detectives on staff at the Trumbull Police Department, and, as best Margot could tell, the only woman on staff was an officer.

Calvin was in his late thirties but still had the jovial jock features and physique to make it look like he'd just left a high school football game to get here on time for work. He was affable, like a golden retriever, and spent more time than was entirely polite pivoting his smile between Margot, Alana, and Sydney.

As he seemed to determine Sydney was closest in age to him, his smile drifted most frequently in her direction. Sydney seemed oblivious to it, or was intentionally ignoring it, which made Margot wonder how things had gone with Spencer on their date. She knew she shouldn't meddle, but she felt like she should ask. For some reason hearing it had gone well would ease a nagging worry that Margot had chalked up to paranoia. It was like having a younger sister—she just wanted to make sure Sydney had had a good time. She didn't need the gory details.

She looked back at Calvin's smiling face. She could imagine that, in a different life and ten years younger, that smile might have turned her head. He was just the kind of guy who oozed charm no matter what he did. Her brother used to say guys like that walked into a room dick first, something Margot hadn't understood until she'd met men like Calvin in person.

He and Darryl joined them at the table, where Greg had set up his laptop with their old projector system and was getting ready to do an overview of the case, along with everything he had learned while he was on his own, all of which would be new information for them as well.

Greg laid out the basics of the case, including a new three-dimensional diagram of the mass grave that had evidently been sent to him by the team at the Body Farm. It was a mock-up, as no ground-penetrating scans had been done of the site, but it gave a pretty detailed look at the depths of each body, their placement, and an even more stark look at the one female victim they suspected had tried to dig her way free.

Margot felt queasy seeing the position of that body from a new angle. She could appreciate the efforts the woman had gone through before succumbing to exhaustion and suffocation.

She had fought to her last breath.

The victims, all still only known by letter and not name, were broken down by date and location, and then the items that had been found with them were shared.

"Can't we do some sort of, I don't know, facial rebuilding on the skulls? I feel like I've seen that somewhere on TV," Barnett said, scratching his mustache idly as he waved his free hand at the projector screen.

"Digital remodeling is certainly available," Andrew said. "Once we have scans of the skeletal remains from the lab in Knoxville, we can submit our request, but there is a substantial backlog of requests for those services at the moment, so we're still going to try to work with some more standard identifying techniques. We'll continue to compile a list of missing persons in the area and wherever possible we'll use the dental X-rays we have access to in order to make comparisons. That should help us weed out some candidates, and hopefully we might get a hit or two."

"Do you plan to release images of the items found with the bodies?" Calvin asked.

"Failing any matches made from dental records and other medical options, yes, we think holding a press conference to share photos of the personal items is a beneficial next step. How equipped is your office to manage a tip line?"

Barnett paled momentarily before adjusting himself to sit higher in his chair. "We can manage the calls, so long as you can help manage the follow-through. I imagine a lot of what we'll get will be from out of state, and that's a bit outside our scope."

Andrew nodded. "Of course."

Greg bumped the slideshow up, and over fifty photos appeared on the screen. Margot struggled to focus on what was being presented, but thankfully Greg advanced the slide again so that the screen showed just a five-year span at a time.

Still, even at five-year intervals there were at least ten people missing per year. And the estimates of the bodies in their grave meant this particular killer—much like Wyatt Holmes—did not have any gender or age preferences, making it exceedingly difficult to weed any potential victims out at this point.

As Greg shuffled through the slides, which also pointed to where their victims had last been seen, Margot saw a few familiar faces, cases that Andrew's team had been working on in their lead-up to interviewing Holmes. The biggest difference was that there were more cases in the past ten years—when Holmes was in prison —that had never crossed their desk because of the time frame.

Margot had trouble imagining that two killers could have potentially been working the same hiking trail for at least five over-lapping years. They needed to know their surroundings so well— how was it they had never come across each other, and didn't know the other existed? Margot knew, from hours spent researching the case, that Holmes had treated the woods near his home like his personal hunting ground. It was territory he guarded zealously, thinking it belonged to him and his pack. How had someone been able to bury seven bodies on his turf without him knowing?

As convincing as he had been when talking to her in person, this was the one thing Margot couldn't quite shake. Sure, as Robert Frost once said, the woods were lovely, dark, and deep, but she wasn't sure she believed it was possible for someone to continually visit Holmes's turf without Holmes ever realizing it.

But the dates didn't lie. There were bodies in that grave Holmes couldn't possibly be responsible for, no matter what kind of logical yoga she tried to do. Someone else *was* out in those same hunting grounds, potentially covering more ground than Holmes ever did. Yet that person came back to that same grave over and over again. Something must have compelled him to return, and, if they could figure out why, that might help them narrow down the who.

While none of the bodies they'd found were fresh, there was still a massive elephant in the room: if Wyatt Holmes hadn't killed everyone in that grave, the person who had could still be out there. That put an added pressure on them to get this case solved, and fast.

Their killer had to be familiar with the area, meaning he might have been a local, or a regular seasonal visitor perhaps. Darryl and Calvin wouldn't love the intimation that someone they knew could very likely be a killer. That never went over great with locals.

They were about to advance to a slide with some of the most recent victims when the female officer Margot had seen earlier peeked her head in the door with a gentle knock on the frame.

"Captain?"

"What's up, Logan?" Darryl asked. There was a warmth to how he spoke to the young officer that made her briefly wonder if the woman might be his daughter. Or perhaps he just had that familial warmth towards his colleagues.

"Sir, there's something I think you need to see. You and the Feds." She nodded at them, and, though Margot could have done without the colloquial nickname, she suspected Officer Logan didn't even realize how dismissive it was.

After a curious shared glance around the table, they got up and followed the young woman out of the room to where a group of other officers were clustered around an empty desk.

"What the Sam Hill is going on here?" the captain asked gruffly, clearly annoyed that his staff appeared to be slacking off on the job while the FBI were present. His cheeks over his mustache were red from frustration.

The officers stepped back, revealing a manila padded envelope on the desk, with something wrapped in plastic sitting on top.

Affixed to the plastic-wrapped item was a Post-it note with a one-line message.

I want them back.

TWENTY-FOUR

There was a moment where everyone in the room just stared at the package, like this was some shared dream they might collectively wake from.

They all knew what the note meant.

"Did anybody touch anything?" Margot asked, shattering the frozen calm that had settled on them and made it so no one seemed able to move or speak.

An officer, no more than twenty, lifted his hand meekly. "It was addressed to the office, I was opening the mail." He gestured to a few other open envelopes on the desk as if he needed proof to back him up. "I didn't know what I was looking at until I read the note."

"Did you touch the paper?" Margot asked.

"I'm not sure. I don't think so. I pulled it out by the plastic."

She nodded. Not ideal, but since he was a cop they would have his prints in the system. Easy enough to rule out against any their UNSUB might have left behind.

Even this detail was a stark reminder of how little they knew.

Because this one envelope changed everything. It confirmed all her suspicions that there was someone other than Holmes out hunting in those woods, and that he hadn't disappeared or moved on to other pastures. He was still out there, and, more importantly, he was watching them.

The thought of it gave Margot the chills.

She didn't know him, and she was used to knowing her killers. Margot didn't know if he was someone who would leave prints behind. If he was, then he wasn't as smart as he liked to think, and that didn't jibe with her impression of a guy who had been killing for more than fifteen years. A lot of what made a serial killer successful was pure dumb luck. But there also had to be an element of real intelligence there, otherwise things would fall apart a lot faster.

Hubris was usually what got them caught. That, or a shift in which side was being granted the dumb luck on any given day: the killer's or the cop's.

Margot knew they couldn't just wait for luck to turn like the tide and shift in their direction, though. He'd given them a gift, and she intended to use it.

"No one has unwrapped the plastic, right?"

A collective round of headshakes went through the room.

"All right, anyone have any gloves? And a couple of evidence bags?"

Officer Logan disappeared and returned a moment later with the items Margot had requested. She handed the gloves out and began donning a pair herself. Smart. Margot liked being around smart people.

Margot approached the desk, slipping her gloves on, and the officers who had gathered around the package with so much curiosity all took a collective step back to give her room. Her own colleagues huddled nearby, watching closely.

She took a seat at the desk and pulled the envelope and its contents towards her. The words on the front of the envelope were in the same assertive handwriting, all block capitals with pressure so intense there were places at the junctions of certain letters where the ink had pooled into darker spots. Margot took the envelope first, checking inside to make sure nothing had been missed, and then slipped it into one of the evidence bags, which she sealed and handed to Officer Logan. "You know how to fill that out?" she asked, hoping her tone didn't come across as condescending. There was a very real chance out here, where crime was so sparse, that the younger officers might have never had a need.

Officer Logan nodded, and filled in the front panel of the evidence bag. Margot carefully peeled the Post-it from the plastic-wrapped item. She checked the reverse side; the only thing present was more leaked ink from the rough penmanship. She sniffed the note, wondering if she might find some clue there. It just smelled strongly of permanent marker.

This she deposited into a smaller bag, and handed over to Logan as well.

Then, as if she had been saving the best Christmas gift to be the biggest surprise, the little plastic-wrapped parcel was sitting in front of her. Her stomach turned just looking at it; deep in her literal guts she knew this was going to be something awful. There was no way it was going to be good; context clues alone could have told anyone that.

Serial killers don't generally send thoughtful gifts to the police.

She quietly hoped it wouldn't involve some kind of ridiculous cypher, because fifty years after the fact some of those sent by the Zodiac killer were still unsolved, which was infuriating. Margot didn't want to have to deal with a killer who thought he was *that* smart.

Working nimbly with the gloves on was a bit tricky, but she managed to unfurl what turned out to be a long strip of cling film, and, once she had gotten through that, their prize awaited.

It was a finger bone.

A complete finger, with all four bones, including the teeny tiny one at the tip.

Margot might not have been an expert in physical anthropology, and she was no doctor, but she knew that bones didn't just stay together like that on their own. They must have been wired together, though the wire was hard to see. These bones were also exceptionally clean. She thought of what they had pulled out of the ground earlier that week, and the skeletons she had seen at the Body Farm just the previous day. Those had been dirty, discolored. This was white, with just the faintest hint of yellowing, and looked as if it had just come from a plastic lab model, not a real human being.

Margot's instincts, though, told her this was the real deal.

She thought about all the clichéd gangster movies where people were sent fingers in the mail to prove that their loved ones could be hurt so much more, and she wondered: did this belong to one of their seven? She knew that, due to the nature of where they were buried and the fact that wildlife had no moral compunctions about eating murder victims, some of the bones from the grave were long gone.

Was one of them missing a finger?

Or was it the worse possibility?

That this belonged to an entirely different victim?

TWENTY-FIVE

Margot sometimes wished she smoked.

She'd taken up a lot of bad habits during the years when she lived shut away in her apartment, riddled with anxiety, saddled with a drinking problem. But she'd never smoked.

Her mom had. It was a habit that she'd picked up during Ed's trial that she had never managed to shake in the years that followed, and maybe that was exactly why Margot had never done it. She knew the way the nicotine clung to everything, the same way sadness clung to her mother.

But sitting out front of the Trumbull police station on a sweet little bench that was straight out of Mayberry, Margot wished she had a cigarette in her hand. It felt symbolically necessary. Otherwise, what the hell was she doing out here?

She was taking a moment to clear her thoughts, and it might not look cool or tough, but fresh air helped ground her, it helped her think more clearly.

She loved her work most of the time. There was a very rewarding element to being able to close cold cases that felt different to solving regular active homicides. There was an element of achieving the impossible in it, knowing that she and her team had managed to do something that detectives and agents before them hadn't been able to, sometimes over the course of decades.

But this felt different, because it was no longer a cold case, it was a harsh reminder that, despite all the work they did, there were always other killers out there adding to the totals. The FBI had actual data on how futile their work was. She and her team were getting close to a hundred cleared cold cases, which felt substantial until she remembered that six thousand homicides went unsolved every single year.

Over two hundred and fifty thousand cases in the country were unsolved.

The work they were doing was a drop in a bucket against a raging house fire that they had no way to put out.

She didn't feel defeated right now, though. An unusual thrill of excitement was building in her the more she thought about this case. Because she and the team had an opportunity here to do something big.

Instead of just talking to a serial killer, they could put one away for good.

You'll never stop them all.

That voice. That nagging voice she'd been hearing since the day her father died. It was so much his that she couldn't help but think of it as an entirely separate entity sometimes, even though she knew it was the same doubt and uncertainty that chased everyone. She had subconsciously let that voice become her father's.

In a way, it was better, because she had rarely listened to her father's bullshit when he had been alive, so why should she start now, when he was coming to her from the great beyond?

She might not be able to catch them all, the voice was right about that. But she could catch one. This felt solvable; she just needed to figure out what she was missing.

And she still couldn't shake Wyatt Holmes.

They had come here because of him. And even though they knew he couldn't have been responsible for all the bodies they'd dug up, Margot was like a dog with a bone—no pun intended. She just wasn't ready to let the connection go.

Someone sat down next to her on the bench, bringing a cup of coffee as an offering. She was surprised to find that it was Greg, because he didn't usually have the emotional range to be the comfort guy. Usually, he didn't even recognize when people were in an emotional space to need comfort.

The coffee, though, was precisely how she made it at the office, so she supposed he was paying attention to some things that happened around him. Greg was just wired differently, and it was part of what made him special. Margot was touched that he had thought of her.

He didn't immediately say anything, just sat with her while she took a sip of her coffee. As far as police station brews went, it wasn't the worst she had ever had, but that was truly like trying to rank the best pap smear she had ever had... were any of them really good or were they all just varying shades of awful? Still, coffee was coffee, and at a time like this it felt like the one act of self-care she was capable of indulging in.

"You spent yesterday looking at a bunch of missing persons cases up and down the trail, right?" she asked.

Greg, who had no coffee, because he didn't drink it, nodded. "Yes. I made a pretty comprehensive list."

This seemed like the understatement of the year given what he'd shown them in the PowerPoint before their meeting had been interrupted.

"In any of those cases, was there a mention of someone contacting the families? Mail, phone calls, something where they were maybe mocking or giving false hope, like suggesting they knew where the missing person was?"

This thing with the finger bothered her, and she didn't think it was something their killer would do in isolation. It was a bold move, sending in potential evidence, drawing attention.

Andrew was already on the phone to Knoxville to grill Dr. Ava on whether or not it looked like any of their victims might have lost a finger, specifically before burial. Though, given their killer's predilection for revisiting the burial site, he probably had ample opportunity to take the finger bones after they were already in the ground. But the cleanliness, the way they had been wired together, suggested to her that this had been something he had been taking care of for a long time.

Was this what he took as a trophy from his victims, little bits of bone that might easily be overlooked after years in the ground? If so, that was a big freebie in helping build his profile. It was hard for killers to keep souvenirs and trophies from their victims if they shared a home with someone. That was part of the reason that killers who took jewelry or personal items might give those items as gifts to their wives or daughters, so they could see their spoils all the time.

Souvenirs were slightly different from trophies. Souvenirs were items a killer would keep private for their own personal enjoyment, to get a thrill of remembrance whenever they looked at them.

Keeping articulated, cleaned human bones around was sure to raise some eyebrows, however carefully they were hidden away, which made Margot think this was likely to be someone who had no live-in partner or relative.

"There was, actually," Greg said, sounding almost surprised by the fact that she was right. He pulled out his phone and went through a few things before finding what he wanted, then handed it to her.

Margot saw a sweet-looking Native American girl, grinning broadly, with one crooked front tooth. Her heart sank, knowing as she did the stats about missing and murdered Indigenous women across North America. The odds had been stacked against this poor girl the moment she left her home alone. There were some groups who were targets for violence, and unfortunately those groups were rarely treated with the same dignity and attention as missing blonde, white girls whose cases happened alongside theirs.

They all mattered, they all deserved justice, but Margot felt a pang of empathy for the girl in the photo because, whatever had happened to her, Margot felt certain it had been passed over by the media and barely investigated by local police.

"That's Daisy Littlewolf, she disappeared while doing a day hike of the trail on her sixteenth birthday. Her family said she was an avid hiker, wouldn't have veered off the trail, and would have gone prepared. She'd hiked the same stretch of trail multiple times in the past and was very familiar with the area. None of her belongings were ever found, and the police ultimately ruled that she was a runaway."

Margot's jaw clenched. Even though she'd known what to expect, it still made her angry to be proven right. "Let me guess, according to her family she had no history of running away and there were no triggers in her life recently to suggest she would have?"

Greg nodded. "They said she was happy, had no conflict with anyone, and was planning to go to vet school when she graduated the next year. Her friends backed that up, which isn't always the case. Said she had no secret boyfriend, never fought with anyone, and had no substance abuse issues at all."

"And someone started to contact the family afterwards?"

Greg took his phone back, tapping at the screen a few more times. "They got a phone call about six months after Daisy disappeared. The caller spoke to Daisy's sister, Jessie, and apparently asked her if she'd like to see her sister again. When Jessie said yes, the caller apparently said, quote, 'Then I can bury you in the same grave.'"

A shiver went through Margot unexpectedly, the chill so sudden it was like someone had run an icy hand down her back. "That feels pretty relevant," she said. "Did he call again?"

"Yes, though this time they were able to record it—they wanted something to take to the police, so they'd been prepared in case he ever called back." Greg tapped his screen, and scratchy audio started to play from the phone.

"Do you think about her a lot?" the voice asked, deep, and

unpleasant. Margot wasn't sure if she was projecting, but just listening to it gave her the ick in a massive way.

"Of course. If you know where she is, please tell us. We won't report you, we just want her to come home." This must have been Daisy's sister, Jessie.

"What if I sent her back to you piece by piece?" There was a dark chuckle. He was clearly quite pleased with his own joke. Margot wrinkled her nose involuntarily in disgust.

There was a little sigh, then Jessie said, "If that's what it takes. We just want her back. Please."

"Why don't you come find her? Come into the woods, like Red Riding Hood. Just watch out for the wolf." Another laugh. Margot felt her rage increasing with every word he said.

"Why are you doing this?" Jessie asked, and though her voice trembled, Margot was in awe of the girl's bravery.

"If you could do anything you wanted, wouldn't you? If no one could stop you, you would do whatever your heart's desire was."

"Where is my sister?" Jessie demanded, ignoring his senseless ramblings.

"She's right where I left her. Don't worry, you'll see her soon."

The recording ended and Margot exchanged a glance with Greg, whose expression didn't give away any of what he was thinking.

"What a fucking piece of work," Margot said, leaning back against the bench and sipping her coffee.

"You think it's the same guy?" Greg asked, putting the phone in his jacket pocket.

"We have no way to know for sure yet. But there's enough there to suggest it's likely to be our guy. I'm going to make damned sure I find out."

"Do you think one of the bodies from the grave could be Daisy Littlewolf?"

Margot stretched out her legs and got to her feet, and Greg followed after her. "There's really only one way to find out, isn't there?"

TWENTY-SIX

Daisy Littlewolf was Victim A, their most recent burial.

Not only did she fit the timeline, having gone missing sixteen months earlier, she was the only one of the victims in the grave who was the right age, and they were able to match her dental records within hours.

One of the seven finally had a name, and the Littlewolf family could go to sleep tonight with at least one kind of answer. They would know finally that Daisy was not coming home. But they would also know definitively that she had never run away, she'd never wanted to leave them.

And once the work on her bones was complete, they would finally be able to bring her home and give her a proper burial.

Of course, the bigger question, one Margot and her team couldn't yet answer, was who had done this to her. The why of it would be a long-lingering thing that no one might ever be able to offer them, but the who was something Margot was determined to discover.

Discovering the body belonged to Daisy also offered more insight into their killer, because Daisy hadn't gone missing anywhere near the grave site. She'd gone missing in Georgia, near the southernmost point of the trail. Meaning their killer had brought her body across state lines and over a hundred miles out of his way just to include her among his collected victims.

It meant someone had been bold enough to bring a dead body all the way up the climb that Margot and the team had made a few days earlier, risking being spotted, and enduring a grueling slog with the added weight of a five-foot-ten teenager who had been, according to photos and records, very athletic and muscular.

Not an easy load to carry by any means.

Margot had dealt with a case during her police tenure that had befuddled the police. A killer managed to bring dead bodies into a national park that closed its gates at night, which shouldn't have been possible, and the how eluded them for a long time. The answer in that case had been almost ludicrously simple, but in this instance Margot felt like the most obvious answer was right in front of them.

He had to have carried Daisy's body; there was simply no other way for him to get her up the trail.

Unless she was still alive when he brought her here.

They now knew that he was fairly dedicated to his burial site, dedicated enough to bring bodies—or living victims—from other states there, rather than burying them where he found them.

Margot now had to wonder what was more likely—that he killed his victims where he found them, then went through the difficult work of transporting their bodies to and from multiple locations, or if he coerced them, kidnapped them, and then killed them closer to his hunting ground.

She hated to admit it, but they were probably going to need to go back to the burial site. If it was a ritualistic place for him rather than a convenient one, there might be more information to be gleaned looking around the grave than just looking in it.

The idea of hoofing it back up there was exhausting, so Margot didn't mention it immediately, but she knew her whole team was probably keenly aware of the necessity. At least they already had their boots with them. That was about as close to a silver lining as she could come up with.

They spent the remainder of their second day in Trumbull pairing missing persons with what little they knew of their victims. Based on gender, age, and the childbearing status of their female victims specifically, they were able to narrow down a list of over sixty missing persons cases to three or four potential candidates per unknown victim. It was a huge amount of information to get through, but with the smaller pool of possible victims they could set to work looking for dental records, DNA profiles, and anything that might help them get a solid match on their remaining Does.

They still had a long way to go before they would know who everyone found in the graves was, but Andrew had decided that Captain Barnett's idea of making pictures of the items they had found with the bodies public could help speed things up, especially if any of the tips linked to the names that were already on their list.

Which was how Margot found herself in front of a mob of reporters, wondering exactly how or why Andrew had selected her for this task instead of Alana, or literally anyone else. She had told him in no uncertain terms that she didn't want to lead the team.

Her name was also associated with a known serial killer, thanks to her participation in a documentary about her father several years earlier. While she wasn't in the spotlight over that anymore, there was no doubt someone would feel the need to call her *daughter of serial killer Ed Finch* in an article or news broadcast.

The lights from the cameras were blinding, forcing her to squint, and putting spots on her cue cards so she couldn't quite read what she had written. Her hands trembled slightly, and she couldn't help but feel like this was a test, or a practical joke. She wanted it to be one of those dreams where she showed up naked to school to take an exam she hadn't studied for. Unfortunately, the buzz in the room and the audible click of camera shutters made it impossible for her to convince herself it was anything other than real.

She cleared her throat and steeled herself. There was a large monitor on wheels behind her. There was no way the police department had anything like this in their budget. It presumably belonged to the school, because the elementary school gym was the only place in town large enough for them to hold the press conference. They'd originally planned to do it outside, but rain had forced them to find an alternative solution.

A hush fell over the room and Margot knew she had their full attention even if she didn't want it.

"Good afternoon, and thank you all for coming. I'm Special Agent Margot Phalen, I work with a special unit in the FBI that helps solve cold cases. As many of you are aware, there was a recent discovery on the Appalachian Trail of an unmarked mass grave site, and we are working to identify the remains of those victims. We have already identified one of the seven victims, though out of respect to her family, and wanting to be sure everyone is notified first, we will not be releasing her identity at this time."

A murmur of obvious annoyance went through the group of reporters. Margot was sure that, even with what she had just said, someone would still ask for Daisy's details.

Perhaps the reason she was here instead of Alana was because she was marginally less likely to answer a stupid question by telling a reporter to get their fucking hearing checked.

But she had no problem aggressively thinking those things.

"At this time, we are asking for help from the community, especially anyone who is living within close proximity to the Appalachian Trail..." She was careful here with her pronunciation, not wanting to get lambasted by local viewers. She recited *throw an apple atcha* in her head. "Please pay close attention to the images we are about to share. These are some of the items we recovered from the site, and if anything looks familiar to you, especially if it is connected to a loved one or someone you know who went missing, please contact our tip line. Don't hesitate, don't worry if you feel like there's only a small chance of there being a connection. We would rather look into something and be wrong about it than not hear from you and have the case continue to be unsolved."

With her soapbox moment over, she was free to turn the media's attention to the slideshow they had prepared, so they could post it on websites or show it in their broadcasts.

Still, Margot couldn't help but feel a slight sense of uneasiness, like they were looking in the wrong direction. She knew how important it was—giving a name to all these people was important. Giving their families peace was important.

But there was now something new to think about, something that she felt superseded their collection of unknown victims. The finger bone in the envelope appeared to have been fresh, which meant there might be someone else out there, someone who may or may not be dead yet.

She couldn't help but feel an anxious pull to focus all of her and her team's energy on that lead instead.

Andrew had argued that, if their guy was watching—and they suspected he was—and he liked to make phone calls, then there was a chance he would reach out to them directly once the tip line opened. His history of calling the Littlewolf family was enough to convince Margot this might actually work, but she still felt like she was wasting her time in this room when there was more important work to do out in the real world.

Once the slideshow of the victims' personal artifacts was finished, Margot steeled herself and returned to the podium.

"I'll take a few brief questions, but please be mindful this is an ongoing investigation, and we can't give out too many specific details at this point. And another reminder that we will not be disclosing the name of our one known victim until a later date."

Another annoyed murmur went through the crowd, but this time it was followed by an onslaught of questions so loud and intense Margot had to steady herself on the podium to keep from taking a step back from the wall of sound.

When it became clear that no one was going to be able to behave themselves and ask questions normally, she started to lose her patience. "Hey, hey. Folks, I know we all want to get our questions answered, but it's only going to happen if we ask them one at a time, okay?" This time she pointed in the direction of a CNN camera, hoping they might be professional enough to show the local stations how it should be done.

She didn't watch the news, so she didn't recognize the female reporter who got to her feet. "Becky Meyers, CNN. I'm just wondering if the FBI or local police are prepared to officially call this a serial killer?"

It was a stupid question very politely asked. Any teenaged girl with a true crime podcast obsession knew this was a serial killer, but Becky Meyers, CNN, wanted Margot to say it was a serial killer because then they could lean into that for their headlines and news crawls.

The team had already discussed this inevitability before the conference had been called, so, while Margot hated having to give the piranhas exactly the salacious reply they wanted, she at least had her answer readily available.

"Yes, at this juncture we are willing to say we would consider this unknown suspect to be a serial killer. The FBI will consider anyone with two or more victims who also meets a specific set of criteria to fall under the serial killer umbrella, and, with seven victims over the course of fifteen years, we believe this person meets all those criteria."

She pointed to another reporter. "Yes?"

The middle-aged man, his skin alarmingly tan, stood and asked, "Can you comment on the cause of death for these victims?"

"Not at this time," Margot said, which was honest, because they still had no idea. "We are working closely with the University of Tennessee in Knoxville, where a team of highly specialized forensic anthropologists are making strides to better give us cause-of-death information in the coming days. We can confirm they were all victims of homicide."

The man made a face at her like he didn't appreciate the stupidity of this answer. Joke was on him, because she didn't appreciate the stupidity of some of their questions.

She pointed to someone else, a smartly dressed woman with

her hair in a sleek Afro bun. "Has your team considered a connection to Wyatt Holmes? Several of his victims were located in this area and he lived not far from here."

At least this woman had come prepared.

"Yes, we actually initially responded to the scene because we believed it might be related to potential unsolved cases from Holmes, but we have since ruled him out as a possibility. There are victims in the grave we have been able to confirm were buried when Holmes was already in prison." She wasn't sure if this would be welcome news. It certainly wouldn't help the average viewer sleep better at night.

"Is there any possibility this person was an accomplice of Holmes?" the reporter asked, obviously looking for some way to connect this story to something the public—especially locally—would be familiar with.

"We have no reason to believe these crimes are connected to Wyatt Holmes in any capacity." Margot almost felt like she should follow her statement with an apology, the reporter looked so disappointed when she sat down.

This continued for a few more minutes with different versions of the same questions being asked, as well as the inevitability of one reporter asking if Margot could give "details" on Daisy Littlewolf without giving her name. Margot reminded him that the general ages and the sexes of all their victims were included in the media kit.

Of course, she had never once indicated which of the seven victims had been identified, so this wouldn't help him narrow things down much, which was her intent.

Finally, she pointed to a reporter who had been staring her down so fixedly it actually made her uncomfortable, to the point where she had skipped over him every time she selected someone to ask a question. His mounting frustration was evident in his ruddy cheeks and focused glower.

"Do you have any reason to believe this killer is a threat to people in the area?"

Margot took a breath. She was surprised this question hadn't been asked sooner, honestly. The moment she had said they believed they were looking at a serial killer, she'd anticipated the press would find a dozen ways to stoke those flames to create a frenzy among their reader- or viewership. She'd been pleasantly surprised that up until now they had largely kept the focus on the victims.

So, when this question hadn't come, she'd let her guard down slightly, which was a mistake, because it took her a few extra seconds to process her reply, which would surely look quite dramatic when played back later.

"We would always recommend caution and vigilance to those who live in areas where a serial killer has been known to operate. From the victim profiles, it should be evident that this particular killer does not favor a particular age or gender in his victims. We are not yet aware if there are any race-based predilections, but from our initial assessments we don't believe that to be a factor for him either." The people they had narrowed down for their potential victim pool were of a variety of races, so even though they hadn't named all their victims yet, there was no implied correlation among those they thought *could* be their victims.

"What we would suggest is that anyone planning to hike the Appalachian Trail consider doing so as part of a pair or group, and that they wear some type of tracking token that someone back home has access to. We would also suggest anyone going for day hikes in the vicinity of the trail, not just in Tennessee but elsewhere, go in pairs or groups, and consider bringing along bear spray as a protective measure. Always, always, we recommend staying aware and alert. Don't wear headphones, and, if you feel like the situation is getting unsafe, turn around, contact someone by phone if you're able, just get out of there."

The room had gone silent as Margot spoke, so her final warning seemed louder than it actually was. She took a deep breath, rearranged her notecards, and then looked back out at the reporters. "Thank you for your time. Please share the tip-line number frequently. I'll turn things back over to Chief Barnett."

She ducked away from the podium, half expecting a last-second burst of new questions to follow her, but thankfully there were none. Barnett would be responsible for soothing the minds of those watching by explaining how the police and FBI were working so well together to solve this case, and he had every confidence they would be able to publicly release victim information soon.

Margot couldn't flee the scene entirely—it wouldn't look right —so she stood with the rest of her team waiting for things to wrap up so they could get back to work.

She thought over her answers several times, picking apart what she'd said, hoping that her real message had gotten through.

It wasn't potential victims she was trying to speak to.

It was their killer.

TWENTY-SEVEN

When Margot returned to her motel with a bag of takeout from the diner in one hand and her key in the other, the last thing she expected to see was someone sitting outside her room.

She paused in the parking lot, eyes scanning the area for her best exit routes. It was a pretty straight shot on her right to get to the motel office, and only two doors down from her room were the rooms of the rest of her team. They would be able to hear if she screamed for help, she told herself.

She at least got to wear her shoulder holster with this outfit, which made her feel more comfortable with grabbing it if she needed to.

Of course, to get to her gun she would need to drop the club sandwich she was carrying, and she didn't want to do that unless she absolutely had to.

Her pulse hammering, she slowly advanced towards her door, ready to run, scream, or shoot depending on what the situation necessitated. All of the rooms at the motel had one chair outside. Margot's anxiety spiked as she realized she hadn't seen anyone just idly lounging outside in a chair the whole time they'd been there.

She moved closer to the figure in the shadows and then

stopped dead in her tracks, trying to decide if what she was seeing could even possibly be true.

"Wes?" she asked, confounded.

Wes was supposed to be on the other side of the country, feeding their chickens and teaching teenagers how to play badminton. It made no sense that he'd be in front of her hotel. It was like her desire to see him had conjured up a ghost of him because she just missed him so badly.

He glanced up at her and smiled. He looked a little bleary, like she had just woken him from a nap, which she very well might have. It would explain why he hadn't said anything when she approached.

"Hey, you," he said, pushing himself to his feet, his tall frame filling the door of her room.

She wondered briefly if any of her teammates had noticed a strange man sitting in front of her door and, if they had, why they hadn't bothered to warn her. But she supposed they might not have seen him, or they might have recognized him and not wanted to ruin the surprise.

Margot hated surprises, but she might make an exception for this one.

She shook off her stupor, closed the distance between them, and wrapped him up in a big hug. "What are you doing here?" she asked, still barely able to believe he'd come.

She hoped no one on her team would judge her for this. A lot of them had people at home they were missing, and she didn't want them to feel embittered towards her. But another part of her, the one she had trained not to worry so much, told her to shut up and kiss the man she loved.

She listened to that part, unlocking the door to her room to usher him inside before planting an eager kiss on his mouth, leaning her whole body into him just because she missed the way it felt to be near him.

He chuckled against her lips, peppering kisses over her cheeks, nose, and forehead. "You've been sounding a little gloomy the last few nights we talked, and it's a Friday, so I thought it might be nice to come visit you. I know you hate surprises, but this one was so last-minute, I didn't want to disappoint you if I couldn't make it work. I got lucky, though, open seat on the cheap to Nashville and the shittiest rental car left on the lot." He smiled, and the warmth of it melted her.

"It's a good surprise. I'll allow it," she replied, setting her food on the small table inside the door, and breaking away from him just long enough to lock the motel door and engage the chain.

Then, she returned to where he was standing, wrapped her arms around his waist, and pressed her face against his chest. The T-shirt he was wearing was soft and smelled of the laundry detergent they used at home. If she closed her eyes, she could imagine they were standing in their kitchen, right after getting up for the day. She was usually awake before him, thanks to the work that was required to keep up their multitude of animals, but sometimes they got to have a quiet moment just like this, and she held on to them like little treasures, things to keep her going when the work got really dark.

Thinking of the animals, she pulled back, looking at him. He wasn't much taller than her, so their gazes were almost level once she'd stopped stooping to snuggle.

"Who's looking after the farm?"

Their home situation was not one that would allow for him to overfill a container of cat food and put out a few extra water dishes. They had several senior dogs who required daily medication, and the chickens needed to be put away every evening for their own peace and protection.

"It's okay. Sadie came for a visit—she was actually the one to suggest I do this."

Sadie Fox was one of Wes's many sisters, and the only one without children. She'd stayed with them for a good stretch during Wes's legal issues the previous fall, and while there had sometimes been a little friction between her and Margot, it usually stemmed from a place of wanting what was best for Wes, which Margot thought was a noble battlefront. Things had warmed considerably since then, and Sadie made frequent visits to the ranch just to spend time with them. Margot thought she might be feeling a bit lonely, but she was such a free spirit Margot had a hard time imagining her settling down any time soon.

Margot sort of imagined that when Sadie finally did find a permanent place to roost, it would be in a little cottage by the ocean, she'd be sixty, and she would live with a woman she called *her roommate* while making windchimes out of seashells to sell to deep-pocketed tourists. Margot wasn't sure why this was her vision for Sadie, but it just seemed to fit, and it made her smile whenever it came into her head.

Sadie knew the farm, and knew how to take care of their animals. She had even received the grudging stamp of approval from Margot's calico cat, Lucy, who liked almost no one but had sat next to Sadie on the couch for about ten minutes once, which was how she demonstrated acceptance.

Knowing she was there—and also knowing that Margot had left behind a laminated set of feeding and medication instructions for Wes—let her ease back into him. Things would be fine for a day or two without them there.

She held Wes's face in her hands, her fingertips tickled by the fine blond stubble that had filled in over a day of travel. His dark-blond hair was mussed, but it was almost always mussed, as if to suggest he had always just finished doing something fun and outdoorsy. It was a change of pace from their time with SFPD, when he was always dressed in nice suits and looked like he was better suited to be a highly paid lawyer than a veteran homicide detective.

Since they'd moved, he had ditched the suits and replaced them with jeans and button-down flannel. Even for work he generally wore khakis and a Willows High School-branded polo shirt. She'd fallen in love with him in his suits, but she found she loved this casual iteration of Wes even more. It was like this had been the final form he was always meant to evolve into. He seemed more relaxed and happier now, but that might have been Margot project-ing, because she so badly *wanted* him to be happy in his life with her.

He had brought a backpack with him, which she hadn't even noticed until he dropped it on the floor next to the door. He moved her carefully in the direction of one of the double beds, his thighs gently pushing her backwards, and she followed where he led her.

Intimacy, real open intimacy, had been hard to achieve for Margot, who had spent her whole adult life shutting herself off from real connections with people. But over their years together, she and Wes had developed a silent shorthand with one another. She knew she could trust him, and he knew never to push the lines of that trust. It meant she could just yield to him in moments like this, and know that her boundaries would always be respected.

He kissed her in a long, lingering way that made her toes and fingertips tingle, and she fumbled with the buttons of his shirt, wondering why anyone needed quite so *many* of them at a time like this. As she grumbled her frustration into his kisses, she felt his mouth curve into a smile, and he put enough space between them to allow him to help her finish the process.

A true gentleman.

She felt her thighs bump against the edge of the bed, and was about to let herself fall onto it, craving the weight of his body on top of hers, when a loud knock at the door made them both go still.

Margot pulled back, feeling dizzy from the kisses, her face certainly rubbed raw from his stubble, and they both waited, rooted in place, as if they might have imagined it and, if they just gave it a moment, the interruptus to their coitus might kindly fuck right off.

Again, the knock sounded, again less a polite rapping, more a demanding pound.

Margot's brow furrowed. She didn't like the way that knock sounded. Based on the dark expression that clouded Wes's face, he didn't like it either.

"Stay here," he said, edging towards the door.

But Margot grabbed him by the arm, stopping him. "Wes,

between the two of us, which one is armed?" she reminded him, gesturing towards the holster still on her hip. That probably would have been uncomfortable if they'd managed to make it to the mattress.

He nodded, letting her pass him, though he stayed right on her heels like he planned to intervene at the first sign of danger. While he knew that Margot was perfectly capable of taking care of herself, she sometimes saw these hypermasculine protective flashes come over him. It was flattering, and in a different scenario, she might have even found it sexy.

However, since the first knock had broken the stillness of the room, her pulse was racing for altogether different reasons. She approached the door from the side, like they had learned in their police days. The last thing you wanted to do was stand in front of a door if someone on the other side was holding a gun.

"Who is it?" Margot asked, trying to keep her tone upbeat, even though she felt anything but.

She hoped she would hear the voice of someone on her team call back to her, because any other option aside from it being someone on her team, would mean that it was someone who should not know she was here.

They waited, the seconds ticked by, and there was no response.

Margot hesitated, then leaned across the door to look through the peephole. This could have been fatal, depending on the circumstances. If someone on the other side had been waiting to see the light in the peephole change, she was giving them exactly what they wanted. But she also couldn't just stay in here all night waiting to see what happened next.

There was no one outside.

While a part of her had known that could be the case, it was still surprising. She exchanged an uncertain look with Wes, then opened the door, her gun still drawn but aimed down at the carpet.

A quick look around outside showed her that no one was waiting in the shadows to jump out at her. The parking lot was almost empty aside from a few parked cars, and a couple of doors down Margot heard a TV playing loudly.

And sitting right in front of her door was a manila envelope, with a dark, heavy-handed scrawl that read:

Special Agent Margot Phalen

The envelope was thick, and obviously contained something much like the one delivered to the police department had.

Margot didn't need to open it to know what was waiting inside.

TWENTY-EIGHT

Andrew Rhodes was a man whose presence was felt in a room, even though he wasn't an imposing size or someone who drew attention to himself. Simply by his existing in a space, the attention would naturally flow to him, which was what happened the moment he stepped into Margot's motel room.

The room, with its two double beds and little countertop kitchenette, had felt almost too big for one person when Margot had first walked in. Now that it was filled, she was beginning to experience a creeping sense of unease, like suddenly all the oxygen in the space was being consumed and there wasn't enough left for her.

She was sitting on the end of one of the beds. Wes, his buttons redone, looking as poised as ever, lingered near the door, wanting to be the first person to get a look at anyone who tried to enter.

So far, those who had passed his gargoyle-like test were Andrew, Alana, and Chief Barnett. Five people in one motel room was three people too many, as far as Margot was concerned. When Officer Logan appeared at the door, toting a camera she didn't look altogether familiar with, Margot felt the immediate desire to walk out the door and keep walking until she was back in California.

It was not a panic attack, but if things continued like this it might become one. She took steadying breaths, and when Wes looked at her for the okay to let Logan in, she gave a tight nod.

Andrew and Barnett were sitting on opposite sides of the little table, both staring at the envelope like they couldn't decide what to do next. Based on their previous encounter with the killer's mail, they didn't need to worry about it exploding, but for FBI agents who had been around as long as Andrew had, the notion of mail that blew up was all too real a concern.

There was also, of course, always the possibility it was loaded with some sort of nerve toxin like anthrax, which had unfortunately proven to be a real thing people needed to worry about.

But Margot knew, and suspected that everyone in the room knew, precisely what was in the envelope.

Since they didn't have access to any high-tech equipment or bomb-sniffing dogs, Andrew had gone about as low-tech as possible in inspecting the package before opening it: he had held a magnet up to it, and when he was satisfied there was nothing metallic inside, he picked the package up—with gloved hands—and took it into the bathroom to open it alone.

Just in case.

The parcel did not explode. When Andrew came back out into the main part of the room, he set the envelope and its contents back on the table for everyone to see. Alana hovered over Margot's shoulder, and they both allowed room for Officer Logan, who had been tasked with documenting the parcel.

The contents were almost identical to what they had received at the police station, but almost immediately Margot knew something wasn't right. The Post-it was in the same blocky writing, but the message was different.

I want them back, or I will replace them.

The words were so large they filled the entire front of the Post-it.

And the plastic-wrapped item, the same size and shape as the finger bones they'd received, was what gave Margot pause.

Whatever was wrapped in this plastic, it wasn't clean, white bone. The dark red, almost brown tone of dried blood was unmistakable, and instead of bone, Margot saw under the wrap only flesh tones.

Whatever was in there was fresh. Or at least it had been when it was wrapped up. Andrew must have been able to tell what he was looking at—he was even closer to it than Margot was—but he didn't hesitate as he began to unwrap it. Soon Margot's hypothesis was proved correct. The plastic wrap unraveled, and a human finger fell on top of the envelope. The blood was dry at this point, no droplets or smears to create dramatic gore, but she was too busy staring at the nail polish to notice.

The one fingernail was painted an icy blue. The kind of shade a teenager might choose.

The shutter-snapping of Logan's camera stopped, and she made a gagging sound. It wasn't loud, but the room was so damn quiet it was the only thing anyone heard. Wes, no stranger to watching officers lose their lunch at crime scenes, opened the motel room door before Logan had even moved. She raised her hand to her mouth and seemed like she was about to apologize, but then the wave of nausea hit her hard and she disappeared through the door. Her retching was audible even though she had run out into the parking lot.

Margot was sympathetic. She didn't think there were a lot of cases in this area that involved severed body parts.

No one in the room commented on it; it was something of a rite of passage that everyone went through at a crime scene once in their career. Even she had tossed her cookies once when she'd been a rookie cop. That hadn't even been a murder scene, it had been a particularly bad car accident. Margot had never seen anything that bad in her life up to that point.

She'd seen worse since, but she'd never thrown up at a scene again.

She felt certain that a veteran cop like Barnett would pull Logan aside later and privately tell her the story of the first time he ever threw up on the job. This, too, was part of the ritual. For her, it had been her much older partner, a guy named Stephens. Just hearing him say she wasn't alone had been enough.

It would have to be for Logan, too, or else this might not be the kind of job she was suited for.

She returned, looking sheepish, but everyone remained focused on the finger, giving her permission to just fall back into place, hiding behind her camera.

With gloved hands, Andrew laid out the finger and note on the envelope and leaned out of the way for Logan to take pictures. Once she had finished, she excused herself and left the room again. Margot felt for her.

"Well," Alana said, letting her breath out in a long sigh. "Margot, I've gotta say I'm glad you were the one at the press conference and not me."

Margot snorted, but it was the first time she had smiled since opening the door to discover the parcel. They were all quietly looking at the finger, trying to make sense of it, when there was a gentle knock at the door. Wes peered through the curtain at the window, then opened the door and ushered Greg inside.

His red hair was flattened on one side, like he'd already been in bed when all of this went down.

"Find anything?" Alana asked, her tone almost bored, like she was anticipating a certain answer. She looked more casual now than Margot could ever remember seeing her, in Lululemon yoga pants and an oversized cashmere sweater. Her nearly white hair was pulled back in a short ponytail at the nape of her neck. She was still wearing a full face of makeup, though, so Margot knew she hadn't been awoken by the drama.

Greg looked as if he still had pillow creases on his face. He shook his head, wearing a disappointed expression. "No. The motel only has one camera, and it faces the road. We're going to take the tape and track any of the cars coming and going from the lot, but if he approached from any other direction then we're not going to see him."

"That's what we get for staying at a motel that Norman Bates would have considered too gross," Alana said, aiming this remark right at Andrew.

Andrew was taking photos of the package on his phone, ignoring the usual banter of his team. "Alana, when you're in charge you can do what you want with your limited budget, but until that day I will continue to book us in to quite literally the only accommodations within a hundred miles of our crime scene."

Alana and Margot exchanged a quick glance. Margot had worried what being put forward for greeting the press might mean, but she felt a strange sense of relief hearing Andrew all but confirm Alana's selection as his replacement. It seemed wrong, feeling lighter when there was a severed body part six feet away from her, but Margot couldn't help her emotions.

"So, we can safely assume he either has a new body he acquired this from or he has a living victim who he isn't quite finished with yet," Andrew said, grounding them back in the case at hand.

"Do you know of any current missing persons cases in the area?" Margot asked Captain Barnett, even though she knew—given where Daisy Littlewolf had gone missing—that this new victim could have come from anywhere.

Still, in her gut she felt like they had to be close. The killer had likely been watching them since the bodies had been discovered, and twice in the span of one week he'd gone out of his way to send or deliver a parcel within the Trumbull town limits. The letter to the police had been mailed with a home-printed label, using the police station's own address for the return address. The only fingerprints from anything on or in the envelope had belonged to the young officer who had found it.

This time, he had delivered it in person, and Margot was willing to bet they wouldn't find anything in terms of fingerprints here either.

The old envelope and this one would both be DNA tested on the off chance he had been dumb enough to lick the envelope, but given how careful he'd been about everything else, Margot already knew the chances of that were somewhere between *slim* and *fuck all*.

This felt like the most tangible clue they'd had this whole time, and it was almost useless to them. The finger *might* have a viable print that *might* belong to someone in the system, but that would just give them one answer. At this point their much more pressing concern was that a serial killer wanted their attention very, very badly, and he seemed to be willing to go to great lengths to get it.

He also wanted his bones back, something that was obviously not going to happen, but that was making him behave irrationally and put himself at risk just to see what he thought belonged to him returned.

They could use that. If he was watching, they could make sure he saw something that would really get his attention. But they would need to be careful how they went about it. Right now, things were looking like this guy, while maybe not local, did not feel out of place spending time in Trumbull, which meant he had likely been here in the past. He wasn't going to stick out.

Margot knew all too well how easily a serial killer could blend into their community. It was something they were exceptionally gifted at, because many of them fell on the psychopath spectrum, which meant they'd already spent a good portion of their lives learning how to mask their differences and mirror the behavior of those around them.

For fifteen years she hadn't realized there was anything wrong with her own father. So it never surprised her that Jim Bob who helped run the church picnic was actually hunting girls in the Alaska wilderness like they were big game, or that Teddy the mechanic who helped change old people's tires for free was actually making skin suits out of middle-aged women.

There was very little that surprised Margot these days, at least when it came to the depravity human beings were capable of.

The scariest thing about serial killers was how many of them looked completely normal, and lived lives that gave no indication of who they truly were under the well-rehearsed veneer. They were good actors by necessity. It was a survival skill.

But that meant that while they were here investigating the case, there wasn't one single soul outside her FBI inner circle that Margot felt confident she could trust. Even lovely Captain Barnett. She knew there was no way they could keep him out of the loop on things entirely—it would sour the relationship with the local PD and the FBI, something they couldn't afford to do at this stage in the investigation, especially when the Trumbull police were the ones running the tip line.

That didn't mean, however, that Margot needed to trust them with everything, and certainly not with their intent to go back up the mountain. In fact, if they played this right and gave the police just enough information, then it might turn out to help them more than hinder them.

For the moment, though, Margot just wanted everyone to get the hell out of her room.

"Andrew, can you bag that up and take it back to the station?" she asked, getting off the bed and heading to the door. She opened it meaningfully. "We can pick this all up in the morning." She did nothing to hide how exhausted she was feeling, and slowly almost everyone else seemed to get the picture, although Alana had to physically steer Greg in the direction of the door before it clicked for him.

Andrew was the last to leave, and gave her a long look before he did. "You going to be okay tonight?"

He knew. He knew what her life had looked like before this, with the half-dozen bolts on her door, and her unwillingness to leave her home alone at certain times.

Her father had told her all the ways she needed to protect herself from people like him, and she had internalized those to a point where she was afraid of the outside world. She didn't let herself form routines. She couldn't even have dinner by herself, out of worry that someone might follow her home.

It had taken her years to break free of those shackles, and to start living her life like an almost normal human being.

Now, everything she had ever feared had been proven true. Someone had used her presence on TV, and the knowledge of the town's limited options for motels, and they had come right to her door.

But Margot didn't feel scared.

She felt more determined than ever to get this guy.

She smiled at Andrew.

"He'd have to be an idiot to try it again," she said. "So, I'm kind of hoping he does."

Andrew gave her a funny little look, then nodded. He had to think she was out of her mind.

Sometimes Margot wondered if she was.

TWENTY-NINE

Despite her bold proclamations to Andrew and the rest of the team about how unbothered she was, Margot was eternally grateful that she had Wes to lean on when they were all gone.

Wes, who knew her better than anyone. Wes, who could read her like a favorite book whose complex passages he had committed to memory.

Wes, who had the best brain for solving murders that she knew.

They lay on the bed together, the mood certainly dampened; she was now content to curl against his side, where her body somehow fit like a key in a lock, and the presence of him was enough to calm her jangling nerves.

She hadn't been afraid when they'd opened the package, or when she realized what all of it meant, but now the shock of it was hitting her and she had begun to tremble uncontrollably, like the air conditioning was on high blast, even though it was off.

Still, the panic attack stayed at bay. Later, when all this was done, she would tell Dr. Singh about how well she'd done in one of the worst-case scenarios he had always told her would never happen.

"A serial killer isn't going to show up on your doorstep,

Margot," he'd told her once, when she'd explained what she was afraid of. "I think, statistically speaking, you've had all the serial killer encounters you're going to have."

That was easy for him to say, but Margot should have realized this was inevitable. You could tell the average person on the street that their likelihood of being attacked by a shark was so low it was almost negligible. But what if that person was regularly free-diving with sharks? The statistics probably changed a little.

And Margot went swimming with the sharks all the damn time.

So, maybe she should have been more surprised by this, but she wasn't. That didn't necessarily make it easy to stomach, but it wasn't going to make her turn tail and go back into hiding.

"We could just go home," Wes offered, though it was one of those polite lies that he knew she wouldn't give in to.

"I would love that," she mumbled against his chest, just enjoying the way he smelled. If she closed her eyes she could almost imagine they were back in their bedroom on the ranch. The illusion was only ruined by the stale-smoke scent of the room, and the lumpy mattress that was making her feel like she was in her sixties instead of her forties.

"Too bad you need to stay here and be a superagent, and get this son of a bitch."

She could hear the smile in his voice even without looking at him. He did that, sometimes, called her superagent instead of Special Agent. From anyone else it might have sounded dismissive or mocking, but from Wes it was endearing. She wished, and not for the first time, he had been able to join her when she had moved to the FBI.

The Bureau was actually remarkably considerate to married agents, and made sure they got posted to the same offices. But they had bent their age restriction rules once in allowing Margot to join even though she was older than their cut-off. They'd also bent the rules in allowing her to spend most of her time working from home. It would have been a bridge too far, asking them to bring in her partner just because she didn't want to work cases without him.

For what it was worth, Wes didn't seem to mind being out of the law enforcement game. Eventually, homicide got to be too much for everyone. It wore a person down, and Wes seemed happier now that he was teaching teenagers to work through their aggression with dodgeball, and helping the boys' basketball team win their first state title since the town of Willows was formed.

That feat had also gone a long way towards getting the locals to start accepting Wes again after his murder accusation the previous year. Because everyone knows murderers can't coach state champs.

Margot didn't care why people had embraced Wes again, she was just happy they had. He was the kind of person who thrived on connection to other people, where Margot knew if she had to be forced into solitary confinement she would probably do just fine, as long as she had a good book and could watch *Bob's Burgers* every now and then.

"Can I poke around at your brain for a bit?" she asked, her fingernails tracing patterns in the white T-shirt he'd put on to sleep in. At home he usually only wore pajama pants, but she couldn't blame him for the extra layers in this questionable motel room.

"Poke away," he said.

"Have you looked into this case at all?" she asked.

"There's not much for us plebs to know at this point, but I've read what's out there."

She hadn't considered that he wouldn't know all the details, she just assumed he would absorb them via osmosis because they were together. She quickly explained what they knew, about the bodies, the timeline, and Daisy Littlewolf being taken from an entirely different state. It was a quick and dirty recap, but it was more information by miles than she had given the press earlier that afternoon.

"I can't figure him out," she concluded, her frustration evident in her voice.

Wes was listening, but he was also twining a piece of her red hair around his fingers. She wore her hair up at all times when working; the high auburn ponytail was almost as much a part of her uniform as any piece of clothing she owned. But there was a brief window before she went to sleep—when she also pulled it up so she wouldn't sweat to death—when she let it hang loose. Wes loved that part of the evening. He would constantly touch and play with her hair, though she wasn't convinced he was even aware he was doing it.

"If it was easy to figure them out," he said, "they wouldn't be so hard to find."

Margot scoffed. "Thanks, Yoda."

He chuckled, the sound vibrating against her cheek.

"You're trying to decide how he's doing it," he confirmed.

"I figure he's either killing them where he finds them, then transporting them twice, which seems awfully fucking difficult. Or he's somehow luring them off the trail and then either killing them offsite, or bringing them to his grave site and killing them there."

"Listen to the evidence. You said one of the skeletons in the grave was positioned in such a way that it looked like she was attempting to climb out."

"Right."

"So she was alive when he buried her."

"Which, Occam's razor and all that shit, means she was alive when he got her to the location."

"That would be the most logical conclusion."

"What baffles me about that, though, is that there were multiple couples or pairs found in that grave. People buried alongside each other at the same time. I can see someone being able to kidnap and compel a single person through the woods. Threats of violence, fear, there are plenty of ways to make someone hike against their will."

"I don't think I've ever used threats of violence. I believe I said, *it will be good for you to get out of the house.*"

"Same thing. But kidding aside, I understand him being able to move single victims. What I don't get is how he could move more than one person at the same time." Though as a general rule, Margot knew that, when it came to violent crimes, the last thing a person should ever do was allow themselves to be moved to a secondary location. It was almost certainly signing a death sentence.

No kidnapper would spend enough time with someone to transport them to a new place just to leave them alive at the end of it. There were probably exceptions to the rule, but Margot knew what she knew, and she knew it was never advisable to let yourself be transported.

"I think it's pretty simple," Wes said. "Threaten the woman."

Margot sat up enough that she could look at him, her brow creased.

"No, don't give me that face," he said with a soft laugh. "Listen to me. The easiest way to get two people, especially a couple, to move together without resistance is to threaten the woman."

"That's the most sexist thing I've ever heard you say."

He rolled his eyes. "It eliminates the wild card, because then he has control over the most important element of the equation. If he did it the opposite way—and I'm sure you'll call me sexist for this, too—by focusing on the man, because the man is stronger, then it overlooks the obvious weakness in the plan."

"The woman is the weakness of the plan? Keep digging that grave, buddy, you can sleep in the barn when I get home."

He smiled again, lifting her hand to his mouth and kissing her knuckles.

"A man is unlikely to leave a woman behind, because he will feel it's his duty to protect her. But a woman will leave a man behind, because she's smarter, and she knows there's a better chance of them both surviving if at least one of them gets away. I think our guy knows that. Maybe because he's fucked it up before, so he knows if you control the woman, you control the power."

Margot stared at him for a long moment, considering this theory. There was a chance he was trying to butter her up, but there was also a chance he might have a real point.

Then what he'd just said jumped out at her.

Maybe because he's fucked it up before.

They'd spent all their time and energy so far looking at potential victims in the missing persons reports, but what if the most important person they were looking for wasn't missing at all?

What if she had gotten away?

THIRTY

The next morning, Wes joined Margot at the police station. He was planning to stay one more night before heading back to the ranch in Elk Creek, and while it wasn't standard practice, Margot felt like they might benefit from having his brainpower on the case while he was around.

Outside contractors weren't unheard of among the FBI, and although he hadn't passed any clearances, all Bureau spouses had been investigated and vetted for national security reasons, so the FBI were aware that he wasn't a lunatic who would use things he learned on the case to sell them to foreign governments or something.

Besides, given how far outside the reach of the Bureau they currently were, Margot figured it was a beg-forgiveness versus ask-permission scenario. When she showed up with him, Andrew merely looked at Wes, then nodded towards the conference room, inviting him to join them.

The local PD took a little more convincing, but once Margot explained Wes's record and years of experience with the SFPD—and his involvement in the Redwood Killer case—they seemed to accept his presence.

The only person in the room who didn't embrace his being

there with open arms was Sydney. She was looking at him like he was there to steal her job. Margot could understand. There were a lot of positions in the Bureau that were highly sought after and turnover was a big thing; agents were frequently moved to different roles and different cities. Sydney's expression said she didn't want Wes to move in and take her spot.

She'd actually been more tense and grouchy since her date with Spencer, something that made Margot think their date had either gone well and he hadn't called her after, or it had gone poorly and she was feeling a bit burned. With all the horrific deliveries and unexpected twists, Margot hadn't had an opportunity to ask Sydney about it, but now that moodiness seemed pointed at Wes.

Margot actually thought it was kind of sweet that Sydney liked her job so much she was willing to give Wes the evil eye throughout their briefing meeting. Maybe later she would explain that, unlike Sydney, almost no one else in the FBI was beating down Andrew's door to be allowed onto the cold case team.

No one was interested in talking to killers who were already in prison, which was the reason so many cold cases lingered for so long.

The work Margot and Andrew had done with Ed Finch had proven that there was public interest in closing those kinds of cases, and that interest had been enough to get their team off the ground and give her a job. It didn't hurt that whenever they solved a serial-killer adjacent cold case, the press was generally much bigger than it could be with other cold cases.

The public, bless them or damn them, loved stories connected to serial killers, especially when it meant learning more gory details about their crimes. This wasn't a new phenomenon. The digital age just made it infinitely easier for people to feed their appetite for those kinds of stories. Margot had seen hundreds of homicides up close and personal, and looked at crime scene images of probably thousands more.

She simply couldn't wrap her head around why people, especially women—who were the most frequent victims of violent crime—would want to spend their weekends with a glass of wine and a documentary about some sort of depraved maniac.

The devil you know, the voice in her head said.

Margot pushed the notion and the voice out of her mind for the time being.

"I want to make a suggestion," she said, drawing the attention of the room to her. With everyone looking at her, she suddenly felt uneasy. "I want us to look for reports of people who were attacked on the trail but got away."

There was a faint mumbling as indistinct concerns over this plan went around the room. Greg was the one who spoke up, looking nervous that whatever he had to say might upset her.

"If our goal is to identify our victims, should we be spreading our resources thin with such a limited scope?" He glanced around, clearly hoping no one else would jump down his throat for asking.

"I'm working on a hypothesis," Margot explained. "I think he brought his victims to the site while they were still alive. And if he was moving his victims to several locations, that means he's taken plenty of stupid risks over the last fifteen years. I think there might be someone out there who has seen this guy, and if there is, isn't she the most important person we could be looking for?"

"Or he," Sydney said, not incorrectly, but also not the most necessary addition to the conversation. She added, "There were male victims as well."

Margot nodded, though based on her discussion with Wes, and the theory he'd put forward, she strongly believed that if anyone had gotten away from their killer it had been a woman.

She didn't want to say that to Sydney, though, who had already made it clear that Wes's presence felt like that of an interloper. Margot saying she trusted his insights more than Sydney's would just be adding insult to injury.

"I think we need to look at reports of hikers who say they were attacked on the trail," Margot went on.

Andrew mulled this over. Finally, he looked down the table. "Greg, you feeling up to it?" he asked.

"Of course," Greg said quickly, though Margot was certain it didn't matter what Greg's workload was like, he would always say yes to Andrew.

"I think the rest of us need to revisit the scene. I've called up the same guide we had earlier; he'll meet us at the trailhead in an hour." Margot was grateful that Andrew had the same idea she had. She kept a careful eye on Barnett and Widdicombe for their reactions. She didn't want to believe either of them were involved in this, but they were local and people would consider them trustworthy. Plus, most people would go willingly with a police officer, which would take some of the mystery out of how their killer so easily persuaded his victims to move around.

Neither of them showed the slightest inkling of concern. Barnett just asked, "We've had a lot of calls since the tip line opened yesterday—how do you want us to approach those?"

"I can stay and start going through them," Sydney said quickly, not even waiting for Andrew to answer. Either she *really* didn't want to go for another hike, or she was just trying to show how useful she could be. Margot had actually thought Alana might volunteer, for both of those reasons. But she should have known her friend better than that, because Alana wanted to be wherever the action was. Even if it meant strapping on some ill-fitting hiking boots and giving herself blisters to do it.

An hour later, Margot, Wes, Alana, Andrew, and good old Spencer Nguyen were all at the trailhead. Chief Barnett had bowed out, but Widdicombe had decided to join them. Officer Logan had tried to volunteer herself, but she was ultimately shot down as they needed all hands on deck at the station to man the busy tip line.

Margot had mixed experiences with tip lines. Normally what they brought in was next to useless, but very occasionally someone actually knew something. She'd seen unsolvable cases get solved because a mother was willing to report on her own son.

After Ted Bundy got caught, police learned that his own girlfriend had reported him to a tip line, though in that case it took an embarrassing amount of time for him to be apprehended after she did.

Margot hoped they wouldn't overlook any good leads that came in just because they might not sound promising. But with a high-profile case like this, there was certainly going to be a lot of chaff to work through. People would call just to feel like they were involved somehow, like it might make a fun anecdote at dinner parties, the time they reported an ex-boyfriend to a serial killer tip line. They would almost certainly get false confessions; there were always some of those to deal with. At least they had plenty of details they'd held back from the public, so weeding out the crackpots would be simple.

It was all just so time-consuming.

Not to mention the thrill and defeat that went along with each tip that seemed like it could lead somewhere but ultimately didn't.

Margot didn't envy the work Sydney had volunteered for. The fact that Sydney had wanted to stay back at the station rather than come on the hike confirmed Margot's suspicions that the date with Spencer had gone poorly and she was looking for an excuse to avoid him now.

Relatable.

She just hoped it was because of a general mismatch, and not because Spencer had done or said anything that crossed a line. She didn't want to break the guy's kneecaps. They needed him for the hike still.

"Howdy, everyone! Hope those boots are all broken in now." Spencer greeted the amassed crew of law enforcement officers like they were Cub Scouts about to get their badges in orienteering. He was bright-eyed and peppy despite the somber reason for them taking this hike, and Margot got the impression he was the kind of guy who said things like *living the dream* and didn't mean them ironically.

Insufferable. How did people get through life being so *happy* all the time?

Wes gave her a look and then leaned over to whisper in her ear, "Every single thing you're thinking is showing on your face right now. You do not have a good emotion filter for your expressions."

Margot had just assumed she had her typical resting bitch face engaged, but evidently, she had turned it up a few notches to disgusted. She did her best to school her features back to a flat, emotionless blank, which probably looked more like mild indigestion, but it was the best she could do unless she plastered on a fake smile, which felt worse.

Beside her, Alana must have overheard Wes, because she was smirking. Between her and Wes there was just nowhere for Margot to escape to. They had an unfair advantage.

"It's just what my face *does*," she protested under her breath.

"You spent too long living alone, it's not your fault," Wes said with a smile.

"The two of you are perfect for each other," Alana said quietly, and Margot wasn't entirely sure if it was a compliment or an insult, but either way it was the truth.

Spencer waved his arms, directing them towards the path and shouting reminders about sunscreen, hydrating, and letting him know if they started to feel hot spots that might turn into blisters. Alana muttered something about her blisters having blisters and it being a cold day in hell before she asked a man for a bandage, but Margot lost most of it as the other woman marched up the trail. Her determination was admirable.

Wes kept pace with Margot at the tail end of the group, with only Widdicombe behind them. The sergeant was just as enthusiastic about the outdoor adventure as Margot would have imagined. For a good five minutes he was actually whistling, before he must have realized it wasn't the ideal thing to do given the scenario and fell silent. But Margot could feel the golden retriever energy vibrating off him, and knew that he was just twitching with the need to start pointing out how much he knew about the local flora and fauna.

With Spencer at the front and Calvin at the back, Margot was in a sandwich of overwhelming positive masculinity, and she was not wired to handle so much cheery enthusiasm. The added difficulty of the hike meant that, by the time they reached the campsite, she would be a deeply foul mood, and if anyone smiled at her she would probably snap at them in a very unkind way.

It was also much hotter than it had been on their two previous hikes, so she was coated in a film of sweat, her hiking clothes sticking to her unpleasantly. She was trying to ration her water so she would have enough for the walk back, but she was sweating so much it was keeping her thirst at an all-time high.

Wes must have noticed her surly discomfort; he offered her water several times on the way up. She rejected it at first but finally accepted when he fixed her with a stern look. The look said, *shut up and drink it, you're being mean.*

Or perhaps she was just projecting.

The water did go a long way towards making her feel better. She hadn't realized just how foggy her brain had become on the way up, and now she felt as if she could actually think straight.

She wasn't the only one looking spent thanks to the oppressive humidity and the exertion of the walk. It was the least convenient crime scene she had ever been forced to deal with—it was a petty reason to hate this killer, but she did.

From a logical place, though, it made something else click for her.

There was no way their killer had carried his victims out here after their deaths. The hike took them almost three hours, and that was with only minimal day-packs. They weren't seasoned hikers, but they were in good physical health. A lone man, no matter how strong, would not reasonably be able to haul a body out here, let alone two.

Margot had known they needed to come out here again with their new killer in mind, and already she felt like it had been worth every arduous step. They had an insight into the UNSUB they hadn't before.

She also realized that Sydney was the smartest of all of them for staying behind, because she got to listen to all the best tip-line calls, drinking coffee, in a nice, air-conditioned building, not sweating her ass off out here.

Margot sat down on a fallen tree, not caring in the slightest if it was covered with wet moss or bugs. She pretended to tie her boots, but really, she just needed a moment to pull herself together. Wes stood nearby, keeping an eye on her but staying out of everyone's way because he wasn't technically working.

Still, she could see the curious look on his face as he took in his surroundings, getting a sense of the area and moving further from her side as he got more and more interested in seeing what he could learn from the environment. That made Margot smile, because it was nice to see him back in his element.

Wes could be in his element anywhere he chose to be, but this, solving crimes, this was something he was so naturally good at that Margot felt more optimistic watching him settle back into it. She couldn't wait to pick his brain when they got back to the motel.

Alana plopped down beside her on the log with a grunt and took a long swig from her water bottle, obviously not caring at all if she had any left for the return trip.

"I want to know why we couldn't have sent one of the eager beavers up here with a video camera and just done this all as a Zoom call," she grumbled.

Margot opened her mouth to reply but Alana lifted a hand to stop her.

"If you're going to say anything remotely logical or reasonable, I don't want to hear it, I just want to be a grumpy bitch."

Wes, even though he'd wandered a good distance away, must have heard this, as he smiled. He knew better than to say anything.

Alana rifled through her backpack until she found a granola bar, and took a big bite of it.

Around a mouthful of ancient grains, she said, "He had to have killed them here."

Margot watched as Andrew, Spencer, and Calvin moved together in a unit, exploring different parts of the site they hadn't looked at as closely in previous visits. Their attention had been so much on the grave, they hadn't really studied the little clearing like it might also be the scene of the crime.

The scene of many crimes, actually.

"I wonder what drew him here," Margot said. "What made this spot feel so special to him?"

"If it wasn't for how far he had to move Littlewolf, I would have said it was a convenient place to find victims. Now I couldn't tell you if I believed he found any of his victims here originally."

"So it has to have a different meaning, then," Margot said, swatting at a wayward mosquito. It was too hot for the bugs to be moving with a feverish flurry, but they were still lingering, drawn in by the sweat and body heat.

They made her think about the science of death. The way flies could find a corpse with such accuracy and efficiency that time of death could be determined just by looking at the generations of larvae spawned on a body. It was revolting, but it was also fascinating, the way nature took care of things like that. The way deer carcasses didn't litter hiking trails, because they were returned to the earth.

When he had buried these bodies, he ensured he would always know where they were. So their killer was kind of the opposite of Wyatt Holmes, in that his bodies weren't left for someone to find—in Holmes's case, the wolves—but rather secreted away so someone would have to know where to look for them.

And it was such a specific and difficult location to bring his victims to. So much effort and forethought had to go into it. Especially for the two pairs of victims in the grave together.

Margot glanced over at Alana. Of the two of them, Alana was

the one who had actually done profiling work. Margot wondered where her friend's mind was right then. Alana had a zoned-out expression on her face, and looked as though she was disassociating from their current situation. But Margot knew there was more going on behind those vacant eyes. She'd seen Alana get into that kind of zone before, literally shutting out the world around her to focus all her mental energy inward.

Margot knew how to make good guesses about her UNSUBs. She could look at all the evidence before her and follow a logical path. Context clues could offer a hell of a lot of insight into a person. But she'd never been able to figure out the mental witch-craft the BSU managed when creating a profile. How the hell could they intuit what kind of car a person might drive, what kind of job they might have? And while those profiles were rarely a hundred percent accurate, they typically got eerily close to the truth.

It was remarkable, really, and probably why only a very select type of person was able to work that job. Margot often wondered if that skillset could be turned off, or if profilers out on dates were always trying to determine a person's social background and potential threat level while sipping beers and sharing a plate of nachos.

It must be exhausting, always looking for someone to turn into a bad guy.

Alana stirred, blinking.

"What are you thinking?" Margot asked.

"What if he didn't force them out here?" Alana asked.

"What do you mean?"

"Think about it. There's an inherent camaraderie associated with hikes like these. A sort of natural trust that comes with being on the same kind of... I don't know... quest?"

"Achievement," Margot said with a soft smile, waving away a fly that kept getting in her face.

"Sure. Well, part of that whole experience is that even though you're doing the thing solo, to all intents and purposes, you meet people along the way. There's an expectation that you're going to have trail buddies for part of the adventure, right?"

"Sure."

"That's how everyone ends up with their trail name, or whatever."

"For someone who didn't own hiking boots before this trip, you suddenly have a lot of insight into the social expectations of long-distance trail hiking."

"I watched *Wild* while we were in Nashville. Reese Witherspoon has the power to teach me anything. After I saw *Legally Blonde*, I briefly considered law school."

"You would have made a terrifying lawyer," Margot said with a laugh.

"I know, thank you."

Margot picked up the threads of what Alana seemed to be suggesting. "So, you think it's possible that this guy finds people other places on the trail, and then sticks with them until they come here? How do we fit Daisy into that, because her family said she was just out for a day hike?"

"I didn't say it was a perfect hypothesis. But we've seen killers escalate before. Maybe he bumped into her on the trail, realized she was only going to be there a short time, and did something rash." She pushed back a sweaty strand of hair and took another small sip from her water, seeming to realize now how much was gone.

"Mmm," Margot said, her gaze following Wes as he crouched down, his fingertips grazing the sandy area where most people would set up their tents. "It's not a bad theory," she said, before Alana could take her long silence personally. "I just think we're missing something. If he was actually just moving up and down the trail until he found someone coming this direction, then he wouldn't have a car nearby, which would change how he approached a situation like Daisy. And I doubt he walked her all the way here against her will. That would have taken days. Weeks. It's a long-ass distance on foot."

Alana nodded. "We'll workshop it." She looked up, blinking into the sunlight that bore down on them. While most of the trail up had been shaded, this site was in a small clearing, so there was no place to get away from the sun unless they headed back into the woods.

"Why this place?" she asked, echoing Margot's own bothersome question.

"There has to be something meaningful here we've missed," Margot said.

"Is it like, a satanic thing?" Alana asked, her voice lilting up at the end in something that sounded dangerously like excitement.

This made Margot chuckle. "Since the Satanic Panic in the eighties, how many things have actually turned out to be Satan-related? Basically none. I'm pretty sure real Satanists are just fighting for equal rights by getting statues of Baphomet put up wherever someone wants to make a public display of the Ten Commandments or something."

Alana briefly looked at Margot as if she had just farted in public, but since Margot found nothing particularly strange about what she had just said, she simply shrugged and moved on. "I'm just saying, as badly as you clearly want it to be something satanic, I don't think you're going to luck out here."

"Nah, this has satanic written all over it, just you wait. We're going to find pentagrams carved into something—"

"Jesus!" came a cry from in the woods.

"Look what you did," Margot started to say, until she realized the cry was coming from Andrew, his deep voice booming across the open clearing.

"What the...?" Alana got to her feet and the two of them followed Wes in the direction of Andrew's voice. Spencer and Calvin were nowhere to be seen but based on the low murmur of voices that got louder as they got closer, Margot assumed they were still with him.

When they found the trio, they were down the slope in the direction of the open grave. The grave site was marked off with bright yellow caution tape, even though it was no longer an active crime scene, because they had moved so much dirt out of the way it had created an open pit that could have been dangerous to anyone who happened to wander well off the beaten path and stumble upon it.

Except, the grave was no longer empty.

THIRTY-ONE

The first thing Margot noticed as she looked into the once-empty mass grave was not the specific details of the body itself. She would register those seconds later.

What stood out more was the Post-it note stuck to the victim's chest.

Margot couldn't read the words, but the bold, dark writing let her imagine them just fine.

I want them back.

Once she moved her gaze from the Post-It, the rest of the scene shifted into focus.

Their victim was a woman in her mid-thirties, white, her dark hair cut in a short pixie cut, and no sign of a backpack, if she had come in with one. She was fully dressed, her flannel shirt still tucked into her moisture-wicking hiking pants. Margot noted she was not wearing a jacket, and she couldn't see one anywhere, which rang alarm bells.

If she had been through-hiking the trail, she'd need a jacket. While daytime temperatures were hideously warm and sticky, the nights got cold, especially out here.

The way the body was positioned it looked almost like she had just fallen in backwards; her arms and legs were akimbo and her eyes still open, a look of eternal surprise etched on her features.

From their position on the slope, it was impossible to see what had killed her. There was no sign of blood on her clothes, and if there was any bruising on her skin from strangulation, Margot couldn't see it from where she was standing.

The one sign of injury—Margot noticed with a sharp intake of breath—was that one of the woman's hands was missing a finger. A finger Margot had seen in her own motel room the night before, if she had to hazard a guess.

She suspected, just based on how generally clean the woman's hand was, that the finger had been cut off postmortem.

How long had she been here? It had been less than a week since their last visit, and there were no visible signs—or smells— that serious decomposition had begun. So, one, maybe two days at the most.

Their killer was keenly aware of their movements, then, which made Margot's gaze dart to Calvin. She didn't *want* to suspect him of anything, but she did wonder if the obvious solution here was that their killer was a cop.

If it was him, though, he was a damn fine actor, because right now he was looking as queasy as someone taking their first boat ride on open water, and the crime scene wasn't even all that grisly, as things like this went.

Margot watched him a moment longer as he paled, then looked away from the body. Was that discomfort or was it guilt?

Or was she looking for too easy an answer? Maybe he was just a cop out here trying to do his job, like they were.

This week had been too tense, too exhausting for her to completely rely on her instincts, but she also knew the only people she could trust out here were the ones she had known coming in. She glanced at Spencer, and saw that he was transfixed by the body. His expression was a mix of shock and confusion, but he didn't seem to be able to look away from the corpse. It was probably the first time he'd ever seen a body. That first time changed people.

She shot a glance at Wes, who was also staring at the crime scene, though he looked like a man who was solving a complex math problem in his head, probably noticing all the same little details she had. When he looked over at her, she jerked her chin in Spencer's direction. As nice as it would be to have Wes's insight into the crime scene, he was the only other person here not actively involved in the case and he could help them out by getting the civilian out of the way.

He understood what she needed without her saying it out loud, walking over to Spencer and placing a gentle hand on his shoulder. Spencer jerked suddenly at the touch, like an electrical current had gone through him. He blinked at Wes as he emerged from his stupor.

"Hey, man," Wes said gently. "Let's go back up the hill. We should let them work." He didn't say anything to imply that the scene might be too difficult to look at or that Spencer couldn't handle it, which was kind.

Spencer nodded slowly and he and Wes disappeared up the hill, leaving just the four of them behind.

"Calvin," Margot said, to get his attention on her and take it off him feeling like he might lose his lunch. "Do you have signal out here?"

Her phone certainly didn't, but perhaps he had a local plan that offered better service in the Smoky Mountains. Who knew? Maybe Dolly Parton had a satellite for locals.

He shook his head, looking apologetic.

Someone was going to need to head back down the path to call this in, and someone was going to need to stay behind. They couldn't just leave an unprotected crime scene out in the open, as there could be hikers coming through at any time. It was hard enough to keep evidence secured in situations like this; the last thing they needed was for some poor schmuck to stumble across it just because he stepped off the trail for a pee.

Call it trust issues or gut instinct, but Margot didn't want Calvin to be the one left behind.

"Go back to the trailhead, or however far you need to go to get signal. We need backup to keep an eye on the trail for hikers, and we could use a helicopter airlift to get this body out of here."

Taking bones back down the path had been enough of a challenge; getting an intact adult body out without ruining any potential evidence on the corpse was too much to risk. They could send the bill for the airlift to the FBI.

Calvin looked like he might protest, but after a moment he just nodded and headed back up the hill.

Though Andrew had been startled enough when finding the body to call out, he had regained his composure almost immediately, and now had his phone out and was snapping photos of the scene.

Margot started to head down the slope, not wanting to waste whatever daylight they had left. With a long hike back down the mountain for anyone not staying overnight, they needed to get a look at the body while there was still time. The helicopter crew, whenever they arrived, wouldn't be able to move her at night, so unless there was a free rescue unit available nearby, they would be here for the night without any real gear, with a killer who knew the woods well hiding God only knew where.

Super.

The slope wasn't too slippery, though it wasn't a cakewalk either, with bits of shale slipping away under Margot's boots and clattering against the rocks on their way down. Still, this time Margot kept her feet underneath her and her eyes firmly fixed on the path that would get her down.

It took about five minutes but finally she was level with the open grave. She ducked underneath the caution tape, then carefully edged her way around the exterior of the pit until she was next to the body. From here, she could better see the woman's face. She had fine lines around her eyes and mouth, which meant she was probably someone who smiled a lot. That realization should have made Margot sad, but somehow it did the opposite. She was grateful to know that while this woman had been alive, she had enjoyed herself.

The woman's cheeks were pockmarked with old acne scars, though they appeared to have been long healed. She wasn't wearing any makeup—why would you on a hike like this?—but she did have a small pair of diamond stud earrings in.

Margot patted her pockets until she found a pair of gloves she'd brought with her. With how much of her time was spent at crime scenes, she almost never left the house without being prepared to safely handle evidence.

"You got another pair of those?" Alana asked, coming to stand beside her, her voice a little airy from the exertion of getting down the steep hill.

Margot did, in fact, have a second pair, but if Andrew started asking, they were going to have to share. She gave Alana the gloves before lowering herself into the open grave. Because the area was so large, it didn't quite have the same feel as she imagined getting into a grave at a cemetery would, but it still had an ominous vibe, like this was somewhere she shouldn't be.

From here she could basically touch the body, though she didn't want to do that just yet. Instead, she moved in a circle around where their victim was situated, just observing. She took out her phone to take a few pictures of the details she had noticed, like the missing finger and the earrings. The earrings told Margot none of this was motivated by a desire to rob these victims, which was something they had already theorized when they had found all the items left with the original group.

But then, where was her backpack? Where was her jacket? Margot didn't like the little things that didn't quite line up. Those puzzle pieces with uneven edges that seemed like they were from an entirely different box.

Finally, when she was standing at the woman's head, looking down at her, she got a good look at the likely cause of death.

She crouched down, angling her head to the side so she could get a better look, and sure enough, the woman's dark hair was sticky with blood. The dirt beneath her was coated in it as well, not that it would have been obvious from where they'd been standing before—the blood had left only a reddish-brown tinge to the dark dirt.

The back of the woman's head had been hit, probably repeatedly, with something heavy, cracking her skull open. It had been a vicious attack, but hyper-localized. Margot wondered if the woman had even seen it coming, or if her assailant had taken her by surprise.

The expression on her face suggested the latter.

When they had found all the skeletons, Margot had wished she could have seen their whole bodies, thinking that somehow would have provided her with all the information she needed. But now she had an intact body and it only came with more questions.

None of this made sense. How had this woman gotten here? How had someone been able to come up behind her and strike her so brutally?

Margot's gaze slipped to the woman's hands. The one missing finger seemed to be the only wound. There was no evidence of defensive marks, and while her fingernails were a bit on the grubby side, there was a slight film of trail dust all over her, indicating that this was just a side effect of it having been a few days since her last shower.

It was as though the killer had popped up out of nowhere and the woman was dead before she even knew what was happening to her.

Alana crouched down on the opposite side of the body. Sometimes, even when she looked like she knew exactly what she was doing, Margot couldn't help but think Alana was out of place. Like she was an actress playing an FBI agent, but had gone so deeply method with it she just never stopped. She looked too polished, even in her cargo shorts and T-shirt, to be doing the same job Margot was.

Alana stared at the body, assessing, considering, then got to her feet. "I want to turn her on her side," she said.

Normally Margot would balk at this idea until they'd at least had the scene thoroughly photographed and the evidence marked out. But these were exceptional circumstances, and no one was coming to make this an easier crime scene to manage.

"Help me roll her and I'll hold her up," Margot said, standing on one side of the body so they could move the woman's weight together. At a glance, their victim was probably a hundred and forty pounds tops, but Margot knew that the phrase *dead weight* didn't exist for no reason. Dead people were just *heavy*, there was no way around it.

She and Alana worked together to roll the woman on her side, and as Margot held the body, the exertion of it making sweat bead on her forehead, Alana looked for additional clues. She untucked the woman's shirt, looking at her back, then nodded to Margot. "Sighs of lividity on her back. I think this is exactly where she died."

Margot had read hundreds of autopsy reports and was no stranger to the city morgue in San Francisco. She knew how to identify the stages of decomp. She knew what lividity meant. The blood pooled in the body as it stopped flowing, leaving bruising where the body had been positioned. If the woman had died somewhere else, or in a different position, the lividity could tell them that. Instead, it just confirmed what Margot already suspected.

They eased the body back into place and Margot patted down the woman's pockets, not wanting to be surprised by anything sharp like a camp knife or syringe, and then she pulled out a slim wallet.

Here, at least, they had something tangible they hadn't gotten with the other victims. When Margot opened the wallet, it was clear the contents were untouched. There was still cash inside, along with a blister pack of birth control pills, showing she was caught up until two days earlier, which gave them another clue as to how long she'd been here.

There was also a driver's license. Margot studied the photo and then looked back at the woman lying on the ground. Her name was Sandra Elkhorn, thirty-six, from Butte, Montana. She was a long way from home, but there were some weathered park permits and camping permits along with the cash, indicating she'd been doing the north to south version of the hike for at least two months.

Margot took off her backpack and pulled out a few evidence bags she had taken from the police station. She put the wallet into one of them, then handed it to Andrew, who had joined them in the pit.

He didn't say much, just wore that same thoughtful, calculating expression they had all had in some version or another since they'd come across the body. He looked at the wallet, then at their victim, and let out a little sigh. He didn't need to say anything. Margot knew what that sigh meant. Until they found this guy, Sandra wouldn't be the last.

THIRTY-TWO

The sun was setting too soon for the helicopter to get there that night, so Andrew, Calvin, and two other officers who had come up as backup volunteered to keep watch over the scene. Margot, Wes, and Alana had hiked out on their own, and barely got back to the parking lot by dusk.

Spencer had left earlier, so Margot wasn't surprised to see that the guide's truck was gone.

Margot didn't love the idea of Andrew being up on the mountain with Calvin, only because her paranoia wouldn't let her relax about any of the locals, but with the other officers there as well she didn't think he was at any risk. Even *if* one of them was their guy, there was no way he'd be stupid enough to try something with so many extra eyes and ears on the mountain. The guys who had come back with Calvin, once he'd managed to get signal to call them, also brought along some basic two-man tents and the necessary equipment to light a fire, along with more water and some food, so no one was going to suffer too badly overnight.

She felt useless going back to the motel, but it meant she and Wes would have time to compare what they had learned from the scene. Margot knew she didn't have any definitive answers yet, but she was curious to hear what Wes had noticed that she might have missed.

He headed out to one of the diners to get them something to eat, while she showered. The sweat and dirt of their hike that day felt so much worse than she had anticipated, like she was chewing on sand and grit, and she was grateful to have it off her.

It felt too early to be in pajamas, and she wanted to be presentable in case any of her team stopped by, so she put on jeans and a lightweight sweatshirt, which would still feel cozy but wouldn't feel weird if someone saw her. She was just pulling on her socks when she heard a soft knock at the door.

She had the TV on, its volume low, to keep an eye on the convergence of media near the trailhead. Things being what they were in the town, there hadn't really been a way to hide what they'd discovered that afternoon, not with the media tuning in to police radio signals. People were reporting live from the parking lot Margot had left not that long ago, but it seemed like local officers were keeping them in check. Hopefully no one was stupid enough to try going up the trail in the dark.

Who knew who they might meet if they did?

She muted the TV and went to the door. She'd told Wes where the key was, but given everything that had happened today, she could forgive him for forgetting it.

When she opened the door, though, she gave a little start of surprise.

It wasn't Wes standing outside waiting for her, but Spencer Nguyen. His truck was parked a little way away, and he had his hands in his pockets and a sheepish, hunched posture. His cheeks still looked slightly flushed, like he'd brought a little of the sun with him.

"Spencer," she said, gathering herself. She hadn't been expecting him and was rattled.

She didn't think Spencer had any ill intent; his body language seemed to suggest he was seeking reassurance. She remembered how hard she had found it, seeing her first body, so she tried to ignore her instincts, which were telling her to shoo him away and lock the door. Wes would be back soon, and he was a lot better at the hand-holding, uplifting stuff that would hopefully make Spencer feel better, maybe chase away whatever nightmares he was going to have that night.

Margot could be empathetic for a few minutes, if she knew she could pass the baton.

"You okay?" she asked when he didn't say anything right away.

He nodded, scraping the concrete pad outside her door with his toe. She cast a glance over his shoulder, wondering if she might spot Wes coming, but he was nowhere to be seen. Trumbull wasn't a big town, but the diners were all a distance away and Wes was on foot.

"Rough day," she said, hoping to encourage him into saying something. It was hard to communicate with a brick wall, no matter how sad that wall seemed to be.

"How do you handle it?" he asked, his voice low, soft. Margot wasn't a hugger, but this seemed like the kind of scenario where someone offered a hug or other comfort.

"I'd say you get used to it," she replied. "But the truth is, I think you more or less just get numb to it. They say that the human body can adapt itself to a lot of things that might otherwise destroy it, and I think that's the brain just protecting us. So my brain figured out a long time ago that you need to be able to look at death and be okay with it, otherwise you're going to lose your damn mind." She offered a small smile, hoping he would find this comforting, but instead he just stared at her, and she realized that perhaps this was the exact wrong thing to say to someone in his situation.

"Spencer, you're allowed to feel anything you're currently feeling. Scared, mad, freaked out, angry, confused. Those are all totally normal things to feel after seeing what you did today. You don't have to be numb to it. I know it's a fucked-up thing to see. It's scary and it's wrong, and no one should have to come to terms with that. But you did see it, and I'm sorry. Just know that that isn't what the world looks like. That's one bad thing, in a whole world of good."

He nodded, let out a little sigh, and then looked over her shoulder into the motel room, like he was hoping she might invite him in.

He seemed like a good kid who just wanted a shoulder to cry on, but she wasn't about to ask him to come into her room. Old habits died hard, and this was one she was perfectly content hanging on to. She didn't want to shut him out when he was obviously going through something difficult, but she couldn't figure out why he had come to her for comfort when just about anyone else on her team would have been better.

Come to think of it, how had he even known where to find her?

She thought this over, recalling all her previous encounters with Spencer. Encounters where they had always met up and parted ways at the trailhead. He had never picked them up at the motel. The front desk—following the situation earlier that week—was under strict instructions not to share their room numbers.

Her hands suddenly felt clammy, and she was distinctly aware that she did not have her gun on her. She'd taken it off when she showered, and stowed it in the drawer beside her bed, because she had foolishly assumed she wouldn't have any need for it for the rest of the evening.

As a chill crept over her, she tried to keep her expression unchanged, and her gaze kept moving to the parking lot, though she tried not to make it too obvious. She was hoping to see Wes come walking up. Actually, she would have welcomed anyone stepping out of their room at that moment. But the lot was silent, except for the electric hum from an overhead light and the muffled sound of someone's too-loud TV from a room a few doors down.

Spencer gave her another sheepish smile, but this time she looked at it with doubt. He had that kind of face, a face that made him immediately likeable and trustworthy. Someone who a hiker on the trail might not think twice about falling in step with for a few hours or days.

"How long have you been doing this?" she asked. "Guiding people?"

He seemed taken aback by the question. His expression faltered slightly, but he regained his composure almost instantly. If she hadn't been looking closely, she might not have seen the slip at all.

But she knew what she was looking for.

She'd spent hours thinking back to family dinners, wondering how she had missed those same little slips in her father. The moment where someone's mask of humanity slips away. It was the same thing she'd spent almost seven years studying when she sat across the tables from serial killers. She didn't consider herself an expert in many things, but looking for those subtle changes in people was one of them.

Now, registering the change made her heart beat harder, though she kept her expression neutral, pleasant.

She thought back to that same day on the trail, the time she had spent staring down Calvin, looking for missteps, wondering if their killer was right under her nose this whole time. Meanwhile she had sent Wes off to hold this guy's hand because he had been so convincingly traumatized by finding Sandra's body that she had felt bad for him.

"Well," he said, coming back to her question at last. "My dad started doing guided hiking in the area when I was about five. I did my first overnight trip on the trail when I was seven."

"How many times have you done the whole thing?" she asked.

"Four." He smiled, looking proud of his accomplishment. "Of course, we did a lot of other local guiding, helped people get a full local adventure in. We specialize in the Smoky Mountains. I've done the full trail as a guide only once—usually people like to do it on their own. Otherwise, I'm sometimes like training wheels; I'll meet them at the start, either north or south, and stay with them until they're comfortable, then I let them do the rest on their own."

Seemed like a great way to find out if someone was hiking the trail alone and have a good sense of their pace, Margot thought to herself.

She was beginning to feel a gnawing sense of worry about Wes.

Had something happened to him? Had he bumped into Spencer on the way back from the diner? Wes would have trusted him, because Margot had given him the impression that was a safe thing to do.

Her hand tightened on the doorknob, her mind wandering to the drawer with her gun, and to where her phone was sitting on the little table by the window. Could she slam the door shut and reach either of them before he forced his way in? How long would it take for someone in the neighboring rooms to hear her if she screamed? She took a steadying breath through her nostrils, trying not to show any emotion while inside she was desperately trying to formulate her next steps.

What if you're overreacting?

At this point, she wasn't sure what internal voice was cajoling her on, but she didn't really like the way it was gaslighting her. That was the problem with what society taught women about safety, that it was better to be polite and sensitive towards men than to trust thousands of years of gut instinct that were screaming at you to protect yourself.

Margot didn't think she was a stupid person, but her brain was sure trying to convince her otherwise in that moment. If she was wrong, she'd deal with that later.

As she was about to close the door a nagging thought crossed her mind.

He can't have killed them all.

This was the same voice, only now she actually paused to consider it. Spencer was in his late twenties. Thirty if she had to push her estimates to the outer limits. The oldest body they'd found in the grave had been there fifteen to eighteen years.

While it was not out of the question for a fifteen-year-old to commit murder—she'd encountered even younger killers—she didn't think the complexity of the crime aligned with a killer that age.

For the first time, she felt a shadow of doubt creeping in, truly making her wonder if she was reading this situation all wrong.

Maybe she *was* being paranoid. Maybe she was looking for hints and signs that weren't actually there.

She glanced at Spencer's face and, in a split second, recognized the mistake she had made.

Spencer lunged, knocking his muscular frame into the door, which sent Margot staggering backwards. She didn't have a chance to get her feet under her, just fell onto the side of the bed, from where she bounced off and hit the stand holding the TV. Pain bloomed in her ribcage, her mind spinning from the suddenness of the attack.

As she tried to catch her breath, she heard the sound of the motel room door shutting, the jangle of the chain lock sliding in place. The sound of the TV being turned up to a deafening level. A news broadcaster screamed into the room about the ongoing search of the Appalachian Trail, reminding everyone about the available tip line.

Margot briefly wondered if there had been any tips called in that they would later realize tied to Spencer.

She also knew this was a sloppy and desperate move on his part. His truck was outside. All it would take was one member of her team to look outside and recognize it and it wouldn't matter what happened in this room. He would be caught.

Of course, Margot would prefer to come out of this alive and be able to hand him over herself. She pushed herself up to her hands and knees and crawled towards the nightstand, but Spencer had the upper hand, looming over her. He grabbed her by her hair, yanking her back to the end of the bed, and kicked her hard in her already bruised ribs.

Her breath escaped in a *whoosh* and the pain was so radiant, so present that Margot felt certain she could trace the link of each individual fracture as it happened. Her eyes watered and it was hard to catch her breath, but she knew the only way she was going to get out of this alive was if she pulled herself together and fought back.

Margot knew how to fight. Her father hadn't given her many

things in life to be proud of, but he'd taught her how to throw a punch, he'd taught her how to defend herself. He'd made sure she understood how to survive in a world filled with monsters like him.

Of course, her father hadn't predicted she would need to do those things in the body of a forty-something woman who could get lower back pain from just doing the dishes sometimes.

But the lessons remained.

Spencer went to kick her again and Margot grabbed hold of his leg. It was hard to hold on with pain lacing through her from the force of the kick, but she clasped onto him like a manacle, then got enough leverage on her upper body to drive her elbow down on the bridge of his foot.

His heavy hiking boots absorbed some of the damage, but Spencer still let out a yowl of pain. Margot used his momentary distraction to pull herself up from the floor, her elbow now throbbing along with her ribs, clawing at the bedding to get herself on her feet, but by that point Spencer had gathered himself enough to make another grab for her.

He wrapped one arm around her throat, pulling back so hard she saw stars and couldn't get her breath. She managed to push both feet up on the mattress and kick back, sending him stumbling to the floor, still holding her. They landed hard, and the first thing Margot saw when she got to her feet was her phone.

She grabbed it, though it was useless at the moment—she'd never have time to place a call before he got to her again—then she saw what was next to it. The heavy, old-fashioned ashtray, which now had a little plastic placard next to it that said

PLEASE TAKE YOUR BUTTS OUTSIDE

Margot took the heavy glass dish without a second thought and wheeled around, hoping like hell she wasn't wasting her one opportunity.

The ashtray met human flesh and bone with a sickening, meaty *crack*. For a moment the momentum of Spencer's assault made him stagger forward a few steps, and Margot backpedaled, climbing onto the unused twin bed to get away from him.

She lifted the ashtray to make another attempt, but then she noticed how slack Spencer's mouth was. The wrongness of the angle of his jaw. How vacant his eyes were.

He slumped onto the bed, still reaching for her, but blood pooled from his mouth onto the mattress. He didn't move.

Margot held the ashtray over her head, her arm trembling from the weight, and as she realized Spencer was no longer breathing, she finally heard the pounding at the door.

THIRTY-THREE

Spencer Nguyen wasn't dead.

Margot took a tiny bit of comfort in that as she sat on the tail end of an ambulance with an EMT prodding at her broken ribs.

Death would have been too convenient. And while perhaps some of the families of their victims would have been satisfied to know he had died as brutally as he had killed some of their kin, it wasn't the same thing as justice. And it wouldn't give them the answers that only he could provide.

Of course, given that Margot had broken his jaw in several places and the side of his face was so swollen he might lose an eye, it might be some time before he started sharing insights with anyone.

He'd have a long time to think, though, because if Margot had her way, he'd never see the light of day as a free man again.

Wes was sitting next to her, and once the EMT was finished poking around and had insisted Margot should go to the hospital for proper X-rays, she let herself sink into his side, not caring how much it hurt to breathe or how many new bruises she was sporting. Wes stroked her hair, pressing kisses into the crown of her head the way she often did to their calico cat Lucy. He had probably apologized to her a hundred times for being so slow getting back, but Margot didn't care. She was just so intensely relieved he wasn't a dead body in the back of Spencer's truck.

When he'd returned, Wes had tried to break the door down. Even though he hadn't gotten there in time to save the day, he was still her hero for making the effort. She thanked God he had come. It made all of the hard edges of her current situation feel softer, more manageable.

Andrew was on the other side of the parking lot, with Alana next to him, as they gave the local police instructions. Margot couldn't hear what Andrew was saying, but she knew he'd be telling them to keep someone outside Spencer's room at all times. Broken face or not, the guy was still a serious flight risk.

The Trumbull police department was spread awfully thin now thanks to this case. Between the officers up on the trail and this new development, it looked like Captain Barnett would be taking first watch just to make sure nothing went awry.

There was no hospital in Trumbull, so the first ambulance—the one with Spencer in it—was heading to a nearby town with a larger population where they could support his needs.

Margot would be following soon after, but she had begged the EMT to give her just a little more time and they had complied, at least for now. When Andrew and Alana finished with the local PD, they crossed the parking lot and joined Margot at the ambulance.

For some reason, as Andrew came to a stop in front of her, Margot let out an unexpected snort of laughter. It came out of nowhere, she hadn't been expecting it, and it *hurt*. She held her ribs and winced, but couldn't quite make the laughter stop. When she finally regained her composure and was wiping tears from her eyes, her ribs and chest throbbing, Alana just stared at her.

"You good, Phalen?"

"No," Margot replied, then chuckled again despite herself. "Really fucking terrible, actually."

"Then why the hell are you laughing?" There was a small smile at the edge of Alana's mouth, like she was annoyed with this but was also fighting the urge to start laughing herself.

"Because I just remembered how the Ricky DeGraff thing ended, and I saw Andrew come over and thought, *We really need to stop meeting this way* and it's not funny but I also can't help but laugh." She shrugged helplessly and wiped away a few more tears that had trickled out.

Alana gave Andrew an exasperated look. "She almost gets killed by suspects twice and she's doing a stand-up routine about it."

Wes, who had let this banter go on while he kept his arm around Margot, clearly couldn't resist giving his two cents. "Her therapist told her she uses sarcasm as a coping mechanism."

Margot elbowed him.

Andrew smiled faintly. "Sounds about right for Margot, honestly." He crouched down so he was eye to eye with her and that same smile softened, turning worried and paternal. "Did he say anything to you? Anything useful?"

Margot tried to recall the short conversation they'd had before Spencer had forced his way into her room. Wes's hand tightened on her shoulder, like he was ready to protect her, even from Andrew, if she needed it.

She said, "He said he's been hiking the trails his whole life, and that he's done guided bits of the trail from both ends, so we know he's familiar with the Georgia end, where Daisy Littlewolf went missing. He would also know who was traveling alone after leaving them, or even know if a couple might be easy to target."

"He didn't admit to anything though?" Alana urged.

Margot shook her head, which briefly made little points of light dance in her vision. She squeezed Wes's thigh as she closed her eyes, letting the dizzy, spinning sensation stop before she spoke. "He didn't mention the case at all. He showed up, acting really torn up about seeing Sandra's body. I don't even know why he chose me."

No one had a ready response for this. Margot was just one cog in the machine of their team. She wasn't in a leadership position, she wasn't the most vocal on the team, and yet she had been the one Spencer had zeroed in on.

She didn't know how to take that.

"There's always a reason," Alana said. "It might not be obvious, but there was a reason that made sense to him."

"Maybe he thought you recognized something in him," Wes offered. "Enough people would have been talking about what you do. Maybe it panicked him."

Margot nodded. Despite everything that had happened to her tonight, she would have loved to have ten minutes across a table with Spencer.

"We're waiting on the warrant for his house—it should come through shortly," Andrew said.

"He said he learned everything from his dad," Margot said, reaching back for the threads of the conversation. "Is his dad still alive?"

"I don't know," Andrew admitted. "We'll look into it."

"I'm coming," Margot said sternly, any edge of the giggles she'd had vanishing in an instant. "When you look at his house, I'm coming with you."

Andrew and Alana exchanged a silent look, but Margot just shook her head. "No, you guys don't get to do that, you don't get to do the *oh, fragile Margot, can she handle it?* thing. I am going to the hospital, I'm going to get my ribs bandaged up, and unless they tell me I'm about to die of something, I will be leaving that hospital and coming right back here. So you can wait a couple of hours to let me finish what I started. I think I deserve that."

Andrew opened his mouth to speak, but Alana put a hand on his shoulder, squeezing. "Yeah, Margot. We can do that."

Margot gave her friend a wan smile, suddenly zapped of all her remaining energy. The EMT who had been hovering nearby seemed to sense the change and swooped in, ushering Alana and

Andrew away. Wes wouldn't be moved; he joined Margot inside the ambulance and held her hand the whole way to the hospital.

As she drifted off with grateful thanks to a heavy dose of painkillers, one question still lingered.

If these crimes went back fifteen years, could Spencer really have been behind all of them?

THIRTY-FOUR

Margot was in no shape to be scouring a crime scene, but despite stern suggestions from several doctors that she should be on bed rest for at least a week, she had signed the forms to say she was leaving against medical advice. Wes had tried to convince her she needed more rest, but he'd also known the futility of trying to change her mind once it was made up. So less than twelve hours after her attack, she was standing in front of Spencer Nguyen's house with Andrew, Alana, and Sydney.

Greg was still at the police station, using what they now knew to trawl through thousands of tip-line calls to try to find any potential witnesses. Margot still didn't know if he and Sydney had uncovered any potential victims who might have escaped. There hadn't been time to ask.

Everyone kept giving her sideways glances of concern, but no one had said anything when she had shown up. And the worst of her bruises were hidden under her clothes, so they didn't even see the really bad parts. Wes had been hard to convince to stay at the motel. She had foolishly tried to tell him he could go back to California and she would be home soon, but he had already called work to take emergency family time for a few days and had confirmed with his sister that she was able to stay longer.

At some point Sadie would come visit them for something other than a major drama, but this would not be that time.

Truly, Margot wanted to be in her bed at home with intense painkillers and perhaps a marathon viewing of *One Tree Hill* to take her mind off things, but she would never have been able to rest easily unless she'd been able to be a part of this.

What the team had learned in the time she was in hospital was that Spencer's father, Nam, had passed away about a year and a half earlier. He'd left Spencer the family home—the one they were currently standing in front of—as well as the family business.

Spencer's mother, Ginny, had died when he was young, according to Officer Logan, who had actually gone to high school with him. She was with them at the house, one of the few officers still available, and her expression was hard to read. She had just learned that someone she had known her whole life may not have been at all the person she thought he was. It was a hard pill to swallow.

There was no way to know what to expect when they went through the front door. Was Spencer living with anyone? Could he potentially be housing an accomplice?

The tension was so thick it could be cut with a knife as Andrew went through the door first, outfitted in a bulletproof vest, as were all the agents and officers behind him.

The last time Margot had been this protected, or at a scene simmering with such uneasy energy, the police had been on the cusp of arresting an entirely different killer. That job had gone down without a hitch, and Margot was hoping this one would as well.

She was forced to wait on the lawn; her injuries denied her the right to a presence inside until it was confirmed to be safe. So she listened closely, her pulse hammering, as the individual cries of *Clear, clear, clear* sounded. Checking each room seemed to take an eternity, but finally Andrew emerged at the door again, holstering his weapon, and waved Margot forward.

Once she stepped through the front door, she felt the pain in her ribs lift slightly—the pain meds were kicking in—and her discomfort was replaced by intense curiosity. She saw a similar change register on Alana's face. She had been all business and intense focus during the sweep, but now she could view the house through the eyes of a profiler.

Margot had never met Nam Nguyen or his wife, but she had met their son, and, while she now knew that everything he had projected to them had been a lie, she also knew this was not the house of a twenty-eight-year-old adventure enthusiast. It felt very much like a house that was stuck in the nineties and early noughties, from the floral couch and loveseat in the living room to the ivy wallpaper trim around the kitchen walls. This was a memorial rather than a space that Spencer had taken on for himself. And maybe part of that was the comfort of being in a house exactly as he remembered it being in childhood, but Margot couldn't help but wonder if another part of it was that Spencer simply didn't have enough personality of his own to *need* to make any changes to the space.

It was obvious that his parents' bedroom hadn't been changed at all since his father died. The space was neat and tidy, the bed made as if they would step into it later that day, but the room itself just felt devoid of life.

Spencer's room was on the other side of the main floor, and here, at least, there were signs of modernity. While the wallpaper was a navy and white pinstripe that made Margot think of the Yankees, the rest of the room was somewhat more suitable for an adult man. The bed was a relatively new IKEA frame with plain sheets and a duvet, all neatly made, as if he had been sure to get everything just so before he left to meet them the previous day. His clothes were all spaced evenly in the closet or folded with military precision in his drawers. In the bathroom, the toothbrush, razor, and face wash were all meticulously spaced on the small counter, and there wasn't even a hint of mildew in the shower.

Margot could practically see Alana constructing a profile for this guy in her mind. She would love to hear about all the insights this kind of environment gave into the twisted mind of a man like Spencer, but unfortunately nothing that they'd seen so far was giving them any actual evidence against him.

The house had no basement, so there was no subterranean lair in which he could hide his nefarious doings. But as Officer Logan stepped into the garage and cleared the space, she turned on an overhead light. Margot, who was standing right behind her, let out a small gasp of surprise.

The Nguyen garage was packed with camping gear.

Margot stepped past Logan, gaping around the space. There had to be at least ten or twelve backpacks, varying from the large distance hiking packs to lightweight ones intended for day hikes. The way they hung from the rafters reminded Margot, with a shiver, of the way some hunters would display their kills. On the metal shelving unit on one wall of the garage were a dozen sleeping bags in varying sizes and colors. The shelf below that had a half-dozen pairs of hiking boots—fewer than with the other items, but Margot could see from the difference in size that these were not shoes Spencer himself had discarded. One pair had bright pink laces.

Alana stopped beside Margot, and Margot turned to see her attention fixed in the same place. "He offered me a pair of boots," she whispered, almost to herself. "When he saw that mine were so uncomfortable, he said he had spares at home that were already broken in. Said he kept a lot of extra equipment to make sure everyone had a comfortable hike."

They both stared at the shelving unit, and Margot wondered which bag belonged to Daisy Littlewolf.

Which belonged to Sandra Elkhorn.

She looked at all the jackets hanging on hooks on the wall behind them and her mouth went dry. She had thought it was strange that so much would have been left with Sandra's body, but that her bag and jacket would be missing.

Now it made sense.

The biggest difference between a trophy and souvenir for a

killer was the souvenir was just for them. A trophy they could give to someone else, so they could see it worn and be brought back to the moment of the kill.

These were the trophies.

It didn't take a lot of mental math to realize that the number of items was greater than the number of bodies they had recovered. Margot felt sick as she counted at least twelve of some items. They knew of eight victims, including Sandra.

There were more, then. Maybe on different trails. Maybe before he settled on the burial site he did.

Margot walked over to a workbench where there were various tools for small repair, and a lot of hiking accessories like whistles, camp tools, and small pocketknives.

She began opening the drawers of the workbench, and in one of them found a framed photo, jammed in face down.

She withdrew it, and her ribs ached from how hard her heart was pounding as she turned it over and rested it on the top of the bench.

Her breath caught as she made sense of what she was looking at.

The photo was taken from a high viewpoint, and was of the sprawling trees of the Smoky Mountains in various shades of fall color. In the center of the photo was a handsome Vietnamese man, his hands resting on the shoulders of a little boy with freckles and a tooth missing from his wide grin.

Nam. Margot could see the similarities between the man and his son, and there was no mistaking that the boy was a baby-faced Spencer.

What made Margot catch her breath and touch the frame with trembling hands, though, wasn't the sweet moment between father and son.

It was the other man in the photo.

Looming large and so imposing that he dominated the picture was the stern, unsmiling figure of none other than Wyatt Holmes.

THIRTY-FIVE

Margot would happily have gone her whole life without returning to Riverbend Maximum Security Institution. She would have been perfectly content never sitting across from Wyatt Holmes again. But this case demanded she put those desires aside.

And this time she had a very different photo to ask Holmes about, and she wasn't going to let him lead her down any rambling garden paths today.

She felt no nerves on taking her seat in the cubicle, and once his hulking form was settled into the chair across from her, she picked up the phone on her side. She found she no longer minded the thick plexiglass between them.

He settled into his chair, looking much more like a medieval drawing of a giant than an actual human man, and Margot felt every bruise and fracture flare in response. But she had no reason to fear him, not from this position. That dulling of her fear instinct allowed something else to fill its place: anger.

She was *pissed* at this man for letting her walk headlong into a situation that was almost the death of her. It didn't matter that he couldn't have known they had hired Spencer. He knew what that grave was, she had no doubt. Yet he'd let her leave here pretending to know nothing about it.

That's not entirely true, the little voice said.

He had just intimated that it wasn't *his* crime scene. She hadn't asked if he'd known whose it was.

She silently told the little voice to kindly shut the fuck up.

She also realized she must have been wearing her inside face on the outside, because Holmes was staring at her with a mixture of confusion and bemusement. She supposed that was a slight improvement on his typically stony, expressionless appearance. He cradled the phone against his shoulder, and it looked like a toy.

Wyatt Holmes stared at her expectantly, unblinking, waiting for her to make the first move.

"How did you meet Nam Nguyen?" she asked.

His lips thinned, but he didn't seem altogether surprised by her question. Then those lips turned upwards in a smile, and she wished they hadn't.

"I knew it when I saw you," he said, shifting his bulk in the small chair to lean forward so he could really look at her. "I knew you were a hunter."

"Well, no thanks to you I almost became the hunt*ed*," she said, not flinching away from his gaze.

This time he did look perplexed. "Nam is gone. You should have had nothing to fear in those woods."

This took Margot aback. She had expected that he had known all of the details, but could he be completely in the dark? Either that or he was just fucking with her again for fun. She didn't trust herself to get a good read on him anymore, not after the last time.

She pulled out the photo she'd found in the Nguyen garage and held it up for him to see. This was no longer a gotcha moment, as he hadn't denied knowing Nam. But she was hoping he would make the unspoken connection. He stared at the photo, no sign on his face of how it made him feel.

"Tell me how you met Nam," she urged.

"In the woods," he said softly. "We met in the woods. And I saw the same thing in him I saw in you." He stared over the top of the photo, fixating on her like she was the most interesting thing in the room, and once again, he smiled that stomach-churning smile.

Margot hoped that face—that exact face—was not the last thing any of his victims ever saw. It was somehow so much worse than his stoic, unfeeling mask.

"So, Nam was a hunter, too?"

Holmes continued to stare at her. "He had the heart of a hunter, but he needed to learn. I was able to show him the way."

Margot let this idea curdle in her belly like bad milk.

"He was your apprentice," she said.

"The mistake you made wasn't believing that I am a wolf, Special Agent. The mistake you made was forgetting what I told you about lone wolves."

Her mouth felt dry and she realized she was still holding up the photo. She set it on the counter, face down so she didn't have to look at it, then met his intense gaze again.

"Lone wolves rarely survive on their own," she said, knowing she was paraphrasing his exact words.

He nodded. "Everyone thought I did what I did alone, and I was fine letting them believe that, because it told me they would never get it. You have to understand the wolves to understand what I did. And the pack, my pack, they made sure I wasn't alone for long."

If Margot had to pick a word for his expression in that moment it would have been *wistful*.

"You taught him how to hunt."

"He knew the woods so well, that's how I knew he was the right fit, the right one to join me. I watched him for a long time. I considered, the first time I saw him, taking him as an offering for the pack, but there was something in here that said *no*." He rapped a heavy knuckle against his sternum. "I knew there had to be a reason for that feeling. I kept watching him. The first time I ever saw him, he wasn't much older than I was at the time, maybe in his twenties." He shrugged once, like it was beneath him to remember immaterial things like age. "When I finally introduced myself to him, told him how those woods were a part of me, he wanted to know more, he was so eager to learn. When he met his mate, things changed between us. She didn't like me, so he spent less and less time hunting with me. But he never stopped hunting."

Margot disconnected herself from the part of her mind that was repulsed by this conversation. She was never going to get anywhere if she couldn't approach this in an analytical way. It was hard, because this case felt exceptionally personal to her now, but it was what she needed to do.

"Do you think he taught Spencer everything you taught him?"

"Nam had his own beliefs. His own feelings about the woods. It wasn't about the wolves for him, he saw the whole forest as having a spirit, and he believed that spirit needed appeasement the same way my wolves did. For a long time, we appeased them both together. Then, he found his own way."

"You knew about the grave."

"There was not much that happened in those woods I didn't know about, Agent Phalen."

"You think the grave was his offering site?" Margot asked, realizing this would be one of the few logical reasons to go to all the effort of bringing so many victims to the same location. She had thought perhaps it was just convenient, but three hikes up there had proven that was hardly the case.

"It isn't for me to understand how someone else honors their gods, but yes, I believe that site was very important to him."

"Important enough for him to share with Spencer?"

Holmes made a scoffing sound, rolling his eyes. It felt so out of place Margot just blinked at him several times. She'd have felt less taken aback if he had lunged at the glass.

"Spencer was no hunter. Nam thought the world of that boy, wanted to share everything with him. But I told him, told him right after that photo was taken." He knocked on the glass assertively, which caused one of the guards to tap on the glass behind him, a warning to behave. Holmes withdrew his hand and showed it to the guard before resting it in his lap again. "I told him the boy didn't have what it took."

"What makes someone a hunter?" Margot asked, not sure if she was asking because of Nam or because of what he'd said to her.

His gaze focused sternly on her. "You know the answer to that. You know it in your gut, where it's more than something I can explain, it's something you feel. I see it whenever I look into your eyes. You play the part, but there's something feral in you. Something that would have no problem snuffing out a life." Margot held her breath. He tilted his head to the side, and all Margot could see in the gesture was the curious expression of a dog. "Have you ever killed anyone before?"

It took her too long to answer.

He nodded, smiled that unsettling smile. "See? I know it when I see it. You know it when you feel it. And Spencer didn't have it."

"That didn't stop him from killing people," Margot said.

"Anyone can kill someone. It doesn't take skill. And he learned a lot from his father."

"Who learned a lot from you."

"A pack shares knowledge. But it also knows when to cut its losses with the weakest members. If they had stayed in my pack, I would have cut that boy loose. I think Nam knew that, too." Holmes looked at her for a long time, then leaned in closer, lowering his voice. "Did you kill him? The boy?"

Margot blanched, but this time she was able to answer. "No."

Holmes regarded her for a moment. "You wanted to, though."

She chewed the inside of her cheek, then, against her better judgement, she said, "Yes."

He sat back, nodding mostly to himself. "And that's why you'll survive. Because a real hunter knows when the kill is worth it."

"Is it ever worth it?" she asked, though she didn't really want him to answer.

He smiled. "I think you know it is."

THIRTY-SIX

Margot understood, logically, that she should not be the one to interview Spencer Nguyen when he woke, but she also had no problem making it abundantly clear to Andrew that she was going to be the one to talk to him whether he liked it or not.

By this point in their relationship, Andrew knew better than to get in Margot's way when she had her mind set on something.

Spencer had been in a medically induced coma for about two weeks before the doctors felt he was recovered enough to be brought out of it. They waited another two days before they allowed any non-medical staff to speak to him, and even though it meant Margot had to fly back from California, she was the first person at the door when that interview was allowed.

Andrew was with her, both so she wouldn't be alone for the interview and probably for liability reasons.

Margot didn't mind. It actually felt nice to have him by her side as she pulled up a chair and sat next to Spencer's hospital bed. Spencer was wearing padded wrist restraints, so there was no way he was going anywhere under his own volition. There was still an officer outside his door every day as well.

When Margot sat, Spencer stirred from his sleep. He got one look at her and recoiled with a jerk, trying to move as far away from her as he could. There wasn't a lot of real estate on his bed to allow for it.

Margot felt an odd swell of satisfaction to know he was afraid of her. She had worried that coming in here might stir something for her. She was no stranger to the effects of PTSD. But instead of fear she just felt a surge of power. He couldn't hurt her.

"Hello, Spencer. I'm glad to see you remember me so well."

His nostrils flared and he yanked his one hand that remained close to her. His attention turned to Andrew, and it was obvious he couldn't decide if he should be relieved or worried to see him there.

"I'm not here to get some kind of twisted revenge on you," Margot assured him. Then she leaned closer, and whispered, "Too many witnesses." She gave him a smile, and she knew based on his reaction it was the kind of smile that would have made Wyatt Holmes proud. That was the only thing that made her reel it back in, settle into her seat, and fold her hands neatly in her lap. "We just want to talk to you, Spencer."

He regarded her carefully, like she might take a page out of his book and make a lunge for him the moment his guard was down. Finally, he seemed to decide that it was safe enough for now, and settled back into his pillow.

"I'm sorry," he said finally. "For what I did to you."

Margot hadn't expected this, and felt herself stiffen in response to it. "Don't do that," she replied. "Because you wouldn't be sorry if you'd gotten away with it. You're only saying you're sorry because you're looking at me and you feel like it's something a normal person would do."

Spencer seemed to consider this, and didn't argue with her. "Okay."

"We found what was in your garage."

He looked up at the ceiling. "Ah. Okay."

She wondered if she had done some damage to his brain when she hit him, because he was giving her such lax replies. But then she remembered the way Holmes had treated her when she first sat across from him. She just needed to ask the right questions.

"Spencer, I want you to tell me what was so special about that spot. Why your father chose to make his... offerings there. Why you wanted us to bring them back so badly."

"You took something that didn't belong to you," he said sharply.

Margot bit her tongue, because her natural response was to remind him that those victims didn't belong to him either. She knew that kind of response wouldn't get her anywhere, though. He'd just shut down again. She could tell that Spencer wasn't all there, despite his ability to function normally alongside others. Whatever his father's reasons for killing were, Spencer had taken them in as gospel and they had shaped who he had grown to be.

She felt a brief moment of sadness for the little boy in the picture, because that boy had reached a crossroads, probably at that point in his life, and he'd taken the wrong path. Now his life was over because of it, and so many others had been lost along the way as well.

"Why was it so important they stay there? Explain it to me and maybe I can help bring them back." It didn't matter if this was a lie. He was so deep into the mythos of that grave site, he might believe her out of desperation.

"You won't understand." He stared up at the ceiling and blinked back tears. It was an unexpected emotion from someone who had done the things he'd done. Margot dealt with a lot of psychopaths in her line of work, but after just a few minutes with Spencer, she didn't think he fit that category.

"Try me. It was important to you, to him. I want to understand why."

"There are stories, stories they tell about why you should be careful in the Appalachians. Don't whistle at night, don't look into the woods after dark, don't trust your ears. My father understood that those stories weren't just stories, they had a meaning to them. They were warnings. And he understood that the only way to keep the world safe was to make offerings to the shadows, to the voices. He knew that a little blood every so often was what was necessary to keep the world safe. He told me that if anything ever happened to him, I needed to make sure that his secrets were protected. That his work was guarded. He told me to keep the tradition alive, or things could be... would be bad. For everyone."

Margot exchanged an uneasy look with Andrew, wondering if he was buying into this fairy tale. The problem was, Spencer sounded awfully convinced of it himself. She just couldn't decide if that was reality, or good acting.

"But why attack me, then? I wasn't going to help you appease any... I don't know... skinwalkers? Old gods? Whatever it was he believed was out there."

"I needed someone to listen, to take me seriously. I needed those bodies back. They weren't yours to take." His voice was thick with anger, his body rigid on the bed. "And because you were the one most likely to see the real me. It was too much of a risk. I needed to keep working."

Margot wished Nam Nguyen was still alive. It was clear that his son had bought into the story he'd been sold, but Margot wanted to know if Nam himself had really believed it, or if he'd just told Spencer what he needed to hear in order to help keep his secret safe. From what Holmes had told her about Nam, it seemed like he might have been a true believer as well. She just would have liked the opportunity to know for herself.

"Tell us how it worked," she said.

"He was always better at it than I was," Spencer said, closing his eyes. "He could follow someone along the trails for miles. Across states, and he would just *know* they were the right one. He would attack them when they weren't expecting it. He was so fast he could take out two at a time before they knew what was coming."

"How?" Margot asked. Dr. Langstrom had narrowed down that blunt force trauma and some knife damage was evident on all their victims, save for Daisy and Sandra, both of whom had no evidence of knife marks on them.

"He had an old hammer. Made from an Indian hammerhead

he found at an antique store. He said it was sacred, said he couldn't hurt anyone with it if they didn't meet the requirements of an offering. He would hit them." He raised his head like he wanted to mime a swinging motion, but he couldn't lift his hand far enough. "Once they were out, he bled them, because the blood was the most important part of the offering."

Margot could picture it, though she didn't need to.

"Why that spot?" she asked.

"He said that was where they would look, where they needed to be fed."

Margot leaned in and fixed him with an unwavering stare. "I'm going to explain to you how this is going to go, all right. I want you to talk me through all of your victims. Where you found them, their names, and how you killed them. You're going to tell me everything I want to know, because if I know all that, then I can explain to everyone else *why* you did it. I'll tell them everything you told me, I'll make them understand."

Spencer's expression changed, and for a moment he looked downright peaceful. A smile played over his lips, and his eyes took on a dreamy, faraway stare.

"For starters, you need to know, I didn't kill them. Not really."

Margot assumed he was about to deny everything, and in her annoyance she almost snapped at him. But then she thought, unexpectedly, of the woman who had tried to dig her way out, the one near the bottom who had fought so hard.

Suddenly, she understood.

"They were still alive when they were buried, weren't they?"

Spencer gave her a long, satisfied look, like she was finally getting it.

"Of course. What good is an offering if they're already dead?"

THIRTY-SEVEN

The man wanted to live in Alaska.

He couldn't have explained why, exactly, but something about the remoteness of it all appealed to him. When he took a break from the person he was on the road, he didn't want reminders of it. The reminders only served to make him hungry again, make him yearn to get back out there.

There were so many opportunities waiting for him.

He felt like, if his day-to-day life was somewhere like Alaska, he could dull that hunger enough. Draw out the time in between so he didn't put himself at greater risk.

There was a lingering awareness in the recesses of his mind that one day his luck would run out. One day someone would put the pieces together, follow the slapdash trail, and maybe, if he was foolish and they were lucky, it would lead them right back to him.

But he'd been doing it for years now, and in all that time no one had come close. There had never been a knock at his door asking questions. No one had ever called his wife to ask her for an alibi.

So far, he'd been very good at it.

The danger came in pushing his luck too far. In going out too often.

His wife had rejected the idea of moving to Alaska outright.

She'd said it was too remote for her. That he was gone so often and she would be left alone with the baby and the bears and nothing else. He had tried to sell it to her as a grand adventure, that their daughter would grow up learning to hunt and fish and explore.

His wife wanted their daughter to grow up with ballet classes and swim lessons. She had no interest in roughing it in the wilderness. With many things in their life she yielded to him, let him make the decisions. But here, she had insisted they would not move to Alaska.

So they lived in Indiana.

Such a nothing state. It wasn't even the kind of place people went on vacation. It only existed, he theorized, to confuse people with Illinois and Idaho on tests of American geography. The joke people had, calling the middle of the country *flyover states*, was how he felt about living in Indiana.

They bought a little ranch house that looked like every other house on their block, and she painted it a color she called Coffee Creamer to convince him it was something other than white, and on weekends when he was home he mowed the lawn and fixed things that she had noticed were broken while he was away.

He played with their daughter when she said he should, and he watched sports on TV when he finished, because that seemed like the right thing to do for a man in his position. A beer and baseball. A beer and basketball. Go Reds. Go Pacers. Sometimes he worked on his car just because it gave him an excuse to be outside and he had the shield of *it's too dangerous for the baby* to hide behind.

He didn't know anything about cars, but he knew you could kill an hour just poking around, as long as the hood was up and you had a greasy rag hanging nearby. The appearance of normalcy was easy for him to present at this point.

Unfortunately, he misjudged when he told his wife he wanted to go to the hardware store and she decided to come along.

"I want to get a few new plants for the living room, and maybe grab some paint for Evie's bedroom. Remember, you said you'd help me do that when you were home." While her tone was light and friendly, her words were a weapon, and she knew precisely how to wield them. She wanted him to know she never forgot the promises he made her while he was away.

All he heard was *I'm listening for the lies*.

So of course he couldn't tell her to stay home, couldn't offer to get those things for her. Which was how he found himself at a hardware store while his wife showed him swatches of paint in dusty pink and pale lemon sherbert hues.

"I want it to be girly, but not *too* girly," she said. "Something she can grow with and then decide on her own if she wants to change it when she gets a bit older."

To speed along the process, he offered her a swatch of an icy lilac hue, something that felt less offensive to his eye than having a pink bedroom in his home.

She didn't immediately dismiss it, but held it among the other shortlist colors. Then she held all three out to Evie. "What do you like, baby?"

Their daughter could barely form sentences and still tried to eat anything she found on the ground, so he found the notion of her selecting her own bedroom color to be absurd. Weren't babies colorblind when they were very young, like dogs? Maybe he was misremembering that. If it was true, then baby toys wouldn't need to be so obnoxiously bright.

Evie snatched the lilac paint swatch from her mother and jammed it in her mouth.

He was barely able to contain the look of repulsion that matched what he was feeling inside. Instead, when his wife looked over at him, he plastered on a smile.

"Guess she likes yours." There was almost disappointment in her tone, an unspoken bitterness that, whenever he was around, Evie seemed to like him better. He wished he could explain that there was no real competition. He didn't care what the baby thought. She was a stupid baby.

"Why don't we do a feature wall in the yellow?" he suggested. "It'll keep the room brighter."

The mood shift was almost immediate. She left him with the baby while she went to get their unmixed paint tins and flag down a teenager to make them the correct colors. He drifted off to another aisle, letting the baby babble away, content to speak to herself since he wasn't answering, and added a few things to the cart that he had come for.

When he found his wife a few minutes later and relieved her of the heavy paint tins, she looked into his cart, her lips pursed in confusion.

She tapped the lid of a large, orange plastic bucket. "Don't you have some of these already?"

He blanched slightly. "A couple, but they're good for keeping the garage clean."

Since she rarely went into the garage, she just shrugged, accepting his explanation. The duct tape and saw apparently didn't bother her. He had mentioned that he wanted to prune the tree in their backyard, so she probably didn't think anything of it.

Maybe someday she would remember this trip in a very different light, but for now it was all just a nice family outing.

They went through the greenhouse, where she selected a few plants for the living room and kitchen, talking the whole time about how they weren't taking advantage of all their south-facing windows. In a way, he was glad for the trip—it gave him practice he was sorely missing to give her the impression he was listening.

The whole time he was just thinking about where he was going to leave this bucket. Where he would set up his next game. Sometimes it took months or years to find the right time or the right person, but he liked to know that he was prepared for the eventuality.

"What do you think of this one?" she asked, holding up a plant with drapey leaves. "It says it's good for beginners."

"Sure," he replied, gesturing to their already full cart.

His mind was hundreds of miles away, thinking about the next time he would get an opportunity to play.

THIRTY-EIGHT

Margot sat on her front porch swing, sipping her coffee and listening to her chickens chatter with one another over the remaining bits of their breakfast. Three dogs were snoozing in various places on the sun-warmed wooden boards. Being down to three was a somber reminder of how short a time they got to spend with their adoptees. It was the one hard thing about taking on seniors.

Sometimes they surprised her and lasted for years. Her first senior dog, Betty, had looked to have one paw firmly in the grave when Margot accidentally adopted her, but she had lived another four years. And sometimes, it seemed like the old ones were just hanging on long enough to have someone take them home so they could pass somewhere safe and comfortable. The shortest adoption they'd ever had was two months.

At the moment, they had three dogs and six cats—the cats, with the exception of Lucy, were not adopted so much as delivered by the cat distribution system. They just showed up, and if they stayed around longer than a week they were fixed and brought into the house. Unlike most of her neighbors, Margot didn't like leaving her cats to saunter free outside. They were in danger of wandering onto the road, or meeting an unpleasant fate with the coyotes that freely roamed her large property. Not to mention they were horrific menaces to the local songbird population.

Lucy was allowed to join Margot when she was outside, because she was more like a dog than a cat and followed her chosen human around, never letting her out of her sight.

Now she was curled up next to Margot on the porch swing, a round ball of calico fur.

Wes came out, his own coffee cup in hand, already dressed to head to the school for an early practice with the volleyball team. He usually got a slightly later start to the day than she did, since his commute was considerably shorter. She still had a three-hour drive ahead of her to get into San Francisco. Today he'd gotten up early to be with her, since it was one of the rare times she actually had to drive into the office—after what had happened in Trumbull it was deemed necessary for them to all meet in person.

Margot had been given time at home following her interview with Spencer and her recovery from the worst of her wounds, but they couldn't put off the work for much longer. There were reports to be filed.

She also had a strong suspicion that she had been asked to come in person because Andrew was planning to use this meeting to announce the team's leadership change. This case had felt like his last hurrah, and her conversations with him over the past month told her that his time with them was winding down.

She didn't want to have to say goodbye to him. If she stayed away, maybe he wouldn't have any choice but to continue working.

Margot knew that childish approach was unfair, though. Andrew had pushed back his retirement for years just to get their team up and running, and she also knew Alana would be a great leader in his stead. It would just be different, and change wasn't something Margot enjoyed.

Wes joined her on the swing, and though he went out of his way not to disrupt Lucy, she still woke, fixed him with a cold stare and jumped down. She didn't go far, just curled up under Margot's feet, but she had made her opinions on the matter very clear.

"Don't take it personally," Margot said, holding back her laughter.

"There is no other way to possibly take it. She loves you the best, she tolerates my existence."

"She's a cat. That she hangs out with us at all means we're lucky. She only vaguely tolerates me, too."

Wes snorted. "If I was gone, she would be sleeping in my spot on the bed immediately, and it isn't because she'd be missing me."

Margot didn't want to consider the idea of Wes being gone in any capacity, but she smiled. "I'm just trying to make you feel better."

"I know she loves you more, you don't need to cover for her." He pulled Margot into his side, the swing rocking gently, and pressed a kiss to her temple. "I get it though. I love you best, too."

"Suck-up." She snuggled into him. There were plenty of reasons she loved Wes, probably more than she could list, more than she would ever be able to recall if asked. She loved him in big ways and impossibly small ones, and there was never a day she didn't feel grateful that he had stuck around long enough to get through all her barriers.

Right now, she loved him because he wasn't coddling her.

He wasn't asking her how she felt a thousand times a day, or tiptoeing around her like she was something fragile and breakable. There were people who might, but Wes seemed to understand instinctively that wasn't what she needed from him.

There had been a time in her life she had done everything she could to avoid falling victim to a killer, because she knew how they worked, and she knew the best ways to protect herself. But those ways had turned her into someone who couldn't *live*. She'd spent years unlearning all of her programming.

It was almost funny that it was only after she opened herself up to the world that she found herself in the exact scenario she'd been hiding from for most of her life.

She thought in the aftermath of it she would be a mess. That she would retreat into her old ways. There was certainly that tedious voice in her mind that said *I told you so*. Her father's voice.

But Margot had surprised herself. She didn't fall apart. Her worst-case scenario had been realized, and she had come out safely on the other side. There were bumps and bruises, some broken bones, and sometimes at night she woke with a start, wondering if someone was standing next to her bed waiting to grab her, but even the nightmares were fading as the weeks went on.

She had learned that, even when the worst came, she could get through it.

Her therapist had been so proud of her that Margot almost felt offended, like he was just waiting for the other shoe to drop. She, meanwhile, was still feeling fine. As fine as someone could be after such an attack.

"Do you think I'm supposed to bring something for Andrew?" she asked idly, pulling her feet up under her on the swing and sipping her coffee, which was now mostly lukewarm. One of the dogs whined in his sleep, kicking out his paws like he was chasing something, before going still and snoring softly.

"It's not his official retirement, is it?"

"He didn't say anything."

"You think he would just bow out without some kind of attention? Just disappear into the ether after a career like that?"

"I feel like Andrew isn't one for wanting a ton of attention focused on him. I also think the Bureau probably won't want to draw a lot of attention to the fact that they forgot to make him retire like six years ago."

She felt Wes smile without having to look at him. "Do you *want* to give him something?"

Margot didn't have an easy answer for that. Andrew had been such an important part of her life for so long, and she couldn't imagine a gift that was appropriate for saying goodbye to someone like that. It felt like the end of an era in a way no other retirement she had ever been through before had.

"We have a really nice unopened bottle of Scotch," Wes suggested.

"Is gifting something you already own tacky?"

"If you think you can find something better at a gas station between Elk Creek and San Francisco you are welcome to try."

"No. You're right. I think that's a good idea."

Still, they sat unmoving a few minutes more until Margot sighed. "It's so much harder to leave in the summer. It's so nice already. Seems like such a waste to spend half my day in a car." Since she wasn't going into the city for a case, she would return home that evening. It didn't make sense to get a hotel room for such a short visit.

"You know what will make it better?"

"Coming home to you?"

"Nope."

She leaned back and looked at him, his expression so goofy and expectant she let out a snort-laugh and finally pushed herself up to her feet. "Yes, I'll get Rocco's on the way home."

Their favorite chicken was about a thirty-minute drive, so she got it whenever she came back from the city, otherwise the trek didn't feel worth it.

THIRTY-NINE

The drive into the city was lovely. Northern California came alive in the summertime. Even though the rolling hills were brown thanks to limited rainfall, trees were in bloom, and there were fields with verdant crops along the way.

She'd lived away from California for a chapter of her life, but she had missed it too badly to stay away. The light and air were just different there than anywhere else she'd ever been. The butter yellow of golden hour, the way the breeze could carry the scent of salty ocean or fresh orange blossom depending on the direction and the day. She loved California, and she'd been happy to reclaim it as her home.

It was part of the reason, too, that she never minded the long drives from her ranch down to the city and back. She loved the Zen quality of watching the scenery pass her by, regardless of the season. When she got to the FBI headquarters in San Francisco, she was in a surprisingly good mood. She had a bottle of Scotch with a ribbon on it in her bag, and, despite everything that had happened over the past month, she felt light, almost relieved.

They were still working to identify the seven victims found at Nam and Spencer's burial site. Besides Daisy, dental records from their narrowed field of potential victims had helped identify four more of the bodies. But that left two, the two at the very bottom, with no names yet. Spencer had told Margot a fair bit in his interrogation, but his knowledge was limited. He knew only a handful of names, and those still needed to be verified.

It turned out he cared very little about who his offerings were, so long as they sated a need.

Dr. Ava had connected their team to a group called the DNA Doe project, who were able to use familial DNA markers to try to find relatives of unidentified homicide victims. They compared the DNA of the victims to that stored in national genealogy databases —from people who willingly submitted their DNA to be tested to find family connections or check for illness markers—to see if they could identify cousins or even siblings of the deceased. The process could be painstaking, depending on how distant the relations were and how degraded the DNA of the victim was.

It was going to be a while before they were finally able to wrap up their case from the Appalachian Trail. But they knew who their killers were. They had been able to tie some of the earlier crimes to Wyatt Holmes—which was their reason for going to Tennessee in the first place—and, all drama aside, they were likely going to consider the trip a success.

Based on the fact they'd found two unknown killers they hadn't even known they were looking for, it was more of a success than they could have predicted.

Despite all that, and even her good mood, Margot felt a pang of melancholy as she filled her coffee cup and headed into the boardroom to await the rest of the team. The only other person already waiting was Sydney.

As usual, she'd come prepared with at least a half-dozen folders, like she wanted to have all her information on hand in case Andrew asked her for some specific detail. He never had, but it seemed like Sydney never wanted to be caught unprepared.

She smiled at Margot. "How you feeling?"

There was no pity or condescension in her tone, which Margot appreciated. She didn't want to be handled with kid gloves by her own team.

"Pretty much back to normal, unless someone makes me laugh too hard, in which case I'm a hot mess express."

"Thankfully I don't think this meeting is going to be a barrel of laughs," Sydney said, adjusting her stack of folders so it was properly squared to the edge of the table.

"How are *you* feeling after all of this?" Margot asked. She was probably the only person at this point who knew about Sydney and Spencer's date, unless Sydney had shared that with the rest of the team.

Margot wasn't going to be the one to tell the others if Sydney hadn't or didn't want to, but she wanted to make sure the other agent was okay. Being in a personal relationship with a killer could really mess with someone's head. Margot would know.

Sydney looked down at the table for a moment, then finally back to Margot. "I feel like an idiot, honestly."

Margot shook her head. "You couldn't have known. None of us knew."

Sydney watched her for a long time without speaking, considering her next words carefully. "I think a part of you knew. Deep down. I think you knew there was something not quite right with him."

"I wouldn't have let you go on that date if I thought, even for a second, you were at some kind of risk."

Sydney waved a hand in the air. "No, I know that. But you can't tell me he didn't make your spidey senses tingle just a little."

It was hard to separate what she knew now from what she had known then, but Margot thought back to that first hike, when Spencer had been so strangely serious about Appalachian folklore. She'd thought at the time that he had just been good at telling a ghost story, but now, with hindsight, what she'd felt in that moment seemed more like a warning.

"I'm worried if I say yes, I'll just convince myself that every person I think is weird might be a killer." She gave a small smile. "And that's no way to live."

There was an unspoken history in that comment that both of them understood completely.

"It's going to give me one hell of a bad first date story," Sydney said finally, giving Margot a smile.

In that small gesture, Margot knew that, while Sydney might be shaken, she would be okay.

She would leave it there.

"Hey, I never asked, and I guess it doesn't matter now, but were there any tips that pointed back to Spencer when you were reviewing the tip-line calls?"

Sydney sat up straighter, her expression warming. "There were!" she said, then realized this response was perhaps a bit too enthusiastic. "There were," she said again, this time calmer. "Though I'm not sure we would have known they were Spencer right away unless that connection had been made for us." She gave Margot a meaningful look.

Yes, good for Margot to be targeted and help them solve the case.

Mighty fine detective work.

Sydney continued. "We actually found one case of a woman who said she was assaulted on the trail by a man she met earlier that morning. That she got close to the area of our grave, and suddenly he started to act erratically, and then out of the blue he attacked her. She said the only reason she got away was that he had grabbed hold of her by her backpack, and she managed to wrestle free of it and leave it behind. She ran like hell and he never caught up with her. She said he told her his name was Trent. When she described him, she didn't mention that she believed he might be mixed-race, just that he was tan, fit, in his early twenties. That was about three years ago, and obviously nothing ever came of it. I think we can now safely assume Trent was Spencer based on the location."

"I bet one of the backpacks in their garage is hers," Margot said, almost to herself. There was a strange relief in that, knowing that at least something in there wasn't tied to another dead body. "What about the other call?"

"A woman called to say she thought one of the items we showed on the broadcast might have belonged to her son. We've been able to confirm that now, with the dental records. Austin Burns, our solo male victim. She said he had hired a guide to help him for part of his trek through Georgia, though she couldn't remember the name of the guide or the company. Said she didn't really think it had mattered, because Austin and the guide had parted ways before he headed into Tennessee."

"Enough time for Spencer to get ahead of him on the trail and meet him right where he wanted him." Margot fiddled with her cup of coffee, marvelling at the planning that Nam and Spencer must have done to get their victims in the right place. Or what Nam had perceived to be the right place to make his offerings.

They would try to keep that information from being made public, but it might come out at trial, depending what direction the defense went. Margot just didn't want that part of the trail to become associated with things like witchcraft or satanism thanks to one man's obsessive desire to appease nature.

Nam wasn't so different from Wyatt Holmes. Margot could understand why they had been drawn to one another.

Spencer, it seemed, had adopted a manic need to appease his father, to continue the work Nam had begun. And he wasn't careful enough or smart enough to keep from being discovered.

She was sure they would still have more to uncover that would point them back to either Nam or Spencer, things that would help build a solid case against Spencer if and when he went to trial. Margot wasn't sure he ever would. There was a strong potential that, thanks to his fresh new head wound, he might be able to plausibly convince a judge he wasn't fit to stand trial, and would get to spend the rest of his life in an institution somewhere.

Margot found that when she considered it, she didn't mind

that, though she knew a trial had more drama, more punch. Families tended to feel at least a bit more satisfied by hearing a jury read a guilty verdict, and she could appreciate that, because it had a finality to it, a sense of closure.

But Margot no longer needed that false sense of closure from a case. She didn't care where he wound up, so long as he wasn't in the outside world anymore. Whether it was a mental institution where he had to wear slippers and get fed pills the rest of his life, or he ended up on the same cell block as Wyatt Holmes at Riverbend, the outcome was the same.

The world was a safer place.

She knew other people might not feel the same, but considering she was one of the few living people who had survived being attacked by Spencer, she thought her opinion might count for something.

The rest of the team filtered into the room. Alana sat near the head of the table across from Andrew, and Greg took a seat near Margot, which implied there would be no presentation with their meeting that day. Margot felt the lump at the back of her throat grow, knowing her suspicions were likely about to be confirmed.

Once their group was in their seats and the door was closed, Andrew got to his feet and stood at the head of the table like he was about to make a stirring toast over Christmas dinner.

"I want to start by telling you how proud I am of what you accomplished this past month," he said, and despite her generally stoic nature, Margot suddenly found it very hard to breathe. "We set out to find justice for two unknown victims we thought might be connected to a killer we already knew. We, instead, have helped solve eight homicides, two pending identification, and we have helped uncover a heretofore unknown father and son serial killer duo. That's why I created this unit. To help find solutions to those cold cases that no one seems to talk about, that have been overlooked." He took a pause, like the magnitude of his words was just starting to catch up to him. He pushed his glasses up on the bridge of his nose, then took a deep breath before he continued.

"I don't think it's a secret that I have overstayed my welcome with the FBI, and, as much as I would love to pretend to be fifty-seven for another decade, my time flying under the radar has come to an end. Not to mention there are a few people in my life who would like to see a little more of me at home and a little less of me out in the field chasing after killers. So I am sorry to say that this is the last case I will be leading with this department, and the last case I will file a report on for the FBI."

Margot swallowed. While they had all known this was coming, there was still a shift in the room. Though no one gasped or acted surprised, she knew they had all hoped their instincts, on this occasion, might be wrong.

Andrew took a breath again, and Margot had to wonder if he was trying to keep himself from getting emotional. He was a bit of a sap—she knew it would be a challenge for him to get through this without at least a few tears. She hoped he would manage it, though, because if he started to cry, she wasn't sure she'd be able to stop herself.

"I'm very proud of the work I've done with the FBI, but of the things I'm the most proud of, this unit is at the top of that list. No one thought what I was trying to do was necessary, but all of you have shown time and time again just how important this work is. What you're doing is hard, it's the kind of thing that wears a soul down, but you show up here every day, and you put in that work, and what you do is important."

Greg was staring at the table, his hands folded in his lap. Sydney was trying her best not to let her feelings show, but Margot could read her as easily as a book. Her expression was a mix of sadness and horror, like she couldn't imagine things continuing without Andrew and now she was going to need to figure out a new plan within the FBI.

Margot knew what she herself would do if the team disbanded. She would leave.

The only reason she had joined the FBI to begin with was to contribute to this team, and she had done that. She could move on to a new chapter if this one ended. But as quickly as she had that thought another rose up and gripped her: that she didn't want to move on. She would miss this work, this team. She wasn't done yet.

"I want you all to know that I've shared your accomplishments with the higher-ups. I've shown them all the numbers, all the closed cases. All the things you've done in almost seven years, and they all agreed that the Bureau will continue to fund the work we're doing."

Sydney let out an audible sigh.

"And I'm also pleased to say that they took my advice on who should step up to fill my shoes. Though hers will be much more fashionable and hard to walk in." He looked down at Alana and smiled. "I'd like to congratulate Alana Yarrow. Or I guess I should say Supervisory Special Agent Alana Yarrow." He applauded, and everyone in the room followed suit, though it was a strange kind of celebration with so few of them.

Alana waved away the praise. She didn't stand. "I am glad to be taking up the mantle, but I don't want to change anything we're doing. I just expect to take a lot less shit from Margot."

Margot smirked. "I make no promises."

"I can't imagine how much quieter my life will be after this," Andrew said, and while it was obviously meant as a joke, a single tear escaped his eye and he hastily swiped it away.

The meeting wrapped shortly thereafter, with no actual debrief on the Trumbull case. Margot left the meeting room, knowing Andrew would find the time to say goodbye to the rest of the team over the course of the morning. She snuck into his office and left the bottle of Scotch on his desk. She added a Post-it note that read

In case we drove you to drink.

Just looking at the Post-it brought her back to the case they'd just finished.

I want them back.

Spencer had been so focused on finishing his father's work, he had made too many foolish decisions. Things that ultimately got him caught.

"You look like you've seen a ghost," came a voice behind her, making her jump. Andrew stepped into his office and set a stack of folders on his desk. Likely some last-minute paperwork that would need his signature before he turned things over to Alana.

"Just... thinking," she said.

"Don't think too hard, Margot, it gets you in trouble. And that gets me into trouble."

She had to laugh at that. "I guess that's not your problem anymore."

He came to stand in front of her, and put a hand on each shoulder. Normally that might bother her, but she had become comfortable with him over the years. She was even able to maintain eye contact instead of looking at her shoes.

"You were never a _problem_, Margot. I hope you know that."

She wanted to say something sarcastic, to brush off the earnestness of his tone, but a lump in her throat made it impossible for her to crack a joke. She looked at him, and for a moment he was in his thirties, his hair dark, no wrinkles around his eyes, no beard. She was fifteen and terrified. In that moment, he was the only solid thing in the entire universe.

The memory passed and she blinked away tears.

"Thank you," she said. "Sometimes you were a real pain in my ass. But thank you. For everything."

He smiled. "I always thought you were going to be something special. I'm glad I was right." He squeezed her shoulders, then in a moment of unexpected tenderness, he pressed a gentle kiss on her forehead. "I hope you know that you're going to be all right, kid."

"I think I do, actually."

Andrew let his hands drop and took a step back, giving her space. "You know where to find me, if you ever need me."

Margot nodded. "Same to you."

A young agent who had just joined their team a month before poked his head into the office, looking uneasy about breaking up the moment. "Agent Phalen?"

"Yes?" She actually appreciated the tension break, otherwise she probably *would* have started to cry.

"Someone just delivered something to your office. It's pretty big, I thought you'd like to know."

"Thanks, Agent Page," she said. She looked back at Andrew once more before following Page out of the office and down the hall to her own. She had the smallest office of all the leads in the unit, but that was fair as she was also on site the least. It didn't bother her to be based out of a glorified closet. At least she had a window.

Sitting in the middle of her already small space was a massive box, marked with stickers to indicate that it was internal FBI mail that should only be opened by a designated agent. She stared at the package uncertainly, wondering what on earth could have been sent to her that would require such a big box.

She used a box cutter to get rid of the outer layer and cut through a substantial layer of bubble wrap. Once the item was unwrapped, Margot simply stood in her office, box cutter still in her hand, staring at it like it was a ghost.

She didn't know why it was freaking her out so much, it was just a big orange pail.

Her heart beat faster as she picked up the note on the top.

We appreciate you offering to help us with this case. Browning PD

With everything that had happened over the past few weeks, Margot had all but forgotten their visit to Browning, which seemed impossible now that she was looking at the bucket again.

She pulled up her chair and sat facing it, the carnage of plastic and cardboard littered around her feet.

Margot had thought she could leave her job if her team ceased to exist, but she knew now that wasn't true.

She couldn't go anywhere until she knew who was behind burying these kill kits.

No matter what it took.

Her work wasn't done yet.

A LETTER FROM THE AUTHOR

Thank you so much for reading *The Wolf at the Door*! I feel so lucky to get to continue Margot's journey, especially visiting some places I've long been fascinated with. I hope you enjoyed it! If you want to join other readers in hearing all about my new releases, you can sign up for my newsletter!

www.stormpublishing.co/kate-wiley

Or for other news and bonus content sign up here:

www.eepurl.com/ASoIz

Reviews are vital to authors, as they can help new readers decide what to spend their time and money on. If you've loved this book and want to read more, I would be eternally grateful if you would consider leaving a review. Even a short review can make all the difference in encouraging a reader to discover my books for the first time.

Getting to write this series has truly been one of the greatest gifts of my life. Between Margot's tenure with the SFPD and now following her with the FBI, I feel like the writing gods gave me such a treat when they sent Margot my way.

If you read that and asked yourself, "What's that about the police?", boy, do I have a treat for you. Before Margot joined the FBI, she had an entire five-book series that delves into her work as a homicide detective and dealing with her own serial killer father. All five books in that series are available now.

Thanks again for being part of this amazing journey with me and I hope you'll stay in touch—I have a lot more planned, and if you keep reading, I'll keep writing!

Kate Wiley

www.katewiley.com

instagram.com/sierradeanauthor
facebook.com/SierraDeanAuthor
tiktok.com/@sierradeanauthor
x.com/sierradean

ACKNOWLEDGMENTS

This series has been a different experience for me from almost anything else I've ever written. By the time the first book is available to be read, I will have finished the first three books in the series. That's exciting, but it also means I have no way to know if anyone likes these books. Since you're reading book two, that means you've likely enjoyed book one, so I hope you'll stick around for the rest of the series.

I like to joke that when it comes to writing a book, whatever part you're currently working on is the hardest/worst. Writing: hard! Editing: hard! Promotion: hard! Writing acknowledgments: hard! But I can say with absolute honesty that having an editor like Vicky Blunden makes the editing part slightly less miserable. I will be forever grateful to her for picking up these books and believing in my writing, and for peppering just enough positivity into her editorial comments to make killing my darlings a little easier.

To the entire staff of Storm Publishing, all my line and copy-editors, all the marvelous promotion staff, everyone who seems to mastermind each release (Alex and Elke, where would I be without you?) and to Oliver for making it all possible. You guys are truly amazing.

To my mom, who seemed shocked to learn I mention her in every single one of these acknowledgments, because she's too scared to read these books (but will watch every single episode of *Joe Kenda: Homicide Hunter*), I love you, I love your support of me, thank you for never being annoyed that I go into recluse mode regularly to get my work done.

The Body Farm in Tennessee has long been a source of fascination for me, and I wasn't kidding in my dedication that I would drop everything to go for a research visit there. But since those visits are hard to come by, I had a little help from the books *Dead Men Do Tell Tales* by William R. Maples, *Stiff* by Mary Roach (the first time I ever heard of the Body Farm), and *Death's Acre* by Dr. Bill Bass. I watched several news stories featuring the farm to try my best to get a sense of the space, but it can be difficult to perfectly capture somewhere you've never been (and can't visit via Google Maps). Any mistakes are my own creative liberties in trying to imagine the outdoor area and labs, so I hope readers and anthropologists alike will forgive me.

And to two fans who picked the first books up last year and updated me *regularly*, forming a two-woman book club in my small town: Niki and Lindsey, I hope you're happy with how this one went.

www.ingramcontent.com/pod-product-compliance
Lightning Source LLC
Chambersburg PA
CBHW011927050726
47591CB00009B/2371